THE FATES OF YORAN

THE CHAIN BREAKER BOOK 3

D.K. HOLMBERG

Copyright © 2020 by D.K. Holmberg

Cover by Damonza.com

All rights reserved.

No part of this book may be reproduced in any form or by any electronic or mechanical means, including information storage and retrieval systems, without written permission from the author, except for the use of brief quotations in a book review.

Want a **free book** and to be notified when D.K. Holmberg's next novel is released, along with other news and freebies? **Sign up for his mailing list by going here.** Your email address will never be shared and you can unsubscribe at any time.

www.dkholmberg.com

CHAPTER ONE

The warehouse in the distance was better lit than Gavin preferred—more than what was necessary for a job like this. He pressed his back against the stone building nearest him. It was a tavern that would normally be boisterous, but it was quiet for probably the same reason Gavin and Gaspar were there.

"Are you going to stay there, boy, or are you going to get moving?" Gaspar asked.

Gaspar hadn't given Gavin much insight about the job, only that it was something important to him. That alone was probably enough for Gavin to agree to take the job, but for whatever reason, Gaspar had preferred to keep it more secretive than Gavin thought necessary.

Gavin looked across the street to where Gaspar flattened himself against a different building. The only part of the old thief that stood out was his shock of silver hair and his flat gray eyes. Otherwise, his faded gray cloak helped him blend in. The building Gaspar concealed himself against was a general store that sold supplies, though it was one Gavin had never visited before.

"*I* don't tell you what to do on *my* jobs."

Gaspar grunted. "You tell me often enough. Like you know better than a man who's worked on the streets for his entire career."

"You worked on the streets as a constable," Gavin said in a whisper. The enchantment that permitted them to speak to each other made the words carry easily, so he knew Gaspar wouldn't struggle with hearing his taunt. "How long were you a thief?"

"Careful, boy."

Gavin shook his head. Gaspar, despite his age, had good eyesight. Hopefully, he would see Gavin's annoyance. He had to suppress it. None of his annoyance was really Gaspar's fault. It was the situation. Staying in Yoran.

The choice had been his, but there were times when it felt otherwise.

"Will the two of you just get going?" Wrenlow's voice broke in between the two of them.

"Stay out of it, kid," Gaspar said.

"You don't need to talk to him like that," Gavin said.

"My job, my talk. Now we're going to do this quietly."

Gavin looked at the warehouse. It was a low stone building with a flat roof, and it occupied nearly the entire block. He stared at it, but they hadn't seen any movement since their arrival. Gavin hadn't expected to. Gaspar had scouted well enough, and as far as he knew, Imogen had taken care of anyone who might be watching.

"I don't know why you really need me for this anyway," Gavin said. "You already have your muscle."

Gavin still didn't know what Imogen was capable of doing. She was a skilled sword fighter—one of the most skilled he'd ever encountered—but he didn't think she had magic. Maybe enchantments, but he hadn't been able to determine whether she had any on her.

"I said quiet," Gaspar growled.

He leaned forward, and then he scurried across the street, moving far more rapidly than Gavin would've given him credit for. Gaspar was older, though Gavin hadn't learned how old. He had served as a constable for several decades, lost a wife, lost his job, and taken up thieving.

Gavin didn't know much else about him. He called Gaspar old, but the man really wasn't that much older than him. Gavin just looked young. He always had. Some days he felt older than he was, though that was mostly a weariness from everything he'd gone through. Since defeating the Mistress of Vines, he had more free time.

Gaspar reached the warehouse entrance, slipped out a lockpick set from his pocket, and made quick work of opening a side door. He disappeared inside.

"You're in. Now what?" Gavin asked.

"Now you follow me, you damn fool. Did you forget the plan already?"

"I was just testing to make sure that you remembered it. You're getting up in years, so how am I to know whether or not you'll remember all of these things unless I question it?"

Gavin darted forward. As soon as he did, a flowing movement came from the side. He twisted, dropping low, and reached for his dagger. The dagger was El'aras made and filled with a strange sort of power. It glowed when magic was used around him.

Thankfully, it didn't glow now.

Whoever approached was not using magic. Not an enchanter, though he still wouldn't put it past one of them to attack. After what had happened with the Mistress of Vines, Gavin remained uncertain about the enchanters and what they might be willing to do.

"Where are you, boy?"

"Quiet," Gavin hissed.

"Now you want me to be quiet?"

Something sped toward him, faster than Gavin could track, but he had trained for scenarios just like this. He rolled to the side and popped up, doing so in the fighting style of Kor. It was a loose sort of stance, but it lent itself well to this type of challenge. He reacted in exaggerated movements, which helped against a much quicker foe.

If he was right, then his opponent would be quite a bit faster than him.

He smiled tightly to himself, resisting the urge to reach for the enchantment stuffed in his pocket. It remained there, untouched, where it would stay.

Gavin had no interest in drawing upon the enchantment

for speed and strength, though he could imagine Gaspar's irritation in learning that he chose not to use something that would grant him a bit of an advantage.

Why use it when I need to keep myself sharp and spar?

It had been far too long since he'd had a worthy foe.

"What are you doing?"

"We have company," Gavin said quickly.

He rolled sideways again as the blur of movement came toward him. He darted after it, swinging low and coming back up, then tumbling off to his side in the same exaggerated manner that was designed to catch somebody who was faster than him. There was always somebody faster and stronger and better, but knowing different styles allowed him to overcome any deficit he had.

According to his old mentor, Gavin had plenty of deficits, despite Tristan trying to beat them out of him.

The blurring movement came straight at him again, and he brought his fist around in a rapid shift of direction. The suddenness of it seemed to catch the person off guard. Gavin punched, and then the person became visible.

He was young, probably no more than eighteen or nineteen, and skinny. Not the kind of person that Gavin would ever have expected to have trouble with normally.

Gavin slammed his open fist into the attacker's throat, knocking the wind out of him. He quickly searched and found what he was looking for wrapped around the boy's neck.

An enchantment.

He looked up quickly but didn't see any sign of other attackers heading toward him.

"Are you coming?" Gaspar snapped at him.

"I told you to be patient," Gavin said.

"You told me to be quiet."

"And you're not being either."

He hurriedly finished checking the man and found no other enchantments on him. The one Gavin had retrieved seemed to be a reasonably powerful enchantment for speed, though perhaps not for strength. Not the way that Olivia had made Gavin's enchantment. Too bad for this boy that he hadn't added an element to help him recover.

Gavin dragged the young attacker off to the side of the road, propped him up against the wall in the alley, and then looked toward the warehouse. He could just make out Gaspar's outline looking out through the cracked door, peering at him.

"You can get going," Gavin said.

"Not without you."

"You still haven't explained why you needed me on this job."

He looked over to the fallen boy, shaking his head. If it was only somebody like that, Imogen likely could've handled it—maybe not as neatly as Gavin and probably bloodier, though sometimes bloody was necessary. But Gaspar or Imogen could've done the job.

"I'm not a thief," Gavin said.

"I don't need a thief. Now get moving."

Gavin inched along the wall, moving deliberately and

watching. Now that he knew there was one enchanted attacker, he had to ensure that there wasn't going to be another. He didn't want to get caught up in whatever was taking place here.

"Keep your eyes open," he said to Gaspar.

"My eyes *are* open."

"What's going on there?" Wrenlow asked.

"Maybe you should be out here," Gavin said.

"I'd like to, but Gaspar didn't want my help." Wrenlow didn't even bother to hide the note of disappointment in his voice.

"You're better off inside," Gaspar said. "Stay by the table. By the books."

"He's better doing what he's good at," Gavin said.

"Would you stop talking," Gaspar muttered.

Gavin laughed softly. "You're just mad that he's sweet on Olivia."

Gaspar grunted. "We are not talking about that."

"Please," Wrenlow said.

"Do I have something that the two of you agree on?" Gavin moved forward, glancing in either direction around him. No signs of another attacker, but there could still be somebody else here. A single person would not be enough to protect an entire warehouse of value, regardless of what lay inside. He didn't know what Gaspar wanted his help for, but he could only imagine that it was worth something significant.

As Gavin started across the street, another flicker of movement came in either direction. Two attackers.

He stopped in the middle of the cobbled street, the stones more cracked than they were in other parts of Yoran, smiling. "I'm going to be another moment."

"Gah," Gaspar grunted, closing the door again.

Gavin didn't have to wait long before the first of the attackers came. When they did, they lunged toward him, sweeping in a blur. Both were enhanced with speed enchantments. Gavin dropped down, punching with his fist toward the first one to arrive, and he nearly shattered the bones in the man's forearm.

Not just enchanted with speed but with something else too.

He popped up, flipping in the air, and landed facing the attackers. The blur darted toward him, and Gavin swept his leg around, kicking outward. He braced himself for a more jarring connection.

His foot connected and crashed into the man, who went down. Gavin followed the movement, driving forward with his other foot. He stomped down on the man's midsection, now visible and exposed, and knocked the wind out of him.

The other person came toward him. Gavin was ready. This was the one who had some enchantment that turned the man to stone, or something else that made him harder to strike. Gavin couldn't do it openhanded. He'd have to use his shoulder. Or a knee.

Gavin braced himself and jumped, swinging both knees up right as the blurring movement streaked at him.

He connected with something. There was a soft, feminine yelp, and Gavin ignored it as he jumped again, swinging his leg around and driving it into the woman's belly. Then she was down. If someone was going to fight him, he was going to defend himself, regardless of gender.

Another of Tristan's lessons.

Gavin hurriedly searched both the woman and the fallen man. He found and stripped them of their enchantments, then dragged them off to the side of the street.

Fighting people with enchantments reminded him of breaking into the Captain's home and what they dealt with when it came to the Mistress of Vines. Could he be responsible? Gavin hadn't been paying that much attention when it came to the Captain, though perhaps he should have. He had allowed the Captain to remain in power, which may have been a mistake. Had he not, though, there would be a danger to the city—a power void that Gavin had been concerned about leaving too open. He suspected even the constables, and Davel Chan, approved.

Whatever this was, Gavin didn't think this was the Captain. He had kept enough tabs that he would've known were he the one responsible.

"Now I'm coming," he said. He pushed open the partially closed door, then stepped through the doorway. There was a faint light inside. "Is that your doing?" he asked Gaspar, nodding to the lantern glowing in the distance.

"I wouldn't have lit that."

"Then they know we're coming."

"Given the mess you made out there, I would say that's a pretty good possibility."

"I didn't make a mess out there," Gavin said, surveying

the inside of the warehouse. It had as low of a ceiling on the inside as he'd expected from the outside. Lines of boxes were arranged throughout. A shelf ran along one wall. The lantern hung from a hook on the ceiling, but there was nothing else here.

He swept his gaze around, looking for any sign of an attacker, but he saw nothing.

They were safe… for now.

"Are you going to tell me what you wanted me for?" Gavin asked.

"Soon enough," Gaspar whispered. He crept forward; his grizzled face wrinkled even more than usual as he stared at the lantern in the distance. He looked from side to side, moving silently.

Gavin followed, now filled more with curiosity than anything else. "You know, this will go a lot easier if you tell me what it is you're up to."

"This will go easier if you stop talking," Gaspar said to him.

Gavin followed Gaspar forward. He really needed to be careful. This was Gaspar's job, not his, and he knew better than to antagonize the old thief. Gaspar had helped him many times on different jobs that he'd taken, and Gavin knew he should really be more appreciative.

"Which one of these trunks are we taking?" he asked.

"None of them," Gaspar said softly. He reached a short door at the back that barely went up to his shoulders, and he wasn't that tall to begin with. He motioned for Gavin to get close.

There was nothing other than the size of the door that was remarkable about it. It was little more than three feet wide by maybe four feet tall. "Go ahead, pick it," Gavin said.

"Do you see a damn lock to pick?" Gaspar asked.

Gavin smiled to himself. "Fine. There's no lock. So what do you want inside of it?"

"Open it," Gaspar said.

Understanding dawned on Gavin. "That's why you asked me to come."

"You're damn right that's why I asked you to come. I needed your special gifts."

"Now they're gifts?"

"I don't know what else to call it. Now go ahead and be this so-called Chain Breaker that you like to keep going on and on about."

The Chain Breaker. A name he had taken after he'd demonstrated his strange and unique ability when he was younger. A name that he should've known meant something more. A name that had told him that he *was* something more.

And yet, now that he operated out in the open, and now that others knew of it and of him, he wasn't quite sure how to feel about it.

"Would you have asked for my help otherwise?" he asked.

"You do have your uses from time to time," Gaspar said, turning his head and looking behind him.

Gavin glanced back too. Two figures came streaking

toward them, and he shook his head. "You want to go ahead and get this, or do you need my help here too?"

"I could use a bit of an assist."

"Just an assist, and that's it?"

Gavin stepped forward. The first attacker came at him and moved with a blazing speed. Gavin stayed in place, prepared for the onslaught of the attack. When it struck, Gavin twisted, driving his elbow down and swinging his leg around.

He hit nothing.

This attacker was better. More controlled.

He should have known that there'd be a change in strategy—and a change in skill.

He couldn't jump very high here. The ceiling was too low, only a few inches above his head. This and the rows of boxes limited his ability to fight effectively. It would limit the speed this person could come at him with too.

Gavin darted off to the side and watched as the blur came at him. He dropped, immediately flipping over and kicking up. He was greeted with a satisfying grunt. The kick sent the person slamming into the ceiling. When they connected, they went crashing down and landed on the ground. Gavin rolled and chopped the side of his hand at the person's neck, knocking them out.

There was still one more.

He popped up and swept his gaze around.

Where are they?

They had to be somewhere inside still. As he looked around, he saw no signs of movement.

"Get over here, boy," Gaspar said.

Gavin looked over toward the door. Gaspar swung a pair of blades in front of him, trying to fend off one of the enchanted attackers that was blurring toward him.

"It looks like you've got this taken care of," Gavin replied.

Most of the time, enchanted individuals didn't blur into nothingness the way that these had. They had to be heavily enchanted or had an unfamiliar enchantment that permitted them to do so.

"Just give me a hand," Gaspar said.

Gavin started forward, but the person he had knocked out—or had seemingly knocked out—grabbed at his foot, tripping him. He stumbled, twisting at the last moment, and crashed into the person across from Gaspar.

He heard a gasp.

Blood dripped down Gaspar's blades, which were plunged into the belly of the young man who stood across from him.

"Dammit," Gaspar said.

Gavin looked down at the boy. He was probably no more than sixteen or seventeen. Young. Bleeding heavily.

Gavin had killed dozens and dozens of times over the years. He viewed it as a part of life. Death was not something he normally feared. Still, in the time that he'd been in the city, he was killing less often than normal and even looked for reasons not to kill. Partly that was a desire to find some other aspect of work, but partly that was because he had come to realize that his skills could be put to use in other ways.

This was the first person he'd killed since the Mistress of Vines.

"It was you or him," Gavin said.

It was the expected response, and the kind of thing that Tristan would've said to him when he was training, but saying it now—and to Gaspar—felt hollow to him.

He hadn't needed to kill.

Ever since dealing with Cyran, Gavin had tried to avoid it. There was nothing gained by hunting people down throughout the city. Not if he wanted to stay here, and surprisingly, he continually debated whether he wanted to stay in Yoran.

"No, it wasn't, and we both know it." Gaspar turned to the door. "Just open the damn door."

He focused on the place of power buried deep within him and called to it—his core reserves. It was something that he had once believed was just tied to additional strength he could access, but he had come to learn was more than that. Magic, probably. He tried not to think about what that meant.

As he called that power up, he filled himself with it and slammed into the door. It exploded with a thunderous crack.

"At least you were useful for that," Gaspar muttered, heading inside.

Gavin followed him, ducking down to get inside the

doorway. As soon as he did, he realized why it was so heavily protected.

"Enchantments," he whispered.

"That's right. Some damn fool thought to sell them here."

Gavin looked back. "Whose are they?" This wasn't the kind of thing to be the work of Zella and her enchanters. Gaspar would have said something otherwise.

"Don't know," Gaspar said, looking over at him. "I caught wind of someone attempting to move them."

That could mean literally moving them or selling them. Either wouldn't be good. "Who?"

"Another thieving crew in the city."

Gavin started to laugh. "So you decided to get there first?"

"It was about making sure we didn't have hundreds of enchantments flowing through the city," Gaspar said.

"There's more to this."

Gaspar looked over to him. "Of course, there is more to this. We've been through what we have over the last few months, and you even need to ask?" He looked over to the enchantments. "Especially after what we dealt with coming from the Captain."

"What are you going to do with them? I'm sure Zella would take them." She'd probably know how to figure out what each of these enchantments did.

"I'm sure she would. I'm thinking of a different approach. I'm going to destroy them," Gaspar said. "I'm not leaving this for the constables, and I'm not leaving this for some other fool. The others don't need this stash."

Gaspar set something down on the center of the floor. It started glowing; a pale orange light radiating off it. It pulsed slowly and gradually increased in the frequency.

"Just a little something that will take care of all of this."

Gavin just shook his head. "You do realize that Desarra—"

"Don't you get her involved in this."

Gavin backed out of the doorway, ducking low.

Even though there were all these enchantments in the room, there was no point in protecting them without having some way to test them, determine what they were, and catalog them.

What do I care if Gaspar destroys all of them?

Maybe it'd be better to have less magic available within the city. The last thing he wanted was for more magic to fill the city. He had already seen just how dangerous Yoran could be with magic, and in his mind, it was better for it to be gone.

Gaspar backed out and motioned for Gavin to move. "Are you going to help me drag these two out of here?"

"I already did what you wanted me to do," Gavin said.

"You don't get to pout on a job."

"I'm not pouting. Usually when I involve you in a job, I fill you in on all the details. And yet, when it comes to your jobs, you don't even give me the same courtesy."

"My jobs don't deal with killing people."

"And my jobs haven't either."

He and Gaspar held each other's gaze, and neither looked away.

"We better get moving, unless you want to see what that enchantment will do," Gaspar said finally.

Gavin flicked his gaze toward the open door. The pulsing from the item that Gaspar had set down continued to intensify. "I can imagine what will happen."

"Then we'd better get moving."

Gavin shook his head. "Fine. But this isn't over."

He grabbed the first man that he'd taken down and flung him onto his shoulder, while Gaspar dragged the other one, leaving behind a trail of blood.

A massive explosion tore through the warehouse, and then it was sucked back in. It left nothing more than rubble behind.

They had barely gotten outside in time.

Gavin stared at the remains of the building. "I could use one of those."

"I'm afraid there are no more," Gaspar said. "That took me a long time to coax out of them."

Them.

The enchanters.

Gaspar *was* working with them. Not that it surprised Gavin.

"Here," Gavin said, dropping the man on the ground. "Now that I've done what you needed, it's your turn. You get to deal with them."

Gaspar shot him a hard-eyed stare, but Gavin ignored it, striding away and leaving Gaspar in the street.

"What was that about? Are either of you hurt?" Wrenlow asked.

"That was him using me."

"Do you want to talk about it?" Wrenlow asked.

"You do realize that he can listen to us."

"I do. I just think that your reaction was—"

"Just stay out of it."

CHAPTER TWO

Gavin leaned on the wall of the bakery across from the Roasted Dragon, looking at the entrance. A dragon carved into the door always caught his attention, the streetlight reflecting off the surface making him think of stories of dragons from his childhood. *Only stories.* There were terrible creatures in the world, but no dragons.

He could go in. Hell, he *should* go in. At this point, he didn't know if he wanted to, though. Maybe his frustration stemmed from how Gaspar had used him, or maybe it stemmed from what Gaspar had said to him. He wasn't sure.

The door to the Dragon opened, and Wrenlow stepped out.

Gavin blinked in surprise. He had muted the enchantment, not wanting to listen to Wrenlow in his ear any more than necessary, but he hadn't been expecting Wrenlow to disappear on him. He figured his friend would've waited for him in the Dragon.

Where was he going?

Wrenlow hurried through the streets, sweeping his head from side to side the way Gavin had taught him. That was about all that Gavin had managed to teach him to do so far. Wrenlow had learned to watch for any pursuers, though he was doing it in a half-assed way. There weren't many people out at this hour, though enough that Wrenlow had to maneuver around a pair of drunks staggering through the center of the street, a pair of lovers leaning on each other, and a group of five men, probably up to no good.

Wrenlow was heading toward the center of the city.

Gavin snorted. The longer he watched, the more certain he was that he didn't know what Wrenlow was doing.

What would Gaspar think of it?

Thankfully, Gaspar was a bit preoccupied right now and would remain so until he dealt with the other thieves they had dispatched. Well, the other thieves that Gavin had dispatched. Gaspar had been silent until Gavin had muted the enchantment as well.

Gavin hurried forward to see just where Wrenlow was going and caught sight of him turning a corner. Wrenlow was heading toward the Captain's fortress and a row of manor homes.

Gavin whistled three times in quick succession.

Wrenlow spun, darting his gaze to either side of him. He shifted his stance and looked like he was ready to fight.

A lot of good that would do him. At least in that stance.

Gavin really needed to keep working with Wrenlow. The boy wasn't going to be able to defend himself if it came down to it. There had been some training, but not as much as what Gavin knew he needed to make him competent.

"Gavin?" Wrenlow said, hurrying toward him.

"What are you doing out here?"

Wrenlow ran a hand through his shaggy brown hair. "I just came to check on something."

"And what would that be?" Gavin asked.

"I came to check on…"

Gavin glanced toward Desarra's home. As soon as he'd started following Wrenlow, he'd known where his friend had been heading. "You can say it. If you're going to pursue her, then you can say it."

He held Gavin's gaze, then pulled his enchantment out of his ear. "You knew?"

Gavin grunted. "Not sure how I couldn't. Why are you sneaking away like this?"

"I'm not…" He shook his head and sighed. "Fine. I'm sneaking. Obviously not well. I don't want Gaspar to know," Wrenlow said.

"Because you don't know if he would approve? It's not like Olivia is his daughter."

"Mostly because of Desarra. I don't want to anger him too much if I…" Wrenlow shook his head. "I don't know what to say." He grinned, and the ink stain on his cheek twitched just a little bit.

Gavin tapped his own cheek, miming where Wrenlow needed to wipe his face. Wrenlow licked one finger and scrubbed at his cheek until the stain was gone.

"You should've looked in the mirror before you came over here," Gavin said.

"I just knew that the job was over, and he was going to be busy, and I figured…"

"You figured that you would take the chance to visit her without him around to question you."

Wrenlow shrugged.

"Does Desarra know?"

"She knows I've sent letters to her sister."

Gavin started to smile before shaking his head. Of course it would be letters. With Wrenlow, that made sense. Gavin had never been one to court through writing, though he had never been one to do much writing in any regard. Typically, either he found someone who liked him and wanted to be with him, or he didn't. That had been the case with Jessica when he'd come to the Roasted Dragon.

"What was your issue earlier?" Wrenlow asked. When Gavin didn't answer right away, Wrenlow laughed softly. "I know you, Gavin. I know there's something going on. Whether or not you want to admit it is another matter."

"You can let it drop."

"I will," Wrenlow said, "but that doesn't change that something was bothering you. Or still *is* bothering you."

Gavin saw movement down the street. He caught a glimpse of Olivia—her long brown hair, her pale blue eyes, and her pale-yellow dress that swished as she moved. She hurried away from her home before moving past two gray cloaked constables patrolling at the end of the street.

Gavin nodded toward her. "It looks like there's your chance."

"I'm sorry, Gavin. Really, I am. Why don't we talk about this later?"

"Why don't we."

"When I get back, I'll keep digging for other jobs. I know we're having a little trouble with them," Wrenlow said.

"We don't need any."

"Isn't that why you have me around? I find jobs for you. We take them. We complete them. And then—"

"I know what the situation is," Gavin said.

"I'm sorry." Wrenlow shifted, turning so that he could look toward Olivia before glancing back at Gavin. "I really should be…"

Gavin nodded. "I know. Go to her."

Wrenlow grinned a goofy, lopsided grin, and Gavin noticed another ink stain on his other cheek. Wrenlow darted off, hurrying to catch up to Olivia.

Everything kept conspiring to keep him here.

First, Gaspar was including him in his jobs, where Gavin had always been the one to summon the old thief into his jobs. Now, Wrenlow was getting caught up with a romantic interest that would be difficult for him to leave. Even Gavin's relationship with Jessica was complicating things. They claimed they were keeping it casual, but Gavin had not chased anyone else since coming to the city, and as far as he knew, neither had she.

This was unusual for him, and it might be the source of his discomfort. There was an odd nature to finding a balance but struggling with it as well. He was used to staying in a place for a little while, but then moving on. That was how he'd maintained his focus over the years. His edge.

He'd been in Yoran for some time now. Long enough to start to set down roots. Long enough that he was comfortable. But comfort brought complacency—a lesson that Tristan had taught him, but it was also a good one. If nothing else, Gavin understood he could not get complacent. He could not get too comfortable. But if he were to stay, what kind of work would he end up doing?

When he had first come to the city, the jobs had been plentiful. Most of them had been done on behalf of Cyran, but not all of them. Lately, he hadn't had any jobs. The only task he really had was to protect the jade egg from the constables and to ensure the enchanters weren't pursued.

Gavin glanced in the direction of the Captain's fortress. Maybe it was time for him to pay the man a visit. If enchantments were moving throughout the city the way that Gaspar had uncovered, he needed to have words with him. Enchantments shouldn't be so freely flowing like that. It was a danger, but maybe not for the same reason that Gaspar feared. It meant that the traditional power in the city had started to shift. Gavin had been around too many places where similar things had taken place and knew the dangers in a power vacuum.

He headed away from the manor houses and away from the Captain's fortress, looking out at the darkened forest. There was a period in his life when he had spent considerable time wandering through forests. This had been another part of his training, but strangely, the memories from before his training were the ones that always stuck with him. He recalled the trees, a cozy home, and the warmth of a fire. All of that filled him with a feeling that he missed out on something, though Gavin could not tell what it was. Some aspect of his childhood, perhaps.

Gavin made his way back toward the Dragon. Every so often, he caught shadowed sight of constables patrolling. He smiled to himself when he saw them. Now that he knew their secret and understood that they had enchantments they liked to keep hidden from the city, Gavin felt as if he had a certain sort of power over them.

As he neared the Dragon, he realized that somebody was trailing him. It was a strange instinct, an awareness of somebody tracking him, but Gavin had honed those instincts over the years. It had kept him alive countless times, and he needed to be careful.

Other than the fight earlier in the day, Gavin hadn't sparred all that much recently. Work with Wrenlow wasn't terribly challenging for him. He had to be careful not to kill Wrenlow at times.

It wasn't that he hadn't continued his training. He always kept his skills sharp by working through all of the movements and forms, but what he really needed was a good sparring session—a fight with somebody as skilled as he was so that he could continue to progress and challenge himself.

The enchanted attackers had given him some of that. Not enough, though. Maybe having somebody trail him gave him a different kind of opportunity. At least he could try to discover why they were trailing him.

He started making a wider circle. As he did, he realized that it wasn't his imagination. There was a dark cloak. A hood pulled up over the cloak. A strange limp. Was there somebody else with them? He didn't see anybody, but that wasn't to say they weren't there.

Gavin switched back around, following the flow of the crowd. He moved carefully, trying not to draw any unnecessary attention to the fact that he had picked up on them but wanting to get a better glimpse of them.

His pursuer had disappeared.

Balls.

Either they had caught him paying attention to them, or he had simply lost sight of them. Regardless, Gavin *was* growing complacent. Just the thing he'd started to fear. He needed a job—something that was *his* job and not Gaspar's, and not one given to him only to use him as the Chain Breaker.

Gavin continued sweeping his gaze along the street, looking for evidence of the person who'd been following him, but he found nothing. Either they had disappeared, which he thought unlikely…

Or they were hiding from him.

Gavin ducked forward, keeping his head down and blending into the crowd. He looked for any hint of the dark cloak, the slight limp, anything to clue him in. He didn't see any sign of them, though they had to be there.

He looped around, making his way back toward the

Dragon. The route was otherwise quiet. There were people out on the street, as there often were, but nobody caught his attention the way the last person had.

Gavin glanced to the rooftops. He wouldn't put it past somebody to scale one of the nearby roofs, hide there, and observe him, but he saw no sign of anybody atop them.

He passed two constables patrolling, and though he glanced in their direction, they didn't pay him much attention either. Neither of the constables had a limp, so he didn't think his pursuer was one of them.

Who was it, then?

He continued making his way along the streets, passing a series of storefronts and warehouses. Gavin looked over them, wondering if perhaps Gaspar might have other places that he had targeted for search. Frustration built within him as he meandered, passing a series of cottages near the edge of the city. Maybe it was just his lack of focus, not knowing what he was after, but increasingly it felt as if it were a lack of purpose.

At the end of the street near the Dragon, he caught sight of the dark cloak in the distance. He watched closely for a moment.

Is it the same person?

No limp this time. The height didn't seem *quite* right.

Gavin darted forward. He reached the Dragon at the end of the street, but they were gone. Gavin spun, looking behind him at the way he came, and still saw no sign of his pursuer.

Something caught his eye near the main entrance to the

Dragon—a couple walking toward the tavern. They were younger, the man with long rust-colored hair and a scruff of a beard, and the woman with pale skin and auburn hair. Gavin moved forward and raised his hand, waving his finger at them. They both shot him a look of annoyance, which he ignored.

He grabbed a folded slip of paper attached to the tavern's door beneath the carving of the dragon's head. It had his name on it.

Odd that somebody would leave a note like this.

He looked around for his pursuer but saw no sign of them, so he unfolded the note and skimmed it.

All of that for a job? Why not just approach me directly and hire me?

He certainly had a reputation in the city, so it wouldn't be altogether surprising that somebody would be afraid to approach him in the open. It might be easier—and generally safer—to come at him indirectly like this.

The details of the job were strange, though. It looked more like a thieving kind of job, the kind of thing that he would've expected Gaspar to take, though Gavin would never say that.

Given the dearth of jobs they had recently, he figured that perhaps it made sense for him to take it. Besides, at the bottom of the page was a symbol for gold, along with the number five.

It was just enough that he couldn't turn it down. Of course not. That would be enough to make sure that he had a good start if he had to leave the city. Not that he didn't have enough funds. He had forced Davel to pay handsomely for the last job, and Gavin didn't even feel any guilt in doing so. It offered him a measure of freedom. Besides, he had completed the job, even if it wasn't the way Davel intended.

If nothing else, having a job that paid well would at least let him feel useful in a way that he hadn't lately. He didn't need to take Gaspar's jobs, and he didn't need to depend on Wrenlow or Jessica to find jobs for him. He could get them on his own, however mysterious this one might be.

He folded up the slip of paper and stuffed it into his pocket. Though he'd been offered the job on his own, that didn't mean he'd do it on his own. When Wrenlow returned, he could look into it to make sure it was safe for Gavin to complete. As safe as necessary, that was. When it came down to it, no job was necessarily safe.

He pushed open the door, took a deep breath of the familiar scent of the Dragon, and immediately tensed.

It shouldn't have felt familiar. It shouldn't have felt comfortable. It shouldn't have felt safe.

Comfort breeds complacency.

It was long past time for Gavin to move past complacency.

CHAPTER THREE

Gavin fingered the slip of paper that had been attached to the door of the Dragon, his mind working through the job that had been left for him. He still had no idea if he would even wanted to take the job, but he tried to think back to the last time that he had come up with an assignment on his own, and the only thing that came to him was what Davel had asked of him when he had come to Gavin to find the jade egg.

Could it really have been that long?

It seemed impossible that had been that long ago, but at the same time, Gavin hadn't been actively pursuing new assignments. That had been a mistake.

Partly that was Gavin's fault. He hadn't been as motivated to pursue other assignments. Not in Yoran, at least. He had been used here. Now it felt as if he were biding his time while looking for information about Tristan, though Wrenlow had failed to uncover any details about Gavin's old mentor. That didn't surprise Gavin all that much. How could it? Tristan had trained him, which meant that he would likely be able to hide from Gavin for as long as he wanted to. He had certainly managed to hide the truth about his death from Gavin.

Gavin had waited at the Dragon for Wrenlow to return, but he'd been gone when he'd gotten up in the morning. He didn't want to wait any longer to find out more details about the job, and his curiosity had been piqued.

He fingered the note again, tempted to bring it out and read it. It shouldn't be so easy to find him or to direct others to him. It had not been like that in any other place that Gavin had visited, spending any amount of time. Only, in Yoran, he *had* become easy to find. And what was worse, no one feared finding him the way that they once would have.

He debated tapping on the enchantment, whispering something to Wrenlow and letting him know where he was going, before deciding against it. Wrenlow was preoccupied. He had gone off with Olivia, and he certainly didn't need Gavin interfering with that.

He was alone.

It was the way that he preferred it, so why did he feel unsettled?

It was this place. It was Yoran. It was everything that he had gone through since coming here. All of that had worked to keep him in the city and had plotted to force him to take action that he had not intended. All of that had turned him into this hesitant person.

He didn't know the address the note had directed him

to, but he had spent enough time in the city that he didn't feel like he needed somebody to guide him. It was on the city's northern edge, near a row of small cottages, the homes small, cozy, and some of them with smoke drifting from chimneys. They were different than the large brick homes found toward the center of the city, or the towering brightly painted wooden manor homes along the western edge. He found Jesser Street as the note directed, and then the intersection with Ihnar Street.

It would be near here.

He fingered the hilt of his dagger, tracing his hand along the El'aras markings on it.

This could be a trap.

There had certainly been enough of them, after all, but the letter had been detailed enough that he didn't think so.

He paused on the far side of the street, his gaze sweeping along the cottages, and tried to look as nonchalant as possible with the occasional person who meandered along the street. A dirt brown dog prowled along the far side of the street, and Gavin noticed it chasing a gray cat. When the dog got close, the cat spun and hissed, swiping at the dog before it yowled and darted away.

Gavin snorted.

It wasn't busy here. There were no shops, nothing to draw people here unless they lived in this part of the city. Anyone here had a reason to eye him with suspicion. His cloak would only draw even more attention, as with the sword sheathed at his side.

It was daylight, which didn't fit Gavin's mood any better, either. He didn't care for operating like this in the daylight. Actions like this were better taken in the dark. Meeting with employers was better done in the darkness.

At least, that had always been his preference in the past.

He counted down the row of cottages until he came to the one where he was supposed to meet his potential employer. A small basket of yellow daisies was set in a windowsill, the only coloration on that building or others surrounding it.

That was the place.

Gavin strode across the street, focusing on his core reserves and reflexively reviewing various fighting styles that he might need to use.

He raised his hand to knock when the door opened.

The face that greeted him was older, graying hair, and with dull blue eyes. She was a good head shorter than him, and he had no sense of a threat from her.

That didn't mean that she wouldn't pose one.

Gavin had too much experience with others who were nonthreatening to believe that she would be completely innocent.

"Are you him?" She spoke in a creaky sort of voice, and she touched her neck, squeezing the gray dress she wore.

"This was you?" Gavin pulled the letter out of his pocket, and he held it out. This was not what he had expected, and certainly not the kind of employer Gavin was accustomed to.

The woman's gaze flickered to the letter and then to Gavin. She seemed to regard him, and something in her dull blue eyes suggested reluctance. "I wasn't sure if you were going to come. She told me that I could ask you, but I didn't know if it was dangerous to ask an outsider for something like this."

Gavin glanced along the street, but no others were moving. It was as if the street had emptied the moment that he had come to this home.

"You want to talk here, or would you prefer meeting somewhere else?"

"I gave you my address. I'm not afraid of you finding me."

Gavin started to smile before catching himself. "Did she tell you what I do?" Gavin held out the note, and his gaze drifted along the surface for just a moment until he came to the letter Z. There was only one person that could have sent this woman to him with that initial.

The only problem was Gavin hadn't expected Zella to send anyone his way.

"She told me that you can find things." She gripped her neck again, and she looked up, meeting Gavin's eyes. There was a fearlessness there, which surprised him.

"Occasionally. That's not all that I do, though."

"But you *can* find things?"

Gavin tried to look past her but didn't see anything in the small cottage that worried him. Not that he really expected to have found anything.

"I can find things, but it would be helpful to know why you need *me* for this."

"Well, she said that her ability to track this kind of item is limited."

"Is that right?"

Zella was a skilled enchanter, and she led the other enchanters in the city. The last time Gavin had dealt with her, he had threatened her and her people because they had been responsible for bringing the Mistress of Vines into the city.

Why would she send this woman to me for help?

"What kind of item is it?"

This time, the woman did look along the street. When she turned her attention back to him, she leaned close. She smelled musty. "The kind that had been forbidden."

"An enchantment," Gavin said.

Her mouth pressed into a thin line. "I wouldn't go looking for it, but I understand that the situation in the city has changed. This item is of value to me."

"Why is that?"

"It was given to me by someone special to me years ago, and I lost it in the war."

Gavin stared at her, keeping his face neutral.

Is that what I am to become? A finder of things?

He had thought it was bad enough before when he had been looking for people, but this was another level altogether. Here he thought that Gaspar had been using him for his magical ability, and he had, but Zella intended to use him for another reason altogether.

It was almost enough to make him refuse.

Almost.

He had been bored, if anything, and having an opportunity to put some of his skills to use—however mildly they might be necessary—seemed as if it provided him an opportunity that he had been lacking. Besides, this might prove an interesting distraction for a little while.

"Tell me what you're missing and what the enchantment does."

"Does it matter what it does?"

"It matters if I am to return it to you."

"Do you really think you can get it?"

Gavin shrugged. "I have no idea. It would help to know what you are after, and what it does, so that I can know what I might need to do."

"I don't know that it will be all that difficult for you to find. I know where the item is. It's the getting to it that's the challenge."

"What do you mean getting to it?"

"She told me that you have a connection to him and that you might be able to use that."

"To him?" Irritation started to bubble within Gavin, and he thought that he understood what this woman, and what Zella, were after.

"Why, the Captain, of course. The necklace is precious to me. It was given to me many years ago, and if I could get it back—"

"No."

"You won't do this? She said that he owed you a debt and that it would be a simple matter for you to ask it of him."

Gavin wasn't so sure that the Captain owed him a debt as it was that Gavin had threatened him, and after having saved his life, he didn't fear the Captain coming after him. But he also didn't like the idea that he would be used for this connection, especially not in such a strange way and for somebody he knew nothing about.

"You still haven't told me anything about this enchantment."

"I've told you that it is precious to me. I've told you that I lost it years ago, during the war, and—"

"You told me about the necklace, but you haven't told me what the enchantment itself does."

The woman nodded slowly. "Of course. It is a memory."

Gavin frowned at her. He had dealt with many enchantments over the years, but more so lately. And in that time, he couldn't claim that he had dealt with any sort of memory enchantment. The idea that there would be one that could be used in such a way left him somewhat surprised. Perhaps he shouldn't be surprised that sorcerers, and enchanters, had many different abilities and uses of magic. Why should he be surprised that they would have one for memory, as well?

"It holds memories, you see. It's precious to me because of the memories that it holds." She looked up at Gavin. "I stored them there, not wanting to lose them, but I lost him anyway."

"What's the memory?"

"My son."

Gavin clenched his jaw. "Are you sure the Captain has this necklace?"

The woman nodded. "I'm sure. I petitioned him years ago, but he ignored me. He accumulated all enchantments back then and has stored them, keeping them from their rightful owners."

"Are you sure the enchantment hasn't faded?"

"It's possible. But unless he has accessed it repeatedly, I think it would be unlikely. I just want to have those memories one more time…"

Gavin sighed. "I will see what I can do."

"The timing is urgent," the woman said. "He has started to move enchantments out of the city. I need you to get it before he takes it where I can't find it again. I don't know what I'd do then."

Gavin frowned. "What do you mean that he is moving enchantments out of the city?"

"I would have assumed you had heard. Zella told me. They have been aware of it and have been trying to prevent him from moving too many of the enchantments, but…"

Gavin was of half a mind to tap on his enchantment and speak to Gaspar, if he would answer. Could that be why he had wanted Gavin's involvement in the last job?

No. If Gaspar had known that the Captain had been moving enchantments out of the city, he would've said something.

Which meant that Gaspar didn't know.

He *had* known about the enchantments, though.

"I will see what I can do." He held out the note. "Five gold coins. As agreed."

The woman nodded her head quickly. "Of course."

He looked at the cottage. It was small. Quaint. And he doubted that the woman had five gold coins. If she did, it would probably be the sum of her entire savings.

Gavin started to back away when the woman called after him.

"Is that it?"

Gavin shrugged. "For now. I'll let you know what I uncover."

He crossed the street, and when he glanced back, the woman was still standing in the doorway, watching him.

He was less concerned about finding a necklace, though he couldn't deny that a woman and her memories of her son pulled at his heartstrings. That was likely the intent. He was more concerned that the Captain moved enchantments out of the city. Here Gavin had thought to neutralize him, at least somewhat. If he were solidifying wealth, then there was a real danger that the Captain might become a different kind of a threat.

It meant that Gavin needed to pay him a visit.

But he wanted to be prepared first.

Maybe with enchantments, though he hadn't necessarily needed enchantments to defeat the Captain the last time. What would be more effective, though, would be information. He needed to understand what was going on.

He tapped on his enchantment as he strode along the

street, rounding a corner, and found the crowd picking up as he entered a part of the city with more shops.

"Wrenlow. I'm going to need your help."

There was silence, and it lasted for a little while.

Gavin had gone another two blocks before the enchantment crackled for a moment, and then Wrenlow's voice came through.

"What is it?"

"We need to meet. Something's going on, and I'm going to need your help."

"What is it? What happened?"

He could practically hear the urgency in Wrenlow's voice. Gavin didn't want to take him away from his time with Olivia, but in this case, Gavin thought that he needed him.

"I'm going to need your help, too, Gaspar."

He had no idea if the thief kept the enchantment in his ear when he was away. Gavin didn't think so, though. Most of the time, Gaspar left the enchantment out, not wanting to be distracted by Gavin and Wrenlow and their conversation. It was almost enough for Gavin to want to reclaim the enchantment from him.

"I haven't heard anything from him recently," Wrenlow said.

Gavin paused. He had reached a large market. A few trees grew along the border, stretching taller than the nearby buildings, as if serving as sentries overseeing the market. A throng of people was here, with more coming and going. A man shoved past him with a cart laded with smoked meats, his round-faced child chasing behind him. It was a wonder the dog Gavin had seen near the woman's house hadn't been drawn here.

Other vendors with carts lined the market, filled with the growing crowd. He passed a few singing minstrels and a troupe of puppetry actors performing a scene with a rapt audience. The air held the mix of smells, from the food vendors to the spice merchants to the florists selling fresh cut flowers.

The crowd made it difficult for him to shoulder his way through. It was times like these when he realized just how much he preferred navigating the city in the dark. At least, doing so at night.

"The Captain has been moving his enchantments."

"Is that why Gaspar has been chasing down different caches of enchantments?"

"Has he?" It meant that there was more than what Gaspar had let on.

"That's what Olivia has told me. Don't tell Gaspar I told you that. Not unless he brings it up first. I don't want him to think that I am betraying his trust, or that Olivia is betraying his trust or that—"

Gavin shook his head, and a short, heavyset man walking next to him shot him a look. Gavin flashed a smile, and the man scurried off.

He realized how he must look walking to the street, talking to himself. A part of him was amused by it, at least as amused as he could be with the irritation within him.

"Just meet me back at the Dragon."

"What are you going to do?"

"I'm heading back to the Dragon. I have to prepare before I go visit with the Captain."

He had no idea how things would change in the city of the Captain manage to acquire more wealth than he already had. Gavin had shifted the power balance in the city once before, keeping the jade egg for himself, leaving it stored in the underground sorcerer's lair where no one else would know to find it.

If the Captain decided to chase down a different avenue for power, what else would happen?

Gavin would be responsible for it.

Not directly, but even indirectly, he had no interest in disrupting the power balance within the city. He complained of sorcerers doing the same thing too often and had no interest in doing the same.

And if the Captain had already started to move enchantments, it was possible that the old woman's necklace would have been moved out of the Captain's fortress by now.

It's even possible Gaspar had destroyed it during the last attack.

He tapped on the enchantment again. "Gaspar."

There was no response.

He waited, listening, looking around at the crowd in the square, before calling out Gaspar's name again.

He was silent.

That wasn't entirely uncommon. Gaspar and Imogen often went off on their own jobs, the same as Gavin had gone off on his own jobs when he had first come to Yoran.

Lately, though, they had been more of a team, working together. Maybe Gaspar didn't want that.

Gavin wasn't sure that he wanted it, either.

He didn't know what he wanted. At one point, it had been to leave the city, but now, Gavin wasn't sure he could leave the city until he knew it was safe. Davel Chan's comment to Gavin came back to him, as it often did when he thought about his time in Yoran.

How could the city truly be safe if Gavin were here?

CHAPTER FOUR

Gavin wiped the bead of sweat off his forehead and grabbed for his shirt, slipping it on as he looked over to Wrenlow. His friend dripped with sweat and took one of the towels that Jessica had stacked on the table next to the cleared out portion of the tavern's main room and used it to dry off his forehead before dabbing his chest.

"I keep waiting for it to get easier," Wrenlow muttered.

Gavin shrugged. "Eventually, I think it will. We just have to keep working."

Or maybe it would be easier if Wrenlow wanted to stop practicing. Not that he was going to say that to Wrenlow, but Gavin hadn't managed to make him anything more than a passing fighter. If Wrenlow came across a run-of-the-mill streetfighter, he might be able to withstand that, but Gavin doubted that Wrenlow would be able to hold up under the kind of threats that Gavin typically found himself facing.

"I've told you I'm willing to practice more often."

"You have to be present to practice." Gavin glanced across the tavern to where Olivia sat in one of the booths, whispering to Jessica. They were the only other two within the tavern.

Olivia was lovely. She had dark raven hair and a youthful face that belied her age because of what had happened when her parents had poured power into the jade egg. Olivia sat with her back stiff, her hands moving, though the enchantments she was busy making were invisible to Gavin from his angle.

She was a skilled enchantress and had already proven her worth several times. She had made him enchantments for speed and strength, and he suspected that she could do other things, if only she had enough time.

Even with enchantments, Wrenlow had not been able to pose much of a challenge for Gavin.

He allowed Wrenlow to use enchantments only at the end of their sparring session and only as a way for Gavin to be tested, if only a little. He wanted Wrenlow to understand that he couldn't become reliant upon enchantments. Enchantments could fail. A fighter should not.

"I've been present," he said. "Quite a bit more than Gaspar, at least."

Gavin grunted, and he looked around the inside of the tavern. There had been a time when Gaspar had seemed overly present, but lately, he had been missing. Probably looking into the enchantments.

"I'm sure he's working on the same thing that we are."

"We could wait for him," Wrenlow said.

Gavin sniffed. "I'm not waiting on Gaspar to go and confront the Captain. This is a straightforward job. I need to go to the Captain, figure out what he's doing with the enchantments, and then find the necklace."

"Only the necklace?"

Gavin hadn't given enough thought. Not yet. Wrenlow was right, though.

If the Captain were moving enchantments out of the city, there might be a need for them to prevent him, or to keep them for themselves. He didn't want to run the risk of him moving something else of value before the other enchanters had a chance to go through it.

If it was just a matter of the enchantments that the constables and Davel Chan had asked him to make, then Gavin doubted he would be all that concerned. If others like this necklace that Gavin was asked to find, he thought the enchanters deserved the opportunity to find it.

They had lost enough already.

He pulled his gaze away from Olivia. He had to stop thinking like that.

The enchanters were not his responsibility. He might've helped them, at least to a certain extent, but they could track down the Captain and demand whatever enchantments that he had of theirs back. Gavin didn't have to do that for them.

"Why don't I start with the necklace, and I will see what

else is going on?" Gavin grabbed his cloak, buckled on his sword and dagger, and glanced around the tavern.

"You're going now?" Wrenlow asked.

Gavin shrugged. "I waited until it was dark, but I don't need to wait any longer."

"You could keep trying to reach Gaspar."

Gavin arched a brow at him. "Or you could come with me."

Wrenlow looked over to where Olivia sat. "If you think that you need me, otherwise…"

"I see."

"I said I'd come. I only wanted you to know I could stay here and help."

Gavin chuckled. "Go ahead and stay here. Like I said. I don't expect much out of this." After stopping at the table, he leaned down and kissed Jessica on the cheek. "I won't be long."

"Just be safe."

Gavin headed out of the tavern, closing the door behind him, and looking back to see Wrenlow sliding into the seat next to Olivia. A wide smile crossed his face.

Gavin shook his head. Jessica's words stuck in his mind. *Be safe.*

He didn't need somebody worrying about him.

He also didn't need to fear that he would let somebody down if he weren't safe.

Gavin certainly couldn't guarantee that he would be safe. With the kind of things that he did, the kind of work he ended up involved in, there was a genuine possibility he would throw himself into danger.

Only Gavin doubted he would find much danger tonight.

The Captain was once somebody he would have been more concerned about. He certainly had been concerned enough when he had broken the Captain's fortress, but this was different. Gavin wasn't looking for a fight.

He strode through the streets. Proper darkness surrounded him, and there was no crowd out in the city like there had been earlier in the day. He slipped the enchantment back into his ear, feeling the cold metal chain that connected the earpiece to the badge that he wore on his cloak begin to warm. Wrenlow wouldn't have the enchantment on now. Not while sitting at the table with Olivia.

Which allowed Gavin to try to reach Gaspar again. He didn't know if Gaspar would even answer, but he hoped that he would.

"Gaspar."

There was no response.

He was probably visiting with Desarra. Or off on some job with Imogen.

The least he could have done was warn Gavin he wasn't going to be available, though.

There was no response.

Gavin reached the Captain's fortress, having tried to communicate with Gaspar a few more times, but had gotten nowhere. There had been no response, nothing coming from Gaspar, which meant that Gavin was off on this job alone.

He paused at the wall surrounding the Captain's fortress, his gaze sweeping along it. It was a tall, fortified stone building with a massive wall surrounding it. An actual fortress and secured well enough there weren't many other buildings around it. The manor homes lining the street in either direction gave the fortress spaces, as if afraid of getting too close to the Captain.

Gavin didn't need to scout here since he had been on the other side of the wall a few times now. He watched for the patrol that he knew to be present but saw no sign of it.

That was odd.

He circled the Captain's fortress, his gaze sweeping along for a moment, but even as he did, he didn't see anything suspicious.

Maybe he was so busy moving the enchantments that he'd sent his guards away.

That seemed unlikely as well.

Gavin reached the main gate. The rectangular iron gate was closed, and as Gavin reached for it, he found that it was also locked.

Maybe the Captain decided that he didn't need anybody standing guard over his fortress. If so, that had been a change for him, as he certainly had kept a watch previously.

Gavin traced his hand along the metal and looked up to the Captain's fortress.

"Gaspar. Wrenlow." He said both of their names into the enchantment, though he wasn't sure that either of them would answer. Gaspar hadn't throughout the day, and Wrenlow was busy with Olivia.

"If you're listening, I'm heading into the Captain's fortress. Something isn't right here."

He focused on his core reserves, feeling that power just below the surface deep within him, as if he were pulling upon some part of his belly where that power was stored. He pushed it out from him and jumped. The jump carried him to the top of the wall. There was a time when Gavin would've thought that he was just a gifted jumper before he understood his magic, what the core reserves meant to him and for him, but now he understood better. He was drawing upon something else and funneling that power out of him in using that power now. Gavin was using magic.

He didn't have any control over it the way that he suspected he would need to. For now, all that mattered was that Gavin could call upon that power, and he could use it when he needed, but he wasn't sure how else he might be able to utilize that magic. If it were El'aras magic the way he increasingly suspected, then there should be a way for him to utilize his magic in the same manner as the El'aras used theirs.

One more thing to learn.

Later, though.

So many things were delayed for him now. All the time he spent in Yoran forced him to put these off.

He looked along the wall but didn't see any shadows moving on the lawn. It was possible that whoever the Captain had patrolling in the yard had enchantments which concealed them, though Gavin didn't see any indications to suggest that anything here was enchanted. Still, he waited a moment. Then another. Then another. If anyone were enchanted in the yard, he wanted to give himself every opportunity to find them and make sure that he knew where they were so that he wouldn't be surprised.

Nothing.

Gavin jumped down, moving silently.

His heart quickened. Just a little, this time with a thrill of excitement that he hadn't expected on this job.

It wasn't that Gavin wanted danger, but he didn't fear it either. He had come anticipating that this would be reasonably straightforward. Ask the Captain what was going on. Maybe he would lie, and Gavin might have to force him to share why he moved the enchantments out of the city, but he hadn't expected that he would find any real danger.

He swept along the wall, keeping his gaze toward the fortress. He didn't see anything there.

It was dark.

That, more than anything, alerted him that something was off more than what he had suspected before.

Gavin crept forward, pausing every so often to look around and see if he would find any evidence of the patrols that had been here before.

As he neared the main door leading into the Captain's fortress, he saw a leg.

He slipped over to the fallen guard. He had a muscular build, dressed in leathers, and still had a sword sheathed.

The several enchantments on his wrist told Gavin he would have been formidable. The man wasn't moving.

He checked for a pulse. There was nothing.

He saw no sign of injury, though.

There were plenty of ways that he could imagine something like that occurring. Gavin knew dozens of different lethal techniques that he could use on somebody without leaving any apparent wound, but it was the nonphysical technique he was more concerned about.

If this was magic…

He focused on his core reserves again.

He had to make sure that he had access to that power.

Gavin unsheathed the dagger. He swept it in front of him, but there was no sign of glowing from the blade to indicate any magic nearby.

That only told him that there was no magic nearby. Not that there was no magic used at all.

Gavin crept forward, and when he reached the door to the home, he pressed, but it was locked.

This was not a time for noise. If there was an attacker inside the fortress, he didn't want them to be alerted of his presence too soon.

Gavin used the El'aras dagger, shoving it into the lock and twisting. He managed to pry the door open. There were probably enchantments set into the door that would keep it locked. Still, the power that existed naturally within the El'aras blade offered a means of carving through those enchantments. They allowed Gavin to slip in more quietly.

And that was what he needed now.

Quiet.

Gavin pulled the door open, looking into the darkened fortress.

He slipped inside, closing the door behind him, careful not to make any more noise than necessary. If somebody had used magic on the door, they might be aware that he had pulled it open. If only the enchanted seals that the Captain had placed, it wouldn't be an issue.

When he had gone only a short distance into the entryway, he found another fallen guard, dressed the same as the last and equally muscular. Gavin checked him for a pulse, but there was none.

He found two bracelets, a ring, and a necklace adorning the man—all enchantments.

Whoever had attacked here had a way of fighting through these enchantments.

The dagger still hadn't started to glow.

No magic, which worried him.

What if I'm too late?

He crept forward.

He had a general understanding of the fortress's layout, though not nearly well enough for him to know where the Captain might be found. When he reached the stairs leading up, he still hadn't found any others, and Gavin crept up the staircase. He moved carefully, quietly, still holding onto the dagger while reaching for his core reserves and prepared himself in case he might need to utilize it.

When he rounded the landing, he paused again, peering up the stairs.

No shadowed forms moved.

He tapped on his enchantment and left it active. If nothing else, he wanted Gaspar and Wrenlow to be aware of what he was doing. That was if they were even listening.

Gavin had gotten too excited about taking a job on his own. That was a mistake.

I've become too reliant on others.

Maybe that was a mistake as well.

Gavin crept up the stairs. When he reached the top of the stairs, he still hadn't seen anyone. He paused at the heavy wooden doors lining the hallway here.

The first one was a closet. He knew that from the last time that he had been here. He pushed it open, peering inside briefly, but saw nothing.

He headed along the hall, checking each door that he came upon, but there was nothing inside any of the doors.

Most of them were bedrooms, and when he had been here before, rescuing Alex, he had worked his way through these bedrooms, searching them until he had found what he needed.

This time, he found nothing.

No one to fight. No sign of the Captain.

Nothing.

He glanced down at the dagger.

It still hadn't started to glow.

Gavin relaxed a little. It meant that he was too late. Whoever had come here had probably abducted the Captain.

When he had finished searching this level, he paused at

the top of the stairs. There had still been no sign of the Captain.

This couldn't be all of it, though. If he had a storeroom filled with enchantments, enough that would have filled the warehouse like he had seen with Gaspar, then Gavin had to find where he had kept them.

He started down the stairs. He paused at the bottom of the stairs, looking over to the body, but there was no sign that anybody else had been there. Gavin was tempted to take the enchantments off the body, but they obviously hadn't been effective in protecting that man, so they would likely do nothing for him, either.

He searched along this level. He found the kitchen, a massive dining room, and what looked to be a banquet hall—all empty. By the time he reached the main entrance, he had started to think that he might not find the Captain or what had happened to him.

There had to be more.

"Gavin?"

He breathed out a sigh, for once not annoyed to hear Wrenlow in his ear. "Wrenlow," Gavin whispered. "Do you remember the Captain's fortress layout?"

"I have it in my book." He could imagine Wrenlow flipping through pages, coming up to the depiction of the Captain's home. "Why?"

"Because the fortress has been attacked."

"Are you sure that you want to stay there by yourself?"

It was almost enough to make Gavin regret having

Wrenlow's voice in his ear. "Just tell me if there are more than the two levels."

"I don't need my diagram for that. There's a basement. I don't have any details on it, though. The sources we had, and that Gaspar was able to uncover, couldn't get us that information. Why?"

"Just a hunch." Gavin swept his gaze around the inside of the entryway. "Where's the basement?"

"There should be a staircase somewhere. Again, I don't have a lot of details. I think there might be an access from the upper level."

"The upper level?"

"That's what I have in my notes. It's why no one had any information about it."

Balls.

He had looked there, though it had been a cursory glance.

He hurried up, already thinking where it would be. When he reached the room that belonged to the Captain, he passed through the large sitting room and made his way into the sleeping chamber.

There was a door along the back wall.

Gavin tested it. It was unlocked.

He pulled it open, and surprisingly, there was a narrow staircase that led down.

"Found it," he said.

Gavin hurried down, holding the dagger out in front of him, watching for any sign of any glowing. If there was anybody using enchantments down here, then he wanted to ensure that he was prepared.

He found nothing.

The stairs were steep and headed down deep into the fortress.

This had to be it.

When they ended, he found another door. This one was massive. Iron. Symbols were worked into the door. Likely enchantments. Gavin tested it and found that it was unlocked.

That was enough to tell him that something was amiss.

He pushed it open and stepped into an enormous room. Rows of shelves and tables had dozens upon dozens of items stacked on them. They were all of various sizes, metal, and glass and wood—likely all enchantments.

This was the Captain's enchantment vault.

A body lay sprawled out near him.

Gavin hurried over.

It was the Captain.

He was a muscular man, solidly built, though older with graying hair. He wore enchantments all along both arms, as well as a chain necklace around his neck. Whoever had knocked him down had enough skill—and power—to handle somebody with enchantments.

Balls.

That meant a sorcerer. It had to.

The Captain wasn't dead. He rolled his head, looking at Gavin.

"What happened?" Gavin whispered.

"Don't let him take it."

Gavin frowned. "Take what?"

"Don't. Let. Take it."

The Captain reached for Gavin's arm, holding his gaze for a moment, but then life faded from his eyes.

Gavin looked up.

Somebody slammed into him, knocking him back, and went racing up the stairs.

CHAPTER FIVE

Gavin got to his feet. As he did, he felt power building. He had no idea how he could feel it, only that he was aware of it. This entire room was a massive vault. He didn't know what the enchantments in the room were, or what the Captain intended gathering them all here, but the fact that he had kept them hidden suggested that they were powerful.

Gavin needed a chance to find the necklace.

But he needed to know who had attacked here.

He looked down to the Captain.

Don't let him take it.

What had the attacker taken?

Gavin looked at the rest of the vault. He could sort through this later. He could find the necklace later.

For now…

Now he needed to find the attacker.

After checking the Captain—he was dead, as far as

Gavin's cursory check could reveal—he raced up the stairs, and by the time he reached the door at the top of the stairs, he found it locked. He summoned the power within him through his core reserves and slammed into the door, forcing it open. It thundered as it crashed open.

Gavin tore through the sleeping chamber, to the sitting room, and then down the stairs. There was still no sign of the attacker.

He reached the door leading out of the fortress.

A shadowed form appeared on top of the wall. They were moving fast.

It had to be a sorcerer, though as Gavin looked at the El'aras dagger, it still hadn't started to glow. If it was a sorcerer, then they weren't using any power.

What have I gotten myself into now?

He pulled the door to the fortress closed and raced forward, reaching the wall, using a surge of power through his core reserves to jump.

When he did, he could feel the power surging within him, and he reached the top of the wall.

He hesitated there.

Where's the attacker?

They were still out there. Somewhere.

Gavin swept his gaze around him.

There.

He saw a shadowed form racing through the streets.

Gavin jumped, landing in a run.

"Wrenlow," he said as he raced forward. "The Captain is dead. I'm chasing his attacker."

"Are you sure you want to do that?"

Gavin ignored that question. "If you can reach Gaspar, I might need his help."

He caught another glimpse of the shadowed form streaking down the street and raced after them. He had to get to them. Somehow.

Gavin ran as quickly as possible, but it seemed as if the attacker made their way even faster than Gavin.

They had to be enchanted, though as he looked down at the El'aras dagger, he saw no sign of glowing.

"What can you tell me?" Wrenlow asked.

Gavin didn't know whether he should be relieved that he had Wrenlow in his ear or irritated. At this point, he needed to just chase the person down.

I wouldn't have found the basement without Wrenlow's help.

Reminding himself of that didn't make him feel that much better.

"Probably a sorcerer. The Captain was heavily enchanted. Whoever got to him took him out quickly."

Not only him but all his guards.

If there was just one attacker, whoever they were was skilled.

A skilled sorcerer in the city.

Why did that strike him too much like the Mistress of Vines?

And another attack on the Captain.

Only this one Gavin had failed to stop.

He didn't feel that much remorse at his death. Especially not with the Captain willingly moving his enchantments out of the city, posing a danger to the delicate peace within the city. Still, Gavin wanted to know what had happened and wanted to find the attacker, if only so he could uncover why the person was operating in the city.

Don't let him take it.

Whatever the sorcerer had taken—and Gavin was convinced that it was a sorcerer—was dangerous enough that the Captain feared them having it.

What could the Captain have had within his vault that would be that dangerous?

Another flicker of movement, and Gavin hurried forward.

Finally, he saw the figure slowing.

Gavin slowed along with them. There was no point in racing after this person until he had a chance to figure out where they were going. Only then would he make his move.

Gavin slipped along the street, trying to see through the cloud of night. This part of the city was older, all stone buildings. Some of them had crumbled, though most remained intact, a sign of the Yoran that once had been. A few streetlights were staggered, though the light they cast was dim and muted. Shadows lingered, spreading outward like a fog in the night. A gentle breeze carried a hint of the forest just at the edge of Yoran, but the scent was buried beneath the stench of the city.

He thought the figure moved toward a home at the end of the street but couldn't be sure. The storefronts in this part of the city were bunched tightly together, which had served him well when needing to run along the rooftops, though a few had too much space between them. The streetlight barely reflected off the glass. As he went farther, the shops began to change over to houses. None of these places was his target, anyway.

"What do you see?" Wrenlow asked, his voice coming through the enchantment Gavin wore in his ear.

He moved carefully, turning from side to side and looking for any sign of movement. He held the El'aras dagger in one hand, which was less obtrusive than the magical sword he also carried. At least with the dagger, he wouldn't draw nearly as much attention from the constables.

"There's a row of houses here," Gavin said. He described to Wrenlow where he'd followed the man.

"There shouldn't be anything out there. Not that I've learned."

"Other than his hideout?"

"That might be true. I wonder what kind of place—"

"Still need to be quiet," he whispered.

Gavin smiled, though he did need for Wrenlow to ease back on the constant chatter in his ear. The enchantment allowed only him to hear anything from that side, though he wasn't sure whether anyone else could overhear their conversation. Certainly, someone might hear his whispering. More than that, Wrenlow continually talking in his ear made it so Gavin couldn't hear what was taking place around him.

He reached the end of the street. So far, there was

nothing but darkness all around him, and he didn't see anything else in the night. The attacker had disappeared.

Gavin gripped the dagger, glancing down at the blade. It hadn't started to glow. For as little magic as presumably existed within Yoran, he'd encountered more than his share of magic users. The blade would expose most of them to him.

But not this person.

"Where are you?" Wrenlow whispered again.

"Near the end of the street. I'll keep looking, but—"

There came a flurry of movement in front of him.

The attacker.

They had taken out the Captain and everyone in his house easily.

He had to be careful.

Gavin spun back against the building. He tried to keep as quiet as he could, dancing across the ground, but his feet dragged a little more loudly than he intended. Gaspar would be disappointed. For that matter, he was disappointed in himself.

A breeze gusted across his face from the suddenness of the movement coming toward him. Instinct, as well as training that had been honed over countless years, kicked in.

He pinned himself back against the wall, focusing on what he could feel, not so much what he could see. In all the times that he'd trained over the years, Gavin had gained some skill hiding in darkness. Learning how to fight in the dark had been one of Tristan's most important lessons.

There came a slight puff of wind.

Gavin darted forward with the El'aras dagger and slammed his fist forward. It met nothing but air. He swung back and swept around in a circle, waiting for a sign of anyone else who might be there. He didn't find anyone.

Again, he twisted.

Again, there came nothing.

Gavin hesitated and ducked a little lower, pushing his head back against the wall. He tried to stare into the darkness, but he couldn't see or feel anything.

"What's happening?" Wrenlow's voice crackled too loudly.

Something slammed into his belly. He tensed and suppressed the pain immediately. He swung his leg out and connected with something. He continued to sweep his leg forward and followed through. Gavin rolled forward in the Sudo technique, then crashed to the ground.

It's too loud. All of this is too loud.

Gavin hurriedly smacked at the enchantment, silencing it. What had he been thinking, leaving it active? He had enough experience with Wrenlow chattering away in his ear, and he should have known better than to keep the enchantment enabled.

Somebody wiggled beneath him.

Gavin lifted them and slammed them back against the cobblestones. He punched rather than using the knife, not wanting to kill. Incapacitation was fine, but nothing more than that. Not until he knew more about why they'd targeted the Captain.

Gavin quickly rolled off to the side, and he lay there for a moment, waiting.

This person was tall and lanky.

Not the person he'd seen in the Captain's fortress.

Gavin didn't notice anyone else near him, but in the darkness…

Not so dark anymore. The dagger glowed softly with yellow light. Magic.

Of course.

He'd suspected a sorcerer had attacked the Captain. This confirmed it.

Gavin borrowed the pale light glowing from the dagger as he looked around him. The light allowed him to see more than he'd been able to otherwise, and it revealed a hint of movement. The shadowed street seemed to press upon him, as if the shadows themselves were ready to attack.

That was all he needed.

He slipped low, shifting his pattern, and dove toward the sign of movement. He rolled onto the other person, who grunted. Gavin needed to be more careful than that.

Gavin jumped to his feet and kicked the downed man. He spun in place, swinging his gaze around. There wasn't anything nearby. Gavin held out the dagger, which continued to glow. He steadied his breathing.

Whoever was using the magic had to be close.

He slipped along the street carefully. In the distance, he caught sight of a dark figure on the far side of the street near a home with a small red awning.

The dagger surged brighter.

He darted forward, moving as quickly as he could. The dagger revealed his presence, but it didn't matter at this point.

All that mattered was that he got to—

Something wrapped around him.

Magic.

Gavin was trapped. The figure on the far side of the street stalked toward him. They were cloaked, and though he couldn't see anything underneath the cloak, he could feel the presence there. The figure continued to wrap bands of power around him, swirling them from head to toe.

Gavin focused on the core reserves of power that existed deep within him. He felt it now as a vast store of energy buried deep within him. Magic energy.

In the time that he'd been in Yoran, he had struggled with trying to come to grips with why he'd have the ability to call upon that kind of magic and what it would do for him. But he had no answers. Unless he had an opportunity to find his old mentor—a man who was supposed to be dead but who Gavin believed still lived—he wouldn't have answers as to why his training had taught him to access power that he was not supposed to reach.

Tristan had never trained those with magic. He had trained fighters. He had trained healers. He had trained poisoners. In the time that Gavin had lived in the barracks and trained with Tristan and the others, there had been no attempt to use magic—nothing other than what he'd been taught and the way he'd been used to break through chains.

Now it would have to allow him to break through something else.

As he held on to that energy, this person—who Gavin believed was a sorcerer rather than just an enchanter—came closer to him.

"You should stay out of my business," the sorcerer said.

"What did you take?" Gavin asked.

Don't let him take it.

The Captain had been concerned enough about whatever had gone missing.

The sorcerer stopped about two paces away from him, as if knowing Gavin might be able to break free. "You should stay out of my business," he said again.

"You don't need to repeat yourself." Gavin breathed out steadily, and he held on to power within him. All it would take would be for him to expand that sense of the core reserves and blast through it.

He had done it before. He had no idea how powerful the sorcerer was, but he had to figure out what was going on. Why would there be *another* sorcerer in the city? Not only that, but why would they be moving at this time of night? And out here?

"I've heard there's someone like you in the city. Someone quite meddlesome," the sorcerer said.

He was the right size and build for the one he'd seen at the Captain's fortress, but had that person had a beard like this sorcerer? He'd been knocked over too fast to tell.

"Meddlesome?" Gavin said. Who was this person? They seemed far too calm for someone who had just broken into

—and killed everyone—at the Captain's fortress. "I'm more than just meddlesome."

He used everything that he could from the core reserves and exploded outward against the barrier. He expected that it would burst him free.

Only it didn't.

The barrier around him bulged, but it didn't shatter.

Shit.

He should have expected it to be more challenging than that.

The sorcerer took a step toward him. Gavin managed to shift his hand just a little bit, enough for him to grab the hilt of the sword he carried.

"Interesting," the sorcerer said.

His voice was deep and carried with it a bit of a grating quality that left Gavin on edge. Too many sorcerers were like that. The man was tall, and he exuded a sense of energy. He had dark robes that draped around him, and his balding head gleamed in the faint moonlight. He held one hand out from him, which Gavin knew meant that he was preparing to use a spell, though Gavin was ready to carve through any magic. With the El'aras dagger, along with whatever the sword could do, he didn't have to worry about the magic of any sorcerer.

"Who are you?" the man asked.

Gavin braced for the inevitable squeeze of power. The bands constricted around him, and he remained ready for the sorcerer to try something different. Thankfully, it seemed as if the sorcerer were mostly concerned about why Gavin could resist the magic.

What he needed was to unsheathe the sword. The sword could cut through magic, and in this case, he'd need to use the blade to escape.

Gavin called upon the core reserves again, summoning them from deep within, and then he exploded outward. The energy around him bulged once more.

He tensed and pulled on the blade, drawing it out of the scabbard. It was free, but the bands of magic constricted him again, preventing him from doing anything with the sword.

The sorcerer took another step toward him, unmindful of what Gavin might be able to do.

Let him feel that way, Gavin thought.

He pushed again, resisting the magic. He was running low on energy, and he didn't know how much more he might be able to withstand. Using that energy, he could resist the bands of power around him, but there was the danger he could weaken himself to the point where he wouldn't be able to fight.

Gavin pushed one more time. The bindings bulged, spreading away from him, and he was able to bring the blade up. He carved through the bindings, parting them on either side of the sword.

The sorcerer gasped. He took a step back, but Gavin slammed the hilt of the sword against the sorcerer's forehead. The bright white light within the blade flickered for a moment before fading.

Gavin dragged the sorcerer back to the edge of the street and looked around. In the darkness, it was difficult for him to see anything else nearby. Maybe he should have left the sorcerer awake long enough for him to use the light of the blade to make sure everything was safe.

He crouched near the sorcerer, who didn't exude the same strength as he had when standing. Maybe there was an element of an enchantment in the way he had used that power. He searched him briefly but didn't find anything on his person. The fabric of his robes was incredibly soft, and there was a hidden embroidery worked within it.

Finally, he tapped on his enchantment. "I caught the person who killed the Captain. I think. A sorcerer."

"Again?" Wrenlow asked.

"This one had a different technique."

"What sort?"

"I'm not entirely sure. He attempted to use a different kind to hold me."

"Attempted?"

"Well, it worked for a little while," Gavin said.

He dragged the sorcerer backward, and Gavin quickly reached into his pouch and pulled out a length of enchanted rope. He tied the rope around the sorcerer's wrists and ankles, binding them tightly, then moved into an alley.

Gradually, the sorcerer started to come around. The sword glowed softly. Gavin crouched next to him again and held the blade up near the sorcerer.

He smiled at him. "You and I are going to have a conversation."

The sorcerer looked up at Gavin and glanced toward the blade, and then he started to jerk on the ropes.

"Enchanted," Gavin said. He lifted the sorcerer, propping him up against the wall. Thankfully, the sword continued to glow. He needed the light to see and to ward off the darkness that he hated. "If you try to wrap me in bands of power again, you'll see that I don't have nearly as much patience the second time. Now, you and I are going to talk," Gavin said again.

The sorcerer snarled at him. "You have made a grave mistake."

"The only mistake I made was not knowing there would be another stinking sorcerer out here tonight."

"You would attack one of the Fates?"

"I'm more than happy to attack fate, though I don't think that's what you're getting at."

"No, you fool. The Fates."

Gavin slammed the hilt of the sword back into the sorcerer's forehead again. He dragged him along the alley as he held on to the blade.

Thankfully, it maintained a hint of light that glowed from it, though Gavin no longer knew if any of that light came from him. He thought it was mostly coming from the sorcerer, though there were times when the blade glowed that made him question whether he was the one responsible for it.

"Are you catching any of that?" Gavin asked into the enchantment.

"I don't know anything about the Fates," Wrenlow said.

"I guess I'm bringing him back to the Dragon to question him," Gavin said.

"I'm sure Jessica is going to be thrilled."

He reached the central part of the street before pausing.

"Why was he out here?" he wondered.

"You want to figure this out now?"

"I need to know what he was after."

The house with the red awning.

What was he after there?

Gavin dragged the sorcerer along the street. Maybe it would be better if he carried him, but with the way the sorcerer had attacked, what were a few bruises?

The street narrowed as he walked, the buildings on either side of him seeming as if they pressed in upon him. The air carried a dampness to it mixed with a foul stink. A cat cried out somewhere nearby, and Gavin tensed a moment. There was nothing else.

He stayed cautious as he made his way down the street, worried that he might need to use the darkness to conceal himself. Most of these buildings were still houses, but not all of them were. Some were larger, and some were much more impressive than others, and all their windows were dark. It didn't take long to find the one with the awning again.

Gavin started toward it, still dragging the sorcerer. He felt something. It was like the wind shifting, nothing more than that, but with the darkness and him already being on edge, Gavin dropped low.

Something whistled over his head.

Gavin grunted in frustration and swept the sword around in a tight arc. It met a hint of resistance and then cleaved straight through it. There was a cry and a spray of warmth.

He grabbed the sorcerer, dragging him toward the building. He wasn't about to pause to think about who he'd killed.

This was *not* how this night was to have gone.

Just question the Captain. That was it.

Things were never as simple as he intended. This was no exception.

He reached the building, still dragging the sorcerer. A soft shuffling movement came from behind him, and Gavin turned, holding the blade up. Through the hint of glowing, he detected five shadowed figures. They wouldn't be more than he could manage, but the noise would be considerable. Even though he couldn't make out all the details, they were of varying heights. Two of them wore dresses, while the other three had on jackets and pants. One of the women had a hat tilted on her head, angled off to the side and shading her face. The shadows that lingered near the figures made them difficult to see.

He glanced down at the sorcerer. He was still out.

The five started toward him. Gavin held out the blade. None of them seemed armed with swords, which almost made it an unfair fight.

"You really don't want to do this," he said.

No one answered, and Gavin shook his head before starting toward them.

He slipped the sword back into the sheath. Then he called upon the remaining energy within him and jumped. The power allowed him to launch up and over those closest, landing in the middle of them.

He dropped down, swinging his leg around and tripping one man, and he caught him in the midsection as he fell. Gavin twisted and spun, and he kicked at another. His heel caught the man in the knee, and he brought his fist up, driving it into the man's face. There was a satisfying crunch as something broke.

Twisting again, he slammed his elbow into another of the attackers that tried to get too close to him. Gavin drove it all the way through and brought his fist back up, catching the attacker in the forehead.

He jumped, using a hint of the core reserves to gain height. He rotated in the air and spun his legs out from him. As he did, he kicked and connected with the forehead of another one of the attackers. Gavin grinned as he landed, though now only one man was remaining.

"You're skilled," the man said.

Gavin smirked. "You have no idea."

"You made a mistake, though."

"What was that?"

"You left him alone," the man replied.

Almost too late, Gavin realized the sorcerer was behind him. Gavin spun and felt something starting to sneak around him. He'd sheathed the sword. He'd also used up considerable reserves.

He called upon a hint of that energy, enough to flow

through him, and jumped. It carried him up and swept him away from the magic trying to wrap around him. Gavin unsheathed the sword in that movement and flipped in the air, carving through the band of magic as he landed.

Somehow, the sorcerer had managed to free his hands and legs, which suggested there was somebody else with him.

Where are they?

Magic made the blade glow brightly, and Gavin spun in place, searching for a sign of the attacker. He didn't see anyone, but they had to be here.

Another burst of power came from behind him. *Another sorcerer?* It would explain how the sorcerer he'd brought here had gotten out so easily.

Gavin darted toward a nearby alley. If nothing else, he needed to figure out what the sorcerer had taken from the Captain. He reached the alley, and power started to build. The blade was glowing, and Gavin swept out with it, slashing at the energy he detected.

The sorcerers turned toward him, spreading out. They glowed brightly. Gavin hadn't seen anything quite like that before.

The first sorcerer grinned at him.

Shit.

A burst of energy exploded into him, knocking Gavin into the alley.

"What's going on?" Wrenlow asked.

"Ambush," Gavin muttered. "It seems as if the sorcerer I

thought I'd contained managed to break free of the enchanted ropes."

"How is that even possible?"

"How am I supposed to know? I'm no sorcerer."

The ropes had been enchanted by Olivia, an enchantress who should've managed to hold a sorcerer with them. When she had bound Gavin in those ropes to test their strength, he had to draw upon a considerable source of power to break free of the bindings. Not that he was more powerful than a sorcerer, but he *did* have experience breaking through bindings. That they would fail against a sorcerer—and so quickly—surprised him.

Gavin needed to try a different approach. Staying here wasn't going to be the safest strategy. He had to get out of here. He could figure out what they'd taken from the Captain later.

Escape first.

The dagger flashed with an occasional pulse of power, suggesting that magic continued to flare. That had to be the sorcerer. Gavin didn't see him anywhere nearby, but he could detect the use of magic reflected in the glow of the El'aras dagger. He could practically feel something as it slammed against the building, though he didn't know if that came from the sorcerer or if there was somebody out there with enchantments. If it was someone with enchantments, Gavin had a better chance of dealing with them. If it was the sorcerer…

He had to be careful anyway because he had limited

reserves of power. Not like the sorcerer, who seemed to have incredible access to magic.

Another blast struck at him.

Gavin raced toward one of the darkened buildings and slammed a shoulder into it, realizing as he did that he'd headed toward the building with the red awning. With a burst through his core reserves, he popped the door open. The room was empty. Gavin backed in. Power continued to build from the sorcerer.

He had to escape.

"Balls," he whispered.

"What was that?" Wrenlow asked.

"I'm not going to be able to get out this way."

"You could take them on."

"I've already used too much energy," Gavin muttered.

"Then run," Wrenlow said.

His only option was to go through the back of the building.

Gavin backed up and felt movement behind him.

He spun, sweeping the sword, and managed to cut through a surge of magic. The blade glowed brightly, and the sorcerer that was there was not supposed to be there.

How did they appear behind me?

Gavin darted forward. He rolled into another room, threw the door closed, and jumped to his feet. The room was empty, much like the last. No decorations. A rug across the floor but no furniture. Nothing other than a window. That was the only other way out of here.

Gavin raced toward the window and pushed it open, and

he looked out into the night. The window looked out onto an alleyway. He paused for a moment, lingering as he looked down, then jumped through the window.

He crept back along the alley. "You need to give me directions from here," he told Wrenlow.

"Where are you?"

"An alley outside of a window off the back of the building."

"What do you want me to do about it?" Wrenlow asked.

"I was hoping you might be able to offer me someplace to go for safety," he said.

There was silence for a moment, and Gavin continued making his way along the alley, looking from side to side for any sign of movement. He didn't notice anything, but he couldn't tell if he was alone or not. For all he knew, he was not. The sorcerer had surprised him—twice. It wouldn't be a stretch to think it could happen again. He listened to the sounds of the street, but he didn't detect anything else out there with him.

Gavin watched the blade to see if it might glow. "Wrenlow?"

"I'm trying to help you, but…"

"But what?"

Wrenlow sighed. "If you're in the part of the city I think you are, I don't see any way for you to go."

"What do you mean?" Gavin asked.

"If you are where I think you are, then there isn't any place for you to go."

Gavin frowned, trying to think of another option.

Shadowed movement came down the alley, and his sword started to glow.

Magic.

The damn sorcerers.

Worse, he was trapped.

CHAPTER SIX

Gavin was in a fenced-in area, the walls towering overhead, and much as Wrenlow had suggested, there really wasn't any way for him to escape other than heading back in to face the sorcerers he detected.

He looked for another possibility.

The sword continued glowing, and it took on an increasing brightness compared to what it had before. Gavin didn't know if that meant the sorcerers were getting close, but he suspected it couldn't be anything good.

"There might be something you can try." Wrenlow's voice came through the enchantment.

Gavin waited. He couldn't see anything on the other side of the walls but increasingly thought that he would have to try.

"If my map is correct"—and Wrenlow's tone of voice suggested that he would be shocked if it weren't—"then if you take the wall to your left, there should be an alley to buildings over, and from there—"

"I'm on it."

Gavin took a running start at the wall, and he jumped, pushing off while summoning power from his core reserves at the same time. The jump carried him up, higher than he would've expected, and he reached the top of the wall more easily than he had anticipated. He landed there, and it gave him a moment to pause. The sword continued to glow, and Gavin scrambled forward, jumping to a nearby rooftop until he found the alley Wrenlow had described.

Gavin backed along the alley as quickly as he could, looking in either direction. He was cautious as he moved through the streets, cautious as he headed along the alley. He gripped the El'aras dagger tightly, watching for signs of the glowing light that signified magic. So far, there had been nothing.

The streets were quiet as well. He didn't know what to make of that, only that with the silence, any movement he made would be noticeable. He had to be careful. He didn't need to be drawing any extra attention to himself.

The wind whistled softly, increasing in intensity since the last time he'd heard it, and an occasional rumble of thunder came in the distance. Maybe there would be a storm. There hadn't been many in his time in Yoran. He didn't know if a storm would help or hinder him.

"Gavin?"

"Just a moment," he whispered. "I think there's something here."

"What is it?"

"Some sort of danger coming my way," Gavin said. He rested his back against a building in the alley, looking in either direction. The alley was completely dark, and he saw no movement. He held out the El'aras dagger but didn't find anything with that either.

"What sort of danger?" Wrenlow asked.

"The kind that involves men creeping toward me," Gavin said.

"What type of men?"

"The dangerous type."

He reached the alley.

Gavin didn't like his odds if there was a sorcerer, not as tired as he felt. The use of his core reserves had tapped enough of his strength that he wasn't sure he had enough to try it again. If it came down to attempting to use it or dying, he would have no choice, but he didn't like those possibilities.

Gavin looked up at the buildings. There was darkness overhead, but he might be able to scale the walls. He had done it before. He'd learned a specific fighting style, Pakol, that helped him stretch out his arms and legs away from him and scramble along that way. The ancient fighting style was all about fluidity and rapid movements, avoiding quick and sudden jolts. The fluidity allowed him to bound his way up the walls, but only if he worked quickly. It depended on where he climbed as well. Gavin wasn't entirely sure that this place was quite as stable as he needed for the technique to be effective.

The blade continued to glow, exposing him. He sheathed the sword. There was no way for him to climb while holding on to the blade, but he couldn't see anything without it. He might be able to feel something or detect anything nearby, but he would have to work quickly.

Gavin pushed off the side of the building and kicked his way up. Climbing that way allowed him the opportunity to scale the side of the building, and he reached for the rooftop.

Something whipped beneath him. Gavin lifted himself up, managing to get above whatever grabbed him right before something else pulled at him.

He rolled onto the roof and sprang to his feet, then started running. He unsheathed the El'aras dagger, wanting something to warn him of a magical attacker nearby. The dagger glowed, lighting his way. Though he knew he should be concerned by that glow, he was still thankful for the benefit it offered.

Gavin followed the slope of the roof. He tried to hurry as quickly as he could, but he stumbled. As he rolled down the rooftop, the thundering of footsteps caught his attention. He tried to brace himself, worried about crashing into the next building or even tumbling off the rooftop, but he skittered to a stop. Thankfully, he didn't slide all the way off. If he had, though, at least he liked his odds. He knew how to twist while falling, and he could careen to the ground without crashing and breaking too much. Besides that, he healed relatively well.

He stood up and turned toward the sound of footsteps.

Somebody was chasing him.

He jumped from one rooftop to the next, clearing an alley. As he did, he paused, looking down at the El'aras dagger. It didn't glow nearly as brightly as it had been before.

Gavin looked behind him. At least three pursuers.

So much for one person responsible for what had happened to the Captain.

There had only been the one, though.

He didn't think these attackers had magic, given how the light of the dagger was fading. That didn't mean they weren't dangerous, though, only that they weren't going to attack him from a distance. He jumped across another alley, racing up the sloped slate rooftop, and then jerked to a stop.

Something held on to him, wrapping around him and keeping him from moving. Gavin tried to lunge against it, to surge past that sense of power, but he couldn't do it. There was too much magic used against him.

He attempted to reach for that core reserve of power deep within him, but there wasn't much left. If he were to pull on it, he didn't know if he could survive the attempt.

He had to try a different technique. He strained again to get free but couldn't get through. Every attempt failed.

Gavin's El'aras dagger started to glow even more brightly.

He needed strength.

"Gavin?"

In his concentration, he hadn't been listening to Wrenlow. Even now, as he heard his friend's voice, he didn't know if he could speak loud enough for Wrenlow to hear him. With the type of magic used on him, it was possible it would restrict him from doing anything—and saying anything.

"Sorcerer," he whispered.

"Where are you?"

"Rooftop."

"Can you do anything?" Wrenlow asked.

"No."

The movement behind him loomed even closer.

Gavin could already feel the magic constricting him. He didn't have enough strength to break the magical bands. All he had was the El'aras dagger.

Is there any way to channel power into that?

"Where on the rooftop?" Wrenlow said.

Gavin took a deep breath, flicking his gaze around. "I don't know. Several streets over from where I was first attacked."

"I'll see what I can do."

Gavin almost laughed, knowing there was nothing that Wrenlow could do to help him. He was alone. Any help Wrenlow might send wouldn't get to him in time.

Power continued to squeeze him, and he fought against it, straining to see if there was any way that he could break free. He continued to struggle, feeling the sense of energy coalescing around him.

The sound of footsteps across the rooftop drew his attention, and Gavin turned his head to see where the footsteps were coming from. As he focused, he tried once more to draw upon the core reserves of energy within him. Gavin called on that, letting that sense of power bubble up within him.

There had to be something that he could do; some way to reach that energy.

The footsteps were coming closer, and the three attackers were moving across the rooftop as well. The combination of the two would be more than what Gavin could withstand.

Irritation filled him—something he might be able to use, to help him summon energy. When it came to calling upon his core reserves, it was all about finding strength.

The band of power around him squeezed even more. Gavin reached deep within him. He held on to that sense of energy, and the power bulged. It was only a little bit, enough that he felt the energy starting to slide. He shifted his arm that was holding the dagger so that he could pull it up. He placed the dagger near his chest.

The blade faced outward, and Gavin held it tightly, squeezing it as the magic pressed against him. He twisted the end of the blade and pushed it slowly forward. Gradually, he could feel the blade cutting through the magic.

The sorcerer who approached him used even more power as he did, drawing upon enough magic to crush Gavin.

Now that Gavin held the El'aras dagger up, he had some control over the blade. He might be able to use that control and find the key to breaking the power wrapping around him.

More power squeezed him again. Gavin ignored it, focusing instead on the dagger. It was the only thing he could concentrate on, the only energy he had. He'd have to use what he could of the dagger to find the strength to break free.

Gavin twisted the blade. He tilted, just enough that he could cut into the spell. As he did, the spell squeezing around him started to shift. And relax.

He tried again. This time, he attempted a different technique.

"Gavin? They shouldn't be long."

"Who shouldn't be long?" he said through gritted teeth.

"Help."

He didn't think he had time to wait for help. Wrenlow would likely have called Gaspar or maybe even Imogen. She might be able to help, but only if she got here in time. He'd seen her handle the Mistress of Vines, so he knew a sorcerer didn't terrify her, but this felt different somehow.

Gavin twisted, forcing the blade forward. It carved slowly, the magic holding him starting to fade, but the footsteps sounded even closer to him. He shoved the El'aras dagger outward, drawing upon the last of his strength—at least, what he thought was the last of his strength.

The magic holding him slithered away. Gavin danced back and dropped low, narrowly avoiding the sorcerer's next attempt at trying to wrap him in power. As he did, Gavin brought the El'aras dagger up overhead.

He rolled down the sloped roof, banging his knee on a metal chimney. He didn't want to stay here any longer than was necessary, and at least having these others near him gave him an opportunity. Gavin took that chance by rolling, and he slammed into something.

He didn't see anything, only felt the resistance against him when he rammed into it. He tried to get back to his feet, but he struggled. Gavin slashed outward with the El'aras dagger. The blade carved through magic, not an attacker. The magic exploded around him, and he tumbled to the side, kicking.

He barely escaped, and he rolled again, this time spinning his legs and sliding down the rooftop. When he reached the edge of it, he dropped to the street below.

Gavin had no idea where he was, only that he had to move as quickly as he could. The sound of pursuit roared behind him as he ran. He ignored that, focusing on sprinting. Only, he couldn't head straight toward the Dragon.

If the pursuers knew it was him out there and discovered where he was staying, the tavern would be attacked. Again. Gavin wasn't going to be responsible for the Dragon getting attacked a second—or, really, a third—time.

What he had to do was take a roundabout way, but even that might not be the most effective. Wrenlow might have called for help for him, but there might be other help he could summon. If only he could reach the enchanters.

They owe me, don't they?

Zella *had* sent the old lady to him. It was because of her that he'd gotten mixed up in whatever this was.

Gavin raced ahead and switched directions. Now, as he was running, he did so with a different purpose. He wasn't heading toward the Dragon but was instead heading through the city, trying to meander as quickly as he could but moving generally toward the enchanters. They were here somewhere.

Gavin held out the El'aras dagger, using the blade to help guide him, worried that there was still a hint of a glow to it. Magic was still out there, which meant he wasn't any safer. Fatigue washed over him, enough that he thought he might collapse, but he had to keep moving.

In the distance, the sounds of the city started to shift. Still, he could hear footsteps behind him. It was dark, late enough that he shouldn't see anything, but he could make out everything around him with the glowing dagger. Even the streetlights in the city had been extinguished for the night.

Gavin rounded a corner, and then he saw the building he sought. As he glanced over his shoulder, the steady sound of movement came toward him. The dagger continued to glow, getting brighter.

This was a mistake.

Gavin raced up to the short door made of darkened oak. None of the buildings nearby had lights on. The only thing that glowed was his dagger. He pounded on the door, worried that this wouldn't work.

"Open up," he said, hammering his fist on the door.

The dagger flashed with sudden bright light. Bands of power swirled around him.

He should've been holding the dagger up to his chest just in case, but he had made a mistake. He'd been using it for light, not protection. Gavin shifted his hands, and he brought the dagger back up, though even that wasn't enough. He couldn't move as the bands of power squeezed him.

Then he felt something else. Another sense of pressure behind him.

He glanced back over his shoulder, his head still able to move. The door was open, and darkness loomed on the other side.

Where are the sorcerers? Where are the other attackers?

Something exploded near him. The power holding on to him faded. Gavin stumbled, falling backward. There was another explosion, and then a third. They came one after another, relentless bursts of power.

He staggered back, collapsing into the building.

He scrambled deeper into the room. The door thudded shut. Gavin rolled over, pulling out the dagger. The room was small and simple, reminding him of the windowed room that he had darted out of while trying to find what he'd been hired to acquire. No decorations adorned the walls, and there was no furniture inside. In this room, there wasn't even a rug.

Just a figure looming in front of him.

Gavin looked up. "Thanks for the help, Zella."

CHAPTER SEVEN

Gavin leaned at the window, looking out. He didn't see any sign of his pursuers. That didn't mean they weren't out there. It just meant that he couldn't see them. Maybe the enchanters had intimidated the pursuers enough to give him space. He just didn't like the idea that he didn't know what was going on.

He also didn't like the idea that he was dealing with sorcery. Again.

It was times like these when he wished that he would have asked Olivia to create another enchantment. One that enhanced eyesight might not be a terrible idea. He refrained from using the enchantment he kept on him to augment his speed and strength. Becoming reliant upon that kind of enchantment could be dangerous if it meant that he'd end up depending upon it rather than his skill. He had trained far too long to lose that.

There was nothing but darkness out there, and as he

glanced down at the dagger, he knew that heading out wasn't quite safe just yet. The blade continued to glow with enough light that he knew he had to be cautious.

"Why have you brought this to us?" Zella asked.

"You're the one who got me involved," he started, pulling the note he still had in his pocket and holding it out to her, "so don't get on my case. Besides, it was the only thing I could think of doing."

"You could have handled it."

Gavin glanced over his shoulder. There were two other enchanters with her. One of them was Mekal, who glared at him, though not with the same intensity that he once had. Mekal looked to be in his mid-teens, though Gavin knew that he was older. His beard had filled in a little bit since Gavin had last seen him, and he had wide-set eyes and a dark shock of hair. He was a few inches shorter than Gavin, though taller than his brother, Kegan.

The other person with her had a youthful face that was unfamiliar to him.

"This is me handling it," Gavin said.

"By bringing danger to my people."

"Well, if it's any consolation, you started it."

Zella cocked her head, looking as if she wanted to say something, but she bit it back. She watched him with her deep brown eyes, her hawkish stare seeming to sweep over him, and he couldn't help but feel as if he wanted nothing more than to back away.

She had dark hair and a sharp chin, and though she looked young, she wasn't. None of the enchanters were actually young. All of them seemed to have frozen in time, the moment the enchantment had swept over the city and torn their families away from them. When power had shifted.

Gavin turned his attention back out to the street, looking through the window. "The Captain is dead. I went to talk to him. Got attacked by one person and followed him. Now there are at least two sorcerers here."

"We have detected three," she said.

Gavin glanced back. "Three?"

She nodded. "Three, but we have been able to erect enough of a barricade around us that prevents them from getting too close."

He frowned. "How long will something like that hold?"

"Long enough."

"Long enough for what?"

"For us to leave," she said.

Gavin smiled tightly. His time around Zella had proven just how strong she was, yet he doubted she wanted to tangle with any of the sorcerers. Despite her confident stance, he didn't think there was anything the enchanters could do against sorcerers like that.

"One of them called himself the Fate. Does that make any sense to you?"

Wrenlow hadn't known anything about the Fates, but Wrenlow wasn't nearly as plugged in to the magical world as Zella. Perhaps she would know something that Wrenlow wouldn't.

Her eyes widened.

"What is it?" Gavin asked.

"Are you sure that's what they said?"

"My hearing isn't bad," he said.

"They said the Fates?"

Gavin nodded.

Zella disappeared into a room at the back of the building, though he could still hear her shuffling around.

"Who is he?" Gavin asked Mekal, nodding to the newcomer before turning his attention back to the window.

"This is Jesol," Mekal said.

"What sort of enchantment skill does he have?" Gavin asked.

He had learned that the enchanters each had their own areas of expertise. Mekal was skilled with animating figurines that he created. Gavin had barely survived when Mekal had used one of those figurines against him.

"Many skills," Jesol said.

Gavin looked back and grinned at him. "Good."

"What do you expect to see out there?" Mekal asked, coming closer.

Gavin shook his head. "Maybe nothing. Maybe something."

"That really doesn't help," Mekal said.

"There were three attackers when I was on the roof, not counting the sorcerer. I figure that any one of them could be here. Of course, I can't see a damn thing, so I can't tell if they're out there."

Gavin continued peering out in the distance. Mekal

joined him at the window and stood alongside him, peering over his shoulder.

"You don't have to stand so close," Gavin said.

"I thought I would help."

"You're not helping by standing there." Gavin shifted his feet, moving over so that Mekal could look out with him.

He turned away from the window. There was no movement. There was nothing.

"I'm sure we could help you see better at night with an enchantment," Mekal said.

"No enchantment," Gavin said, tempting as it was.

"What do you have against them?"

"I don't have anything against enchantments, per se. It's just…" Gavin still preferred not to use enchantments if he could avoid it. There were only a few he trusted—like the one that allowed him to communicate with Wrenlow. If that failed, he didn't feel like he would be as lost as he might be were he to come to rely upon an enchantment for sight or speed or strength.

"You don't like us much," Jesol said.

Gavin glanced over at him. "I don't know you much. It's not a matter of liking or not."

"But you *don't* like us," Jesol said again.

Gavin grunted and looked around the room. The space was mostly empty. It had several enchantments around it. Because of those enchantments, they would be safe. He wouldn't have to worry about an attack, though there remained the possibility that he would still have to fight, were someone to come.

He waited for Zella to return, hoping to find out what she knew about the Fates.

"Have you heard anything about the Fates?" he asked, turning to Mekal.

"No, but I'm not as connected to that world as she is."

"That world?"

"The magical world," Mekal said.

"Why not?"

Mekal shrugged. "I suppose because I just haven't been as connected to it over the years."

Gavin wondered if Zella tried to protect her people, preventing them from accessing that world. It would make a certain sort of sense. Having more people involved in the magical world put them in danger—at least within Yoran. Other places wouldn't be nearly as dangerous.

He started to turn back for the window when Zella came from the back room.

"What is it?" he asked.

"I need to know more about this person you claim was here," she said.

"Not claim. Is here. Killed the Captain."

"You told me it was one of the Fates."

"Right, but what is that?"

"It doesn't make sense," she said, a deep frown creasing her face. "The Fates are a council of sorcerers. *The* council of sorcerers."

Gavin smiled slightly. "What?"

"Yes, and they are powerful. Dangerous. And they have

never come to Yoran before. They control magic everywhere. Like fate. They're *the* Fates."

"Then maybe it's not one of the Fates. Somebody like that wouldn't come here to take on the Captain."

"If they claimed that they were, then they were. There is incredible danger to any sorcerer who falsely claims to be one of the Fates."

"That doesn't make any sense," he said.

"Sense or not, it's the truth."

Gavin sighed. "So we have another sorcerer here."

"So? That's the only thing you can say? I'm telling you that it's one of the council of sorcerers, and your reaction is 'so.'"

"Well, you also said that they're not supposed to be in Yoran."

"It's not so much that they're not supposed to be here, it's that they've never been here before. If they have turned their attention to Yoran…"

Gavin frowned. "What makes you think they haven't been here before?"

"Because we've been left alone," she said.

"The city hasn't exactly been left alone," Gavin said.

"Not the city. Us. Enchanters." She glanced at the door, mouth pressed into a tight line. "Sorcerers and enchanters have a complicated relationship, and if they are here, they will try to use us. The same way the Mistress of Vines attempted to use us."

Gavin frowned even more. Neither Mekal nor Jesol were saying anything. "They may not know you're here."

"They may not have known before, but by you coming here, by us helping you, we've now alerted them, if reaching the Captain didn't do so already." Zella sighed, turning her attention toward Mekal. "Go make preparations."

"How many?" Mekal asked.

"As many as you can. I'm afraid we will need all of them."

Mekal glanced over at Gavin for a moment before turning and heading away.

Gavin shook his head. "It can't be all that bad."

"I can tell you what I know about the Fates," she said. "I don't have much experience with them. Most of us in Yoran don't, but what I do know is that they are harsh masters."

"Listen, Zella. I've explored much of the world, and I've seen plenty of harsh masters. I've been to Cambal, where the sorcerers rule. I've been to Bogot, where there's another type of magical rule. In both places, the leaders are ruthless, and they lead with violence and anger." And that wasn't even saying anything about when he had been hired to bring down the Tanran. She had been brutal, no different than so many other sorcerers who decided they could rule. "At least there's peace here. Now."

It was a relative peace, and Gavin knew that. The constables didn't chase the enchanters the way they once did, though Gavin wasn't so naïve to believe that everything had been resolved.

Zella narrowed her gaze at him. "You might've been to those places, but what I'm telling you is that the Fates are worse. I don't know as much as I probably should about the Fates. What I do know is that there are three of them. That we know of. There might be more, though they don't share their identity. Each is a sorcerer of incredible power. And ruthless. One does not simply become a sorcerer of incredible power without an element of ruthlessness. They rule over the Sorcerer's Society with power and authority, and they use that for them to rule over the other places you have mentioned. If one of the Fates has come to the city, they all may have. They are ruthless, after all, and I have a hard time thinking that one would allow another to claim whatever prize they are after on their own."

Prize?

Don't let him take it.

Gavin's brow furrowed. He had not been to some of those places in a while, and yet he still couldn't imagine that what she suggested was real. Given that he wasn't plugged in to the magical world all that much, he had no idea what was real and what was not. He didn't think that there was some sort of hidden ruler, though what did he really know?

"I doubt the Fates are here for you."

He wasn't sure, though.

Zella sighed. "And here I thought the Mistress of Vines was as bad as it was going to get." She turned to Jesol. "Watch the window."

"What about you?" Gavin asked.

"I have to go make my preparations."

She left him, and Gavin stood there for a moment, staring all around him. There wasn't anything for him here, and he couldn't help but feel as if he shouldn't stay here any longer.

"What are you doing?" Jesol asked.

"I think it's time for me to go," Gavin replied.

"She didn't say that you could go."

Gavin smiled at him. "Listen. You're new. At least, you're new to me. If you want to live, you're going to leave me alone."

Jesol pulled himself up, holding his gaze on Gavin. "You don't scare me."

"Then you haven't been paying attention."

Jesol eyed him for a moment, and as Gavin reached toward the door, the El'aras dagger started to glow. Gavin shook his head. He darted off to the side and twisted the blade, bringing the hilt up into Jesol's midsection and knocking the wind out of him.

Gavin stepped back, letting Jesol fall. "Like I said, you haven't been paying attention."

He reached for the door and pulled it open. Out in the street, darkness surrounded him. The magic that caused the El'aras dagger to glow had faded. There was little left of it, and he didn't see anything else he needed to be concerned about.

Gavin jogged along the street in a roundabout path, weaving his way toward the Dragon. He was troubled. If the Fates were as bad as what Zella said, then they were dangerous.

Don't let him take it.

What had the Fates been after?

Gavin wanted nothing more than to rest, but he didn't think he would get that chance. He slipped around through the alley, heading into the Dragon a different way. He didn't want to use the main entrance on the off chance somebody was watching and was aware of what he was doing.

When he stepped in, a strange surge of energy washed over him. It was an enchantment—and it was a new one. He stepped into the main part of the tavern and found Wrenlow slumped over a table, resting.

The Roasted Dragon was a comfortable and cozy tavern. With the hearth crackling and the heat of a considerable flame glowing inside, there was something quite welcoming about the place. Tables were scattered around, far more than needed these days. There had been a time when the tavern was busier, a time of music and dancing and activity, but ever since the El'aras had attacked, the tavern had fallen silent.

Jessica sat in a chair near one corner, the fire crackling warmly next to her, but she looked weary. Her chestnut-colored hair was pulled back in a braid, as usual. She wore an apron, though the only people she cooked for these days were Gavin and Wrenlow, and occasionally Gaspar and Imogen. Even that was increasingly uncommon.

"What's going on?" Gavin asked.

"You," she said, jumping to her feet, heading toward him. She punched him in the chest.

"What about me?" he asked, rubbing the spot she hit.

"You've been silent."

Gavin remembered he'd forgotten to turn his ear enchantment back on. "I've been a bit distracted." He was tempted to tell her about what happened but decided it would be better to share it one time with everyone.

"Just because you've been distracted doesn't mean that you don't have an obligation to us," she said.

"I'm not trying to ignore you," he said.

"What happened?"

"Let's talk when Wrenlow is awake." He looked around. "Do you have any food?"

She glowered at him. "You come into my tavern after having disappeared for most of the night, and the first thing you ask about is food?"

Gavin leaned forward and kissed her on the cheek. "I suppose I could ask about ale," he said.

She punched him in the chest again. "What happened?"

"Nothing. Well, maybe not nothing. More than what I expected."

"The last thing we heard, you were trapped on a rooftop."

"That wasn't the last time," Gavin whispered.

At least, he didn't think it was. The last time he talked to Wrenlow, he had been running through the streets and trying to figure out a safe place to go. It was right before he had gone to the enchanters. Only, now that he was here, he wondered if perhaps he should have been more forthright with Wrenlow.

Gavin headed toward the kitchen, and Jessica followed. The kitchen of the Roasted Dragon was a large space that had once been a bustling place of energy and activity. The smell of bread baking still permeated the kitchen, and several loaves rested on one counter. Two massive stoves lined the far wall, and a cabinet situated on the opposite wall had all the items that Jessica used in her cooking and baking. All the cooks that she'd once hired had stayed away after the attack.

He started working through the cupboards. Most of the time, Jessica had some food here, and whether it was dried food or leftovers, he didn't really care. At this point, the only thing that Gavin wanted was to find something to eat.

She ignored him as he sorted through cupboards. He grabbed some dried meat, then one of the loaves of bread, which he stacked onto a plate. He headed back out into the tavern's main part and took a seat at one of the tables near Wrenlow.

"Well?" she asked.

"Well what?"

"Are you going to talk about this?"

"I told you, when he comes around," Gavin said, nodding toward Wrenlow's sleeping form.

"Why?"

"Because I don't really know what to make of it."

"Gavin—"

"Whatever's happening might be dangerous," he said, then took a bite. "I don't know enough about it to be able to say with any certainty, but from what I can tell, there are dangerous sorcerers in the city. One of them killed the Captain, probably to take an enchantment."

Jessica sighed. "These days, there always are sorcerers."

He looked over to her. "But that hasn't always been the case, has it?"

She frowned, shaking her head. "No."

"Even though Yoran is not a place of magic, it seems like magic has converged upon it."

Wrenlow started to stir, coming around and groaning. His lean face was clean-shaven today, and his pale blue eyes flicked from Gavin to Jessica for a moment before settling back on Gavin. He had a smudge of ink on his shirt, and there would likely be some on his fingers. Wrenlow always buried himself in his books. He took notes on all the different informants he'd gathered, coordinating them and trying to keep them organized. It was something that Gavin very much appreciated.

Wrenlow looked up. "Gavin?" he asked, squeezing his hand over his ear. "Are you still there?"

"I'm right here," Gavin said. Wrenlow's voice was loud in his ear, but it was also coming from across the room, creating a strange effect.

Wrenlow blinked and looked at Gavin. "What happened?"

"Well, it seems as if there is at least one incredibly dangerous sorcerer in the city, maybe three of them, and from what the enchanters tell me, they're powerful."

"You went to the enchanters?"

"I needed help, and I went to them to give me a chance to get away."

"I tried to send word to them, but…"

"You sent word to them?" Gavin asked.

Wrenlow nodded. "I figured that if anyone could help you with the sorcerer, it would be the enchanters, but I didn't realize you were dealing with more than one sorcerer."

"I didn't know I was either." Gavin took another bite of bread, chewing slowly. "We need to go back and look at everything we've done since coming to Yoran. Now with the Captain dead, I'm starting to become concerned about everything that's happened."

"Why?"

Gavin cocked his head at Wrenlow. "You need to wake up more. Your mind isn't working."

"My mind is working quite fine," Wrenlow said, rubbing sleep from his eyes. "I just don't really understand what you're getting at."

"Think about the jobs that we've had most recently. Cyran. The El'aras. The Captain and the Mistress of Vines. Now there's more than one sorcerer here, one of them incredibly powerful."

"You escaped from the most powerful sorcerers in the world?" Jessica asked, pulling the chair over and turning it toward him.

"I had help," Gavin said.

"If they're that powerful, then you shouldn't have been able to escape."

"Like I said, I had help."

"We need to get Gaspar involved," she said.

"He'll probably hear about it from the enchanters anyway."

Gavin finished eating, leaned back in the chair, and looked over at the fire. His mind raced, working through the jobs he and Wrenlow had done in the time they'd been in Yoran. Many of the jobs had been straightforward, but they'd all been on behalf of Cyran. What Gavin knew about Cyran was that he had been trying to gain power, wanting to improve his position.

Gavin had been tasked with removing the Risen Shard, but not only that. Cyran had hired him to remove other threats throughout the city. There was a merchant, and Gavin had believed that he had been smuggling children from the city, forcing them into slavery in the south. It was a reasonable conclusion based on the information that he and Wrenlow had managed to acquire at the time, but now…

What if there had been something more to it?

Even something as obvious as that should have been left him questioning.

Gavin had removed another man who had some sway in the city. A wealthy businessman, though even now, Gavin still didn't know what he had been involved in. Maybe that was a mistake. He should have questioned more. He should have tried to understand everything that he was asked to do.

What if Cyran was somehow looking for something to impress the Fates?

Gavin wouldn't know without contacting the El'aras. He reached into his pocket and pulled out a marker. He flipped it over in his hand, twirling it on his palm.

"What are you doing?" Wrenlow asked, coming closer.

"Think about it," Gavin said. "In the time we've been here, with all of the magical goings-on that we've dealt with, there seems to be one connection."

"What connection is that?"

"Me."

He squeezed the marker. Anna had given it to him as her way of allowing Gavin to summon her for help, though he'd never attempted to use it. Maybe now was the time. Only, the moment he did, he would bring the El'aras into the city. He doubted Anna and the El'aras would move quietly—or discreetly. The El'aras lived beyond the borders of the kingdom, beyond any of the free cities. They staked claim to lands outside of the forests, mostly because it was safer for them. Too many people viewed their magic as dangerous, which it was.

Is that what I want?

He slipped the marker back into his pocket. Jessica visibly relaxed.

"What is it?" Gavin asked.

"Nothing. It's just… the last time they were here…" She swept her gaze around the Dragon, her hand clenched to her belly, where she still had the scar from the attack. Her eyes settled back on him.

"It's not going to be the same next time," he said.

"You don't know that. You don't know anything about them."

"I know enough," Gavin said.

She shook her head. "You only *think* you know enough.

When it comes to the El'aras and the kind of power they possess, I don't think anyone can truly know."

Gavin kept his face neutral. He was at least part El'aras, though he had no idea what that meant for him. And he never would've believed it were it not for the El'aras visit and discovering that he had this magical connection to some deep part of himself.

Perhaps Jessica was right. There was no way for him to know the El'aras. Not without calling them back.

Gavin got to his feet and started to pace. "I need to know what they took from the Captain."

"And like I said, you need to reach out to Gaspar," she said.

Gavin stopped in front of the fire, staring at the flames.

Maybe he did need to go to Gaspar, who had contacts that he could use. Contacts that might be necessary. Not only that, but Imogen came with Gaspar. He needed someone not afraid to help him take on a sorcerer.

Jessica slipped out of the Dragon without another word.

"Why do I get the sense that you're more troubled than you're letting on," Wrenlow said.

"It was something Zella mentioned. That the Fates were responsible for all of the magical maneuvering in the world."

"And you believe her?"

"I don't have a reason not to, and given that she seemed to believe it, I at least have to consider the possibility," Gavin said. "I don't think the enchanters have much experience with the magical world, but they might have enough to know certain things I don't." He looked up at Wrenlow. "You and I have dealt with many different magical beings over the years, but there are limits to what we know about magic."

Wrenlow smiled. "Thankfully."

Gavin began to pace again, and his mind started piecing through the jobs he'd taken over the years—specifically, the year he'd been in Yoran. A different job came back to him, an early job that he had done for Tristan.

He had returned to Tristan, having stolen a small ceramic bowl.

"How did you feel when you took it?" Tristan had asked. He was older than Gavin, though Gavin had never learned by how much. Tristan had seemed considerably older than him during the time when Gavin had studied under him, though that might've just been his imagination.

Tristan had dark hair with streaks of gray running through it. He wasn't a large man, though he was stronger than he looked. Faster too. He always defeated Gavin. There had only been one time where Gavin had gotten close to stopping his teacher, and that had been when he unloaded all the power of his core reserves into attempting to stop him.

Gavin had been inside of a small room, with a hearth much like the one in the Dragon. The room had been decorated well, with the paneled walls painted a deep brown, and statues and paintings all around it. A plush carpet had covered the floor. Gavin always remembered carpet, as the barracks had none, and it always struck him as something warm and inviting, regardless of the truth of that matter.

"Scared," Gavin admitted.

Tristan smiled at him, as he always did when Gavin said he was afraid.

Gavin waited for the inevitable strike. Not only did he know that he shouldn't always acknowledge his fear, but he also knew that he shouldn't always admit it to Tristan. Only, in this case, he thought that it was necessary.

"Fear is natural when you're dealing with this," Tristan said. "You did well."

"I barely got out of there," Gavin replied.

"But you got out."

Gavin glanced at the bowl. "What is this?"

"A signifier of your ability," Tristan said.

Gavin studied the ceramic bowl. It was painted a pale blue, and there were strange markings along it, letters he couldn't read. In hindsight, Gavin knew the bowl was El'aras in origin, though he didn't think the home that he'd broken into and stolen it from had been an El'aras home.

"Did you face any particular challenges? Anything more than what we had discussed?"

Gavin shook his head. "There was a trick to getting in the door."

"What trick was that?"

"You said I had to focus on my core strength to open it," Gavin said.

By then, he had already broken through the leathers and had begun to break through chains, demonstrating his ability to shatter things around him. At the time, Gavin had thought it was only a matter of knowing the power within him was part of his core reserves, but now he wasn't so sure. Now he didn't know whether there was something else, some other way that Tristan tried to test him. Perhaps Tristan had already known that he had the power within him, some sort of magic.

Tristan nodded. "And it worked."

"It worked," Gavin said.

"What about when you were inside?"

Gavin smiled. "There wasn't anyone there. We didn't have to worry about it."

That had been his concern when he was breaking into the house. Tristan had warned him that there might be one of three different people home, and if they were, then he was to dispatch them. Gavin had no hesitation dispatching people when it came to the kinds of jobs that Tristan assigned him—but in this case, to simply steal a bowl—Gavin didn't think there was any reason to do so.

He looked down at the bowl and traced his finger along the surface of it. "All that trouble, just for this. What is it?"

"I already told you. It's a marker."

"A marker of what?"

"Fate." Tristan didn't look up. He stared at the bowl for a long time, saying nothing else.

Gavin shook his head, tearing himself away. In all the jobs he'd taken for Tristan, that was one of the strangest. It hadn't been all that difficult. Gavin had been forced to use his core reserves—possibly magic—to break into the door, but nothing else. He hadn't needed to kill. He hadn't needed to fight. All he'd needed to do was take the bowl.

He thought about Tristan's response and how he had

acted, and he still didn't know what to make of it. Perhaps there was nothing to it.

Since learning that Tristan still lived, Gavin hadn't gone after him yet. He needed to, mostly so he could figure out why Tristan had concealed his own death and resurrection from him.

He took a deep breath and let it out. The door opened, and Gaspar strode in with Jessica, followed by Imogen. Jessica tugged on her brown braid, pulling it around to her left shoulder, biting her lip as she studied Gaspar and then Imogen.

Imogen remained quiet, as usual. She took up a position near the door, though she nodded to Gavin. She was short and thin, and her dark hair always shielded her eyes, giving her a mysterious quality.

"What is this?" Gaspar asked as he laid eyes on Gavin.

"Something new. The Captain is dead. A sorcerer attacked."

Gaspar glanced to Imogen. "Dead?"

"And he was moving enchantments. Probably even responsible for those you pulled me in on."

"That bastard," Gaspar muttered.

"Now we've got something worse to deal with." He told them about the Fate and what Zella had said.

"What makes you think he's sticking around? If he got what he's after, that might be it."

Maybe. Gavin couldn't get past what the Captain had said.

Don't let him take it.

But take *what*?

"I don't think he's done. He was going somewhere when I caught up to him."

Gaspar watched him for a long moment before nodding. "I will see what I can find from the enchanters."

"Thank you," Jessica said.

"After I get some rest, I'm going to see if I can find where they were going," Gavin said.

Find the Fate, figure out what he took, then…

He didn't know.

If he had to face the Fate again, would he survive?

CHAPTER EIGHT

Gavin sat up. He had needed a little bit of rest, and he rubbed the sleep from his eyes. He was still tired, though not nearly as exhausted as he had been before. At least now he didn't feel as if he had been using his core reserves to the point of emptiness. He dressed quickly and came down the stairs into the tavern and looked over at Jessica. She sat alone, a stack of papers in front of her. She leaned forward and rested her elbows on the table as she rubbed her temple. Her apron was draped over her shoulder, and again she looked tired. Weary.

He approached and took a seat across from her. "What are you doing?"

"I'm going through my debt," she said. "Ever since the attack, I haven't been as profitable as what I need to be." She looked up at him, smiling tightly. "I do have debtors, Gavin."

"I could help."

She laughed softly. "Help with what? Paying for my

tavern? No. I'm responsible for it, and I'm not going to have somebody else do anything I should be doing for myself."

Gavin nodded. "I understand."

"Do you?"

"I understand you want to be independent and to make sure you're able to cover your finances."

She shook her head. "It's more than just that, Gavin."

"What else is it?"

"Eventually, you're going to leave here. You don't have to deny it. We both know it's true. When you do, I'm not going to be able to depend upon you taking care of me."

Gavin leaned back. He had considered leaving several times before. Each time he gave it much thought, he realized that perhaps now wasn't quite the right time for him to depart. Something else always came up, prompting him to stay. It was almost as if he were meant to be in Yoran. Maybe it was more that he needed to be. Cyran had certainly coordinated things so that Gavin ended up in the city, and ever since then, odd things had been happening that were forcing him to stay.

"I don't know that you ever depended upon me taking care of you," he said.

"Perhaps not quite like that, but I've allowed myself to become more dependent on you than I typically would be."

Gavin looked around the tavern. It was empty and late enough in the evening that he would've expected to find the tavern full—at least when he had first come to Yoran. Before the attack, the Dragon would've been occupied with various patrons, a musician or two, and servers making sure that everyone had the food and drink they needed.

Recently, none of that had been the case.

"Don't worry about me," she said. "When you decide to move on, I'm going to be fine."

"I know you will be," Gavin said.

She smiled at him. "I'm stronger than you give me credit for."

"I haven't tried to say you weren't."

"I know you haven't," she whispered.

"What's that supposed to mean?"

"It's just that you act as if you have to protect me, but that's not necessary."

"When the tavern is attacked because of me, I feel like I'm responsible for it." He hesitated. This wasn't the conversation he intended to have with her, but maybe it was overdue. "Would you prefer I leave now?"

She looked down at her hands for a moment before glancing up at him. "No."

Gavin swallowed. "I…" He wasn't sure what to say or how to say it, knowing only that he felt as if there was something more he needed to be telling her. For now, he simply said nothing. "I suppose I need to figure out where the Fate was going."

She nodded. "I'll be here." She glanced around the tavern before looking back down at the table, then started sorting through her papers.

Gavin took another look back at Jessica before heading out onto the street. He wandered past a general store. He started toward the part of the city where he'd been attacked by the Fate when he saw something that made him slow.

Shadows loomed in the distance, swirling around the street like a fog. Several constables patrolled near it. The fog seemed to move... and then one of the constables dropped.

The fallen constable didn't get up.

Gavin hurried over to the fallen man. He was still alive. His skin was cool, almost cold, and though he had a bracelet on either wrist—enchantments, surely—he had nothing else on him that would identify him as a constable.

Dark shadows swirled around him, pressing on either side.

He pulled the constable to the side of the road, propping him up against a nearby building. He needed to get the man help. This would also be an easy way for him to ingratiate himself with Davel Chan, especially given the tension between them ever since the attack on the Captain's home. Gavin needed to keep peace—at least as much as possible, considering how he had possession of the jade egg, something the constables wanted back from him.

A shout echoed down the street. *The other constable?* Gavin checked on the man, making sure that he was fine, before darting forward.

When he rounded a corner, he found another constable —probably the other one he'd seen—lying on the ground, resting near one of the streetlights. Much like the other, this man twitched.

What was going on?

The constable was alive, though his skin was not cold like the last one's had been.

Gavin checked him over, searching for any sign of other injuries, but found nothing. Either he had been jumped, hit in the head, or…

The El'aras dagger started to glow softly.

Or has it been glowing the entire time?

Gavin hadn't been paying attention to it, which meant that it likely had been glowing. He simply hadn't noticed.

Balls.

Could this be the Fate?

He got to his feet, sweeping his gaze along the street. It was too dark for him to make out much of anything, almost supernaturally so. Could there be any sorcery presence here? He held on to the El'aras dagger, though it didn't glow nearly as much as what he feared it might. As he swept the dagger around, he searched for movement within those shadows. He couldn't find anything.

Gavin slipped down a nearby alley, scrambled up the wall, and crouched on one of the nearby rooftops. He lowered himself so that he blended in with the darkness as he surveyed the street.

It didn't take long before he saw movement. A single figure strode down the street, darkness swirling around them.

A sorcerer. It had to be the Fate that had attacked Gavin the night before.

Gavin watched for a few moments before jumping to the

next building, and then to the next. It didn't seem as if the Fate had seen him.

Yet.

He jumped to the next rooftop, still watching the sorcerer as they strode along the street. They seemed unmindful of his presence. Still, whatever magic they used to make the darkness swirl around them was impressive.

Gavin smiled. He would move quickly, to catch the sorcerer and question them. He needed to know everything about why they were in the city.

He jumped down from the rooftop and landed on the street, then darted forward. He held on to the El'aras dagger before changing his mind and sheathing it. He grabbed the sword instead. The dagger might be easier for him to maneuver in tight quarters, but the sword would be more beneficial against a sorcerer. They knew magic, but they didn't know traditional weaponry.

Especially as it glowed under the magic that the sorcerer used.

He reached the spot where he had first seen the shadowed figure. Gavin started to slow, sweeping his gaze around the street. It was empty. Stone storefronts pressed inward, and the occasional breeze pulled at a few signs. A small tree interrupted the flow of buildings here, a spindly bells tree that Gavin knew to avoid, much like the buildings seemed to avoid it.

Where had he gone?

He checked his pocket, making sure that he had another bundle of enchanted ropes. Hopefully, these would work better than the last, and he could wind them around in a better pattern.

He reached another intersection and paused, looking in either direction, but he didn't see anything. Night was dark around him. Darker than it should have been.

Somewhere distant, someone cried out.

Could that be another constable?

Why was the Fate attacking them?

So much for the Fate leaving after getting what he wanted from the Captain.

Gavin was on the periphery of the city, which abutted the forest. Most of these cottages were smaller, more run-down, a few in need of roof repairs, and obviously owned by those without nearly as much wealth. It was a wonder that the constables even patrolled it.

Another shout. This one was closer.

He raced forward. The dark fog swirling around him looked something like smoke, though it was denser than any smoke he'd seen before. He held out the sword, sweeping it in front of him as he ran, the glowing light carving through the darkness and guiding him forward.

He found another constable, then another, and then another.

Gavin looked up.

Three constables down in one part of the city?

Where was the sorcerer?

He raced forward after checking each of the constables, making sure that they were all still alive, and stopped at the edge of the forest.

There was no sign of anything or anyone.

One of the constables behind him cried out, and Gavin turned back. He wanted to chase the sorcerer into the forest, but at the same time, he also felt as if he needed to help the injured.

Even if it meant helping one of the constables.

"I'm going to find you," he whispered to the Fate.

Wind suddenly gusted around him, and it seemed as if the forest whispered back.

He had to find where the Fate was hiding—before anything else happened.

Gavin crept forward, following the flow of traffic on the street. The crowd seemed smaller, with people hurrying along on their tasks without looking around themselves the way they normally would. Could the people detect the presence of the sorcerer? He'd not noticed that with sorcerers in the city before, but then Gavin hadn't paid attention to it, either.

None of the constables had been permanently injured, though he had waited by them until other constables on patrol had arrived. He gave them space as they found their fallen colleagues, careful not to linger. He didn't want to be blamed for what happened but wanted to ensure that somebody arrived to bring them out of the streets. It wouldn't do for another sorcerer or somebody else to suddenly appear and attack them.

He still didn't have an answer as to what had happened or why the sorcerer had attacked constables. Gavin had searched for evidence of additional attacks but found nothing. No other constables were injured. There was no other sign of the strange sorcerer, and no other glow from his sword or dagger to indicate magic used around him.

It was now early morning, and his few hours of sleep had restored him enough that he at least thought he wouldn't have to worry about getting overpowered by somebody. If he were to come across the Fate, at least he had enough strength—and core reserves—that he might be able to call upon the power so he could break free. Not that he wanted to have to do that, plus he didn't think a sorcerer would attack openly in the middle of daytime either.

Regardless, he kept the hood of his cloak over his head, keeping himself concealed. He swept his gaze along the street, looking for any sign of movement, but he didn't see anything.

The only thing he was aware of was the sense of activity in the city. It was not typical for this time of morning. Or maybe it was. Gavin didn't come out in the mornings often.

Gavin hadn't realized the home he'd been heading toward the night before had been so close to the market, but as he followed the flow of traffic, he thought it convenient that it had been. At least Gavin had some additional concealment this way. He moved as quickly as he could, staying as covered as possible.

The sounds of the city around him were almost overwhelming. It was part of why he enjoyed working at night, under cover of darkness and in relative silence. The only distraction in nighttime was from listening to Wrenlow in his ear, but even that wasn't terrible.

Gavin breathed in. The smell of the city was different in the daytime as well. At night, there was almost a sense of coolness to the air, which seemed to wipe away the stench of bodies and filth and everything that crowded around him now. But there was an energy here now, and he couldn't help but find everything slightly entertaining, from the merchants pushing carts along the street to the street performers tumbling or dancing to the people shopping.

He veered off down a side street, away from the market. Gavin reached the building the Fate had been heading to the night before, then paused across from it. The red awning was there, much more visible in the daytime. It was different than the other buildings.

Why this place?

Perhaps that was the better question.

Gavin watched for a while but saw no one, and he hurried across the street. He tested the door, found it locked, and jammed a knife into it. He twisted the knife and popped the door open. It wasn't nearly as effective as the kind of lockpick that Gaspar used—especially since the old thief could relock the door, something Gavin's technique wouldn't allow—but it did the job.

Once inside, he closed the door and started to shuffle through cupboards in the kitchen. It was a small home and easy for him to sort through quickly. No other furniture and no decorations were found here. Dust clung to the air, filling his nostrils, and everything that he touched seemed to kick up even more dust. Empty. The main part of the house was empty as well.

He headed to the back room, where he'd been forced to go out the window, and he paused at the window. At least he knew he could go through the alley if it came down to it, but he didn't see anything otherwise.

Only, there *was* something.

A faint outline on the floor.

He crouched down and began to work his knife into the seam of the crack that he saw. The blade wasn't sharp enough. Reaching into his sheath, he pulled out the El'aras dagger and tried that, leveraging it into the crack. Gavin wiggled the dagger from side to side to see if he could lift the trapdoor—at least, he was increasingly certain that it was a trapdoor.

The El'aras dagger managed to get deeper into it, and he pried, mindful that he might blunt the dagger. El'aras blades were incredibly sharp. Gavin worked his way around the trapdoor, carving through the cracks. The dagger wasn't strong enough.

The sword.

Gavin unsheathed it, and the sword fit into the crack. He slid the blade around the edges, and he leveraged it. The trapdoor started to open.

His heart hammered. This was a sorcerer's lair.

This was where the Fate had come.

Gavin knew of other similar lairs. It seemed dangerous he would come across another one. He continued to work the sword into the trapdoor and felt the door start to pull up. When he could get his fingers underneath it, he pried and lifted the door.

He held the sword down into the hole. There was no glow from below.

At least there was no sign of the Fate.

Gavin moved carefully down the ladder, holding the sword in one hand, prepared for a waiting Fate. He paused at the bottom of the ladder. The darkness stretched in front of him. Gavin moved forward but didn't see or hear anything. The shadows started to swallow him. The farther he went, the more the light from behind him began to fade, ultimately plunging him into complete darkness.

The smart play would be getting help.

He'd seen what would happen taking on one of the Fates.

But if he surprised the Fate before anyone else was hurt...

He slid his feet along the stone, holding the sword out, but there was no movement. Gavin paused when he felt something press in on him, squeezing and pushing him back. It was a strange sensation, a magical sensation. He had no idea what it was, only that he could feel something out there and around him. It left his skin tingling, the hairs on the back of his neck on edge, and an uncomfortable tension inside of him.

Then he found a door.

Or rather, the door found him.

He crashed into it and bounced off. Gavin held his nose, stifling a cry.

He reached out and felt the door. Its handle was curved, forming almost a complete circle but with some waviness to it. Holding on to it left him with a tingling through his hand. Gavin squeezed the handle briefly before releasing it. He tried again and twisted it, but the door was locked.

It reminded him of how he had to try to jam the dagger and the sword into the trapdoor. Could he do something similar now? He started to run the blade of the El'aras dagger around the perimeter of the door but didn't find anything.

Maybe there was a way for him to force it open.

Not necessarily with magic... *or perhaps with magic.*

Gavin called upon the core reserve of power within him. That might be all that he needed to do. As he focused on that sense of energy, he shoved his shoulder into the door.

The door resisted him.

Gavin tried again, ramming his shoulder into the door over and over. Each time he did, some resistance around him faded. He continued to slam his shoulder into it. The door creaked, then groaned, and then it finally crashed open.

It was dark.

No Fate here.

He took in a slow breath, noticing that the air had something of a pungent aroma. Gavin swept the sword out in front of him, probing as he took a step, then another. There was no glow to suggest any hint of magic. He needed to figure out some way to illuminate the room.

He stepped in and moved slowly, probing forward. Finally, he came across a table. Gavin ran his hand along the surface of the table carefully. His hand bumped something. A lantern.

He grabbed it, twisted the handle. The lantern started to glow with a pale white light, though he hadn't lit any oil or anything inside of it. Some sort of magical lantern.

Gavin held it out.

The light revealed a curved room. Walls sloped overhead, stretching high above him. Gavin couldn't see far into the darkness, but the light of the lantern gave him barely enough of a way to perceive the peak of the ceiling.

The air had a strange odor to it. Each time he took a breath, he couldn't shake the feeling that the odor was lingering in his nostrils, as if trying to work its way deeper into his mouth.

He swung the lantern from side to side, quickly assessing whether there was anything else there. Whereas Gaspar was quick about determining if there were any items of value in a room, Gavin was much more skilled at searching for threats. No sign of the Fate—or why he would have been heading here the night before.

Gavin paused in the middle of the room, where the odor seemed more pungent. He couldn't find the source, so he stepped deeper in. It was much larger than he would've expected, certainly larger than the lair in Cyran's home. He stepped toward the back room, then he saw it.

He knew immediately what it was.

A body, but so far decomposed it wasn't even identifiable as a body. Velvet robes hung around it. As Gavin came close, the smell still struck him, and he had the sense that the smell had been contained for ages. It was almost as if it had been bound here so that it wouldn't assault anyone.

This had to be a sorcerer—the one who owned the home.

Could this *be the reason the Fate had come?*

Gavin needed to check the sorcerer's body. He reached his hand into the cloak and felt inside the pockets, but he didn't find anything. He nudged the sorcerer's body, and the bones collapsed, dust spewing up. Gavin brought his shirt up over his mouth.

He nudged the body with his foot, pushing it off to the side. It covered nothing but more stone.

Gavin stepped forward, heading deeper into the room, sweeping the lantern around. He turned the brightness up, and the magical lantern glowed more intensely, pushing back the darkness.

He glanced down at his El'aras dagger. Surprisingly, it glowed as well.

Magic was here.

Gavin dimmed the lantern again, glancing down at the dagger.

The glow persisted.

So much for surprising the Fate.

Gavin stepped out and closed the door. He still didn't see anything.

In the light of the lantern, strange symbols on the surface of the door caught his attention. Gavin traced his hand across them. He held the dagger up to the door, and he frowned for a moment. The writing on the dagger was similar to the writing on the door.

El'aras? Why would the El'aras have helped create these doors?

Something sounded nearby.

He had to keep moving.

Stop the Fate.

Gavin hurried toward the trap door, and the sound came again. The brightness of the dagger intensified.

Gavin reached the ladder leading out of this crawlspace. He started up slowly, and the sound came once more. This time from overhead. As he neared the top of the ladder, he prepared himself to fight the Fate.

The trapdoor slammed shut above him.

Gavin shoved his shoulder up against the trapdoor but couldn't move it. He tried again and again, but each time he met resistance. The ladder was cool to the touch; an old wood slick and worn down over time. If there was somebody out there, he liked his chances better fighting rather than hiding.

He pushed on the trapdoor again. He focused on his core reserves, concentrating, and then he shoved. With a surge, he felt the trapdoor starting to move.

Then the ladder cracked.

Gavin dropped down a step. He could no longer throw his shoulder into the trapdoor the way he had before.

Whatever he had detected was up there still—either that or the sorcerer who'd caused his El'aras dagger to glow was using some sort of magic on the trapdoor to make it so Gavin couldn't escape.

Gavin shoved again.

The step beneath him cracked again.

Gavin dropped again.

The Fate had to have sealed him in.

He was stuck.

At the bottom of the ladder, he looked up at the trapdoor overhead. There were no markings on it, much like there were no markings on it from above. It was simply a door.

He tapped on the enchantment. "Wrenlow, are you there?"

There was silence.

Gavin looked up at the trapdoor again. The glow of the dagger persisted, giving him enough light to see more clearly, although the magical lantern light allowed him to be able to peer above him too.

The answers weren't out there, and he didn't know if they would be in the room where he had emerged. There had to be some other way out from here. Not just the trapdoor, but an alternative exit. What sorcerer would have given themselves only one way out? Or why would the El'aras, given what he had seen on the door?

Gavin made his way back to the room. He looked at the door again, noting the El'aras symbols and writing. He pushed it open and wrinkled his nose at the smell. Why was the odor still so fresh in here? If the body were old and had been there for a while, why would he still smell it quite so profoundly?

And what reason had the Fate for coming here?

As far as he knew, there was only one way in and out of a sorcerer's lair like this.

"Wrenlow?" he called into the enchantment again, and again he didn't know whether Wrenlow was listening to him. Maybe he couldn't hear him. Or worse, maybe the enchantment had somehow been severed because he'd come down to the sorcerer's lair.

Find a way out, then find the Fate again.

Gavin set the lantern down near the dead sorcerer as he explored. He headed to the walls, searching in a pattern as he spiraled generally inward. There had to be something else here. Another way out.

"Wrenlow, if you're there, I need help," he whispered into the enchantment.

He was so accustomed to having somebody with him these days.

Gavin crawled across the ground, holding the dagger out, sweeping it from side to side. Maybe there would be a crack or something along the ground to guide him. He found nothing. He held the dagger closer to the sorcerer's body, and the light started to glow even more brightly.

Gavin frowned, looking over to the door for a moment. As he did, he realized the symbols that were present on the other side were also present on this side.

The dagger was glowing a little less brightly than it had been before; the distance from the sorcerer's remains seeming to dim the light. Using the lantern might help. Gavin brought it over to where he stood near the door. He twisted the handle so that the light blazed more brightly. He studied the markings on the door. They were El'aras symbols.

For the most part, the door gleamed with reflected light. But the lower section seemed duller, as if it had been touched. *Or scuffed.* Gavin leaned down, studying it. From a lower vantage, as he held the lantern out, he couldn't even see the slight change in sheen to the door.

He shifted the lantern from side to side but didn't see anything more. He jabbed at the section of the door with his dagger.

The door hissed.

Balls.

He held the dagger to the door more cautiously than the last time. The door hissed again. He lingered for a moment, getting even lower and holding the lantern out so that he could see if the spot where he touched the dagger to the door would change anything. Gavin brought the dagger up to the door on one of the higher sections, but nothing happened. Bringing it back down lower, closer to where he saw the dull areas, he noticed the hissing sound again.

Only in a certain small section of the door did it make that sound. He couldn't even tell if it came from the dagger or if it came from the door. Gavin pushed the dagger against the hissing door, and he listened for a long moment, waiting for something to change. It continued to hiss, the sound building around him.

He took a seat, studying the door. He couldn't read the El'aras writing.

If the dagger made it hiss, what would happen with the sword?

Gavin unsheathed the sword, but it didn't hiss at all. Of course, there weren't the same markings on it, though it still had other El'aras markings. He pushed the sword forward, pressing the blade against the door. Rather than a hissing sound, there came a soft grinding.

The blade blazed brighter again.

He started to pull it back, but he couldn't. It was almost as if the sword locked in place, preventing him from doing anything with it. Gavin jerked his hand back, trying to withstand the changing nature of whatever was happening, but he couldn't.

He pushed the sword forward. If he wasn't going to pull the blade back, then if nothing else, he would force it farther forward. The blade glowed, and something unexpected happened.

The symbols on it changed shape. They glowed in a way that matched with the door, which started to grind again.

The door began to roll open—differently than how it normally opened. The part where the sword touched the door rolled slowly, pulsing with a hint of brightness and a surge of pale light.

An opening formed to the right of the door, not within it.

Withdrawing the sword, he stepped into the darkness.

CHAPTER NINE

Once Gavin stepped inside, another grinding sound came from behind him, and he spun around, the lantern light allowing him to see that the opening that had formed was rolling back into place.

Gavin held out the lantern and turned back around, but he could barely see anything. He detected shadows ahead. These days, it felt as if he were noticing shadows moving all around him, though none of them were obvious. Nothing along the corridor. Instead, he turned around and focused on the door itself.

Gavin was sealed inside. Only, as he looked at it, he wondered if he truly was. The inside of the door had similar symbols as what he had seen on the other side. It was almost as if the El'aras writing matched up with the sword.

He looked down at the blade. It still glowed, though it was dimmer than it had been before. He had taken this from Cyran's home—from *his* lair.

Had Cyran known what he possessed?

Gavin crept along the hallway, the sword still glowing with a soft light. The hallway ran parallel to the other hall. Could it be that the sorcerer's lair led to more than one location? Would Cyran's lair lead to more than one?

The walls were smooth, almost perfectly so, and certain areas of the wall caught the light reflected off the lantern, shining it back at him. Gavin stopped and noted a symbol that reminded him of the ones he saw in other sections of the hallway. Those symbols seemed to matter.

"Let me know if you can hear me," he said into the enchantment.

There was still no response from Wrenlow, and the silence around him felt even more stark with the heavy darkness around him. Gavin twisted the lantern, and the brightness shone along the corridor. It looked to stretch an impossibly long distance beneath the city.

He reached a branch point in the tunnels that veered in either direction. The tunnels extended away from him, darkened both ways. A soft breeze blew, though Gavin couldn't tell where it came from. It carried the stench of foul water mixed with decay.

The sword started to glow a little bit more brightly when he pointed it in one direction, so he turned and headed that way. He moved more carefully. Every so often, he caught sight of something along the tunnel, and he didn't know if it was a reflection off the walls or if it was something else. He swung the lantern around, but he never caught them with the light. The walk through the tunnels seemed to take an impossibly long time, though it never veered off. It headed straight, and thankfully, he had the lantern with him.

It seemed almost as if eyes were watching him. That had to be his imagination. Thankfully, he wasn't trapped here in the darkness. He crept forward, and the sword continued to glow more brightly with each step.

Finally, he found an end point. A door.

The door was different than the last one. Whereas the other one had been almost oval and had rolled in and out of place, this one was rectangular and filled the wall in front of him. The same El'aras writing that had been on the other door existed here as well.

Gavin ran his finger along it, marveling at the complexity of the writing. The lettering had symbols that seemed to be squished together, forming words and sentences. Many of the symbols were far more complicated than any that he saw elsewhere, and certainly more complicated than the typical writing within Yoran. He traced his finger along the letters. Some of them looked to be a jumble of geometric shapes, triangles and squares, and circles. Others were more like swirls, and still others looked to be rune-type symbols that could be patterns and pictures more than actual letters. All of them were intricate, and he couldn't imagine taking the time to write them out like this.

It was far more detailed than what had been on the other door. This one reminded him of the El'aras dagger, more so than the sword he now carried. He held the sword up and pressed it against the door, but nothing happened. He tried the dagger next, but even though the writing on both the sword and the dagger looked similar, neither attempt made any sort of difference in coaxing the door to open.

On a whim, he flipped the blades over and tried their other sides. The writing was different on each side of the El'aras dagger, as was the case with the sword. When he tried, nothing changed.

It was strange that it had worked with the other door. Stranger still was that the El'aras dagger had caused the hissing sound. Maybe he could try something else. Gavin brought them both together. That didn't work either.

Perhaps this door wasn't meant to be opened by him.

He backtracked. When he reached the branch point, he headed in the opposite direction. It took a while before he reached that portion of the tunnel, and he was not surprised when he had to walk or what seemed another impossible distance before reaching the end of the hall. Gavin couldn't even imagine how these tunnels had been built in the first place. Somebody had taken considerable time to dig them out. Not only time, but given how smooth the walls seemed, he couldn't help but feel as if it had taken power—magic, probably.

He reached another doorway.

This one was circular, though there were lines within it. Gavin took in the El'aras writing much like he had on the other door, and he held the dagger up to it. It started hissing. He brought the sword out and held it against the door, waiting for any sign of movement.

Slowly, the sword started to take on a faint glow. The

glow began to intensify the longer he held it there. He pushed it farther against the door, waiting. For a moment, nothing happened. Then the door started opening.

In a spiraling fashion, the lines created a circular pattern as it opened, twisting into darkness. Gavin lingered for a second before moving the lantern forward, and he could make out a room on the other side.

Once he stepped inside, the door closed again. The combination of the sword and the lantern shone brightly, making it so that Gavin was better able to see everything around him.

The room was enormous. The walls were all made of smooth stone, not stacked block like many of the buildings in Yoran. It looked like the room itself had been carved out of the rock beneath the city. There was a dampness to the walls, and he heard a tinkling of water. He felt a breath of air whisper across his cheeks—a breath that was stale and damp, and one that lingered in his nostrils. This room was shaped similarly to the one he had just come through, only this one seemed to be filled with artifacts.

The shelves lining the walls were packed full of items. The table was cluttered with various relics. *Sorcerers'* relics. The items resting on the table were intriguing. He would almost have called them enchantments, but Gavin had never seen any enchantments with such detail. Some of them looked to be carved out of stone or metal, with intricate inlays. He traced his finger along one cylindrical item, which looked something like a bracelet, but as he ran his fingers along the surface of it, he couldn't tell if it truly was a bracelet or if it was simply a sculpture. It reminded him of the enchantment Olivia had made for him, but only vaguely. The enchantment was a poor replica of this.

At one end of the table, he found three small sculptures, each of which looked like an animal. They were like the items Mekal enchanted. There was what was obviously a wolf, though the snout was slightly shortened and scrunched in. There was a strange humanoid creature that was covered in what looked like fur. The third sculpture resembled a man with his legs curled in toward his body, his arms wrapped around himself. The pose reminded Gavin of how he had often been forced to sit while Tristan worked with him, training him to escape.

Everything on the table had a feeling of power to it. Everything here struck him as something that Zella would love to get her hands on, but he also suspected this was the kind of place that Cyran had wanted to find. Now that Gavin knew who and what Cyran really was, he had little doubt that Cyran would take the power of a place like this and manipulate it in his favor.

This had to be what the Fate was after.

He searched for a doorway. Once he figured out how to get out, he could return if he wanted to. The far side of the room had a door.

Gavin paused in front of the door and tried it. Locked. Focusing inwardly, he used the sense of the core reserve power he had and jerked on the door. The lock snapped, and he pulled it open.

He stopped in the hallway. There was nothing there. He

followed it until he reached the end, where he found a ladder. He climbed and paused when he reached the trapdoor. Gavin braced himself for anything that might be on the other side.

He pushed. Resistance greeted him. The wooden ladder creaked.

The resistance didn't feel the same as it had with the other one. At least in this case, he didn't think a sorcerer was holding a magical spell against him, keeping him from opening the trapdoor.

He continued to push, though rather than shoving forcefully, he pushed carefully. He kept his shoulder leveraged up against the trapdoor and squeezed, while imagining all the things that might be on the other side.

For all he knew, it was an empty room, though if it were anything like what he had found in Cyran's home, it would have been covered by a rug. Maybe that was what he pushed against.

He had to be more forceful. Bracing himself with his feet on either side of the ladder, Gavin gave it a hard shove. The door exploded up. He made a point of holding on to the El'aras dagger and poked his head up, but he didn't see anything out there. He scrambled down the ladder, grabbed the lantern, then headed back up.

Gavin swung the lantern around what appeared to be a small room. All stone walls, barely ten paces in each direction. It was otherwise empty. Why had it been so difficult for him to force the door open?

He found the answer when he approached one of the

walls. A large trunk rested nearby, toppled over. Gavin tipped it upright and looked inside of it. A few items were in the trunk, most of them broken ceramics. A section of cloth likely had once been wrapped around the ceramics. There was a slender blade, which he wrapped in cloth and stuffed into his pocket. It didn't strike him as anything altogether significant, but if it was near a sorcerer's lair, then it might be meaningful.

Gavin surveyed the room for a moment before flipping the trapdoor closed. He moved the trunk on top of it once again. There wasn't much evidence that the trap door was even there with the door closed and the trunk in place. Considering what he knew about it, though, and its ties to sorcery, he supposed that he shouldn't be altogether surprised.

Approaching the door, he listened for a moment. He doubted there was anyone here. If there had been, the noise of the trunk slamming against the wall would've caught their attention. That it hadn't done so suggested that the home was empty.

Gavin tested the handle, relieved the door was unlocked. He pushed it open slowly and glanced out. There was nothing and no one there. Whereas the other rooms had been in homes—or, in Cyran's case, in some sort of healer's enclave—this looked to be little more than a warehouse. It was enormous. The room in front of him sprawled much farther than Gavin would have imagined. He used the lantern to better see what was there, but he couldn't make much out.

Instinct warned him that something wasn't quite right here, though so far, he had seen nothing out of the ordinary. The only unusual thing he found was that this warehouse was here at all.

He started along the rows of shelves. It occurred to him that he still hadn't heard anything from Wrenlow. He didn't know whether the sorcerer's lair made it so that he couldn't hear anything, or if it blocked the enchantment.

Get outside into the open and head back to the Dragon.

Those thoughts stayed with Gavin.

He didn't see a doorway. As he moved through the rows of shelves, he noticed a soft shuffling sound. Gavin spun, holding the lantern out, but there was nothing. Maybe that shuffling was his imagination.

He moved quickly and came across an opening in the shelves. A doorway wasn't far from him. As he neared it, he noticed the shuffling sound again. There was something off about that. Gavin couldn't tell quite what it was, only that he felt as if it were trailing after him. Whatever was there came closer.

He hurried forward. The door loomed in front of him. The lantern glow illuminated it and revealed El'aras symbols on it as well. That couldn't be a coincidence.

Of course, Gavin knew that none of this could be a coincidence.

The shuffling came closer, and he raced toward the door, threw it open, and ran outside. The moment he was outside, he felt foolish. He turned back toward the building.

He looked for the sound of shuffling that he had heard

but saw nothing. As he started to turn, he noticed a hint of smoke trailing out of the building. It was faint, and in the daylight, it was difficult for him to know if the smoke came from the building or simply drifted toward it. What he needed was to head back inside to investigate further.

He didn't recognize the sign that was shaped like a man leaning over a table with an animal crawling across the tabletop, but as he peered along the street, he knew where he was. He could just make out the building's crumbling stone topping a small rise that he'd been told once housed the sorcery school. When closer to it, Gavin could imagine young sorcerers running through the now overgrown lawn, flittering about with magic and spells.

It was the opposite side of the city from where he thought he would end up, quite a way from where he had been in the first place.

Gavin backed to the opposite side of the street, and he stood for a moment, looking around. He didn't see anyone nor any sign of movement. Certainly nothing that would make him think he had emerged someplace dangerous.

"Gavin?"

Gavin breathed out. He felt a little embarrassed about how relieved he was to hear Wrenlow's voice. "I'm here."

"Something has—"

Wrenlow fell silent.

"Wrenlow? If you can hear me, I'll be right there."

CHAPTER TEN

He approached the Dragon slowly. There wasn't anything about it that screamed that he would find a problem, only the fact that Wrenlow had fallen silent. He'd tried using the enchantment, but there had been no answer.

Gavin reached the alley leading toward the Dragon. He walked by, keeping the hood of his cloak over his head, moving past the tavern as if it hadn't been his destination. In doing so, he chanced a look around, sweeping his gaze everywhere. Then he finally turned the corner.

He thought he saw something behind him, though that flutter of movement may only have been his imagination. Gavin could no longer tell. Given what he'd gone through so far today, he felt as if he were overreacting to everything. He looped all the way back around, heading toward the Dragon from a different direction.

He could still make out the tavern in the distance, but as

he watched, he realized there was something strange about it.

Constables.

Gavin frowned. The constables left them alone. Ever since the last attack, they'd ignored the tavern, making a point of completely avoiding this area.

Was that why Wrenlow had fallen silent?

He approached the Dragon from the back street. He didn't want anything happening to the Dragon. Not only because he cared about Jessica, but the tavern had grown on him.

When he reached it, he paused for a moment and looked around, but he didn't see anything. The constables had to be patrolling and waiting for him to come through. He reached an alleyway and headed to the end of it. He kicked his legs out to the side and scrambled up the walls, using the narrow buildings to give him enough of a grip as he climbed to the top.

Once on the rooftop, he crawled forward, moving carefully. What drew his attention was not on the street as he'd expected. This was on the roof level with him. On the opposite roof, the constable looked below, probably watching for him. Gavin scrambled back down and reached the alley, keeping the hood of his cloak up as he crossed the street. He then scaled up to the rooftop from another alley. He crawled along, heading toward the constable.

Gavin slipped as quietly as he could. He approached the constable from behind and smiled. "This is an interesting place for you to get some sleep."

The constable turned around and started to back away, but Gavin jerked the El'aras dagger free and shoved it toward him. It glowed slightly. Enchantments? "You and I are going to have a conversation."

The constable's gaze darted past Gavin.

He wasn't alone.

Gavin spun and kicked the second constable's legs out from under him. This one wore a gray cloak that blended into the rooftop. He had a long dagger, though not El'aras as far as Gavin could tell. He stayed on his hands and knees, the dagger gripped in one hand, watching Gavin.

"Two of you?" Gavin said. "Doesn't Davel know I don't enjoy being observed like that?"

"Davel is well aware of what you like. And he's also well aware that it makes little difference when it impacts his responsibility to the city."

Gavin turned slowly at the familiar voice. "Davel Chan."

Davel Chan was short and stout, with dark hair, thin wrinkles along the corners of his eyes, and a tight-lipped smile. His wide cheekbones carried just a hint of a beard, as if he had simply neglected to shave for the last few days rather than intentionally grown it. He had on a thin cloak over the gray jacket and pants worn by the constables, along with a small pouch strapped to his waist. He carried no weapon, but given that he would have enchantments on him, Gavin wasn't surprised by that.

"Gavin Lorren. I shouldn't be surprised you observed us, but I must admit to feeling a little impressed," Davel Chan said.

"Your men aren't the best at concealing their presence."

"I think we're better than you give us credit for."

Gavin shrugged. "If you think so, but I still found you."

"And I found you."

"I presume that one or more of you are in the Dragon?"

Davel cocked his head to the side, frowning. "What?"

"It's nothing," Gavin said. Perhaps the constable didn't know Wrenlow had observed him. "What do you need?"

"What makes you think I need anything? Perhaps I'm only checking in on you."

"I think we're both aware of how that went for you the last time," Gavin said.

He was tempted to reach into his pocket for the enchantment for speed and strength. Facing the constables, he often felt as if he needed to have more of an advantage than he did. Not that he feared that Davel Chan would attack. They had an uneasy alliance, at least for now. Chan needed him for access to the jade egg to make enchantments.

"Careful," Davel said, his gaze flicking from one constable to the other.

"You don't want them to know?"

"There's no purpose in them knowing anything more than they need to," Davel said.

Gavin glanced over to the constables. They watched him, both now armed, as if ready to attack. Two constables weren't enough to eliminate Gavin. Davel would know that as well. Which suggested that they were enchanted.

"Are you here because of what happened to the

Captain?" he asked. He shouldn't be surprised that Davel would learn so quickly.

Davel frowned. "What happened?"

He didn't know.

Between that, and the strange attack he'd seen, he would have expected Davel to have known. "Why *are* you here?"

"For what we agreed on. That you would provide access to the egg when requested."

Gavin shook his head. It wasn't about the Fates. "I didn't agree to that. It was your request, but I never made any claim I would honor it."

Davel watched him, a dangerous glint in his eyes. "You understand the repercussions if you choose not to permit access."

"Maybe I don't. Perhaps you should remind me."

Davel slipped closer to him, the enchantments making him move more rapidly than Gavin could. He didn't like the idea of battling Davel on the rooftop, even though he didn't think he would be at too much of a disadvantage. Davel was skilled, but Gavin had already proven his ability in countering him despite his enchantments.

"You know what will happen," Davel said.

Movement near the street caught Gavin's attention, and he hazarded a brief glance. It was a mistake.

Davel pressed a knife up to Gavin's belly. "The egg."

Gavin didn't move, though he wasn't sure that he really needed to move. Even though he had a knife to his belly, he doubted that Davel intended to use it. Besides, it wouldn't be the first time that he had a knife jabbed into his belly.

"There has been magical movement in the city," Davel said. "Sorcery. I know you don't care too much about that, but we have had stability within Yoran for decades."

"Only because you betrayed those who align themselves with you," Gavin reminded.

"You weren't here," Davel said.

Gavin smiled. "I wasn't, but that doesn't mean I don't know what happened."

There was another slight movement along the street, and Gavin glanced down, trying to gauge what it was that he saw. At this point, with Davel holding the knife up to his belly, it didn't really matter whether Gavin turned his attention to anything down below. If Davel wanted to attack him, he would do so.

Gavin knew better than to ignore things that caught his attention. He knew he'd seen some sort of movement. He stared for a moment before finally pulling his gaze away, and he looked over at the two constables.

They weren't here because of the Fates. Not directly.

Which meant Wrenlow had reached out to him for another reason.

He turned his attention back to Davel. "I can get you access to the egg but not right now."

"That also wasn't the agreement."

"The agreement wasn't that you would get unlimited access," Gavin said. "The agreement was that you would *have* access. I get to decide when and where, and I get to decide how it happens." He started to stand.

Davel followed him, continuing to hold the knife up against Gavin's stomach.

Gavin shot him a look. "Unless you intend to use that knife against me, I would place that back in your sheath."

"The same way you haven't replaced your dagger in your sheath?"

Gavin glanced down, smiling. "You mean this one?" He shoved it slightly forward, driving it toward Davel's side. The El'aras dagger pressed up against his side enough for the point to bite into the flesh.

Davel winced, jerking away.

Gavin backed away, sliding the El'aras dagger into its sheath, grinning briefly at Davel. "Send word of when and where you want to meet."

"You know where I want to meet."

"I'm not coming to your barracks."

"Do you really think I will do something to you there?"

Gavin shrugged. "I wouldn't put it past you."

"You have been granted safe passage in the city. Isn't that reassurance enough?"

Gavin glanced toward the other two constables. "No. Send word where you want to meet, and you'd better keep the number of constables down. Otherwise, you might find that the egg isn't nearly as accessible as you hoped."

Gavin slipped back, holding on to the dagger. The blade glowed softly.

How long had it been doing that?

Long enough.

The Fate.

Davel glared at him, but Gavin ignored it, reaching the edge of the rooftop and dropping down. He lingered for a moment on the street and looked for any sign of movement. Something was not quite right.

He glanced overhead. The constables—other than Davel—had moved toward the edge of the rooftop and watched him.

Let them.

There didn't seem to be anything near the Dragon, though he had to be careful. Circling around, he reached the alley and slipped the El'aras dagger out of the sheath to see if it was still glowing. Unfortunately, it was.

It wouldn't be because of the constables. They might have enchantments, but they weren't enchanters. As far as Gavin knew, there shouldn't be anyone here who used that kind of power.

Maybe he'd made a mistake not encouraging Davel to follow him in.

An idea started to come to him. Gavin darted forward, and he walked through the door leading into the kitchen of the Dragon. He paused a moment. The kitchen was empty and smelled of bread, though he saw no loaves anywhere. A single lantern glowed softly in the center of the kitchen, resting on one of the counters. The air was cool, evidence that the ovens had not been lit recently. He smelled no roasted meats, no vegetables, and no ale. All of it reminded him just how little the Dragon had been working as a tavern recently.

When he reached the door leading out into the tavern,

he waited another moment, looking out. The Dragon was quiet. He didn't see any sign of Wrenlow or Jessica or anyone else. The dagger still glowed.

He opened the door and slipped along the back wall. He didn't see anything, but experience had shown him there were times when he might not see what was there. He crept toward the back staircase.

When he reached the door leading up to the rooms, he pressed his hand on it, then continued moving around the tavern. Reaching the fireplace, Gavin hesitated.

He tapped on the enchantment.

"If you're there, give me some sort of alert," he whispered.

He didn't hear anything.

Could something have happened to Wrenlow?

The Dragon had been attacked too many times because of Gavin, and he knew he needed to be cautious and move carefully, but at this point, he had no idea whether there was anything to be concerned about. It might only be him overreacting.

He continued around the wall. "Wrenlow?" he whispered.

Gavin slipped the El'aras dagger into its sheath and switched over to the sword. When he unsheathed it, the blade blazed with a bright white light.

He turned slowly in place, looking all around. He hesitated a moment, then he took a step forward. Pressure built around him.

There it is.

He'd been waiting for a sign of magic. There was a faint shimmer at the corner of his vision, something that suggested the sorcerers had somehow shrouded the entire inside of the tavern in a way that prevented him from seeing what else was here.

Tricky.

Gavin took another step forward, shifting the sword so that it gradually cut through the power holding him. He didn't want to use it too abruptly and play his hand too quickly, but he needed to use it in a way that allowed him to step forward so that the sorcerer couldn't hold on to him.

Gavin dragged the sword with him.

Then he felt tension. The pressure around him was different, though he remembered that feeling. It came from the floor, wrapping around his feet, working its way up his legs, reminding him of what he had experienced the night that he'd been attacked by the Fates.

Which meant the Fate was here.

CHAPTER ELEVEN

Gavin took a moment to focus his breathing. He needed to gather himself to ensure the Fate didn't use his power against him and prevent him from breaking free. He reached for that deep part of him. These days, he found himself reaching for the core reserves far more often than he ever had before. It was like a pool buried deep within him.

When he had trained while younger, learning how to access that power, it had been some distant part of him that he had understood to be there but only accessed when he needed it. Emergencies, essentially. These days, Gavin found that everything became an emergency.

What had happened to Wrenlow and Jessica?

There might have been others in the tavern that had been impacted by the Fate as well, and he would have to offer them protection. Gavin didn't see anything here. The only thing he was aware of was a persistent sense of pressure slowly snaking around him.

The more he felt it, the clearer he was that the sensation twisting around his legs continued to build, working up around his chest, slowly easing into position, making it so he could barely move.

It started to constrict.

As he pushed against it, he could feel a strange barricade as it bulged, though didn't break. He was the Chain Breaker, and that was the strength he needed to get free of the Fates. Invisible power continued to constrict, and a shadow separated from the rest.

Gavin gripped the sword as the shadow came toward him.

"Where is it?" a voice asked.

Gavin couldn't make out the source of the voice. Everything was shadowed around him. They were using some sort of concealment upon him, making it so that he couldn't find what they were doing or where they were.

"Where is what?" Gavin found getting the words out to be more difficult than he would have expected.

The shadow came closer and stepped into his field of vision. It was the same bearded Fate he had seen the night before. "You made a mistake attacking me. I will have it."

He had a strange voice and a deep, booming quality to it. Gavin almost smiled to himself. It had to be magically enhanced; something like an enchantment.

It made him wonder how this sorcerer's voice would

sound without the enchantment. Probably weak. A man who needed to enchant his voice would be afraid.

Gavin knew how to handle someone like that.

If only he could break free.

The strange sword was powerful enough that Gavin thought that it should carve through the magic. Only, as he attempted to push against whatever the Fates did to him, Gavin found the resistance more than what he could withstand.

"I don't know what you're talking about. You're the one who took it from the Captain." Gavin grew increasingly annoyed with the Fate. He still couldn't make out much detail of the sorcerer, but he could feel him as he pressed against Gavin. There was a strange odor to him as well. "How much longer do you think you can hold me?"

"I have much experience holding others. You are no more challenge than anyone else."

"I am Gavin Lorren, the Chain Breaker."

The sorcerer chuckled as he stepped closer. "You have believed yourself to be the Chain Breaker, but this is no chain." The power continued to constrict around him, feeling almost as if it were something alive. It slithered along his skin.

Gavin could no longer hold the sword out from him, rendering it useless. Any attempt to free himself from what he detected was pointless. There was nothing that he could do.

The sorcerer held him. "You will find that it hurts less when you stop struggling."

"I'm not going to stop."

"Then you will suffer. As your friends suffer."

Much like the sorcerer had said, when Gavin stopped struggling, the constriction around him began to ease. He could still feel it writhing, almost as if it were trying to work its way around him and gain a better position, but it no longer hurt.

"What did you do to them?" Gavin said.

They must be here somewhere.

How had he found us?

It hadn't taken him that long to get here when Wrenlow had called for him.

"They thought to fight. They made a mistake, and they will pay for it."

"If you do anything to them—"

"What do you think you can do with these threats of yours, Gavin Lorren?" The sorcerer took a step toward him, and the energy coming from him persisted, building even more. "What do you think you are capable of doing? Anything you can do, I have already prepared for. Now. Where is it?"

Gavin realized that he didn't really know anything about the Fates. Nothing other than what Zella had shared with him, and she had not known nearly enough. There were at least three, though he was dealing with only one. At least, that Gavin knew about.

What if there were others here?

He started to focus on his core reserves, trying to prepare for the possibility that he might have to use even more of that power that he had answers faded. If there were more than one of the Fates present in the city, Gavin wasn't sure what it would take for him to break free.

The Fate leaned toward Gavin, pressing his face up against him. Darkness still shrouded him, making it difficult for Gavin to see anything, as if the sorcerer intended to keep him in the dark.

Gavin strained once more against the bindings. He called upon his core reserves, but that strength had already started to fade after everything he'd been through. As he pushed against the strange binding, it constricted even more tightly around him.

The sorcerer chuckled again. "I must admit that it is quite enjoyable to immobilize you in such a way. I will have what you have stolen from us."

Gavin grunted. He tried to turn and shift the sword, but even that wasn't going to work. The only thing that he could move was his head, and he could barely even twist toward the sorcerer.

"What makes you think I have anything?" Gavin asked.

The sorcerer chuckled once more, taking a slight step back as he watched Gavin. "You will share with me."

Gavin prepared for the increased squeeze of power around him. He had to summon the core reserves within him—he was convinced that he could break free once he did. He pushed against what the sorcerer wrapped around him. As he did, Gavin could feel the barrier start to slip.

The sorcerer took a step toward him, now standing only a step away, and the power wrapped more tightly around him. Gavin could still move his head. He jerked it forward in a sharp movement, cracking his forehead against the sorcerer's.

The sorcerer cried out, backing away.

The barrier around Gavin suddenly slipped. He darted forward, slicing through it, and he thrust his sword into the sorcerer's belly. The shadows fell from around the sorcerer, and suddenly he became visible as he pulled away from Gavin.

He was a slim man, nothing like the first sorcerer Gavin had seen. His jet-black hair ran in waves down to his shoulders. His eyes were lined, the only evidence of age, and his thin lips pressed together in a tight frown. The dark robes he wore were similar to the other sorcerer's.

Where are the others?

Wrenlow and Jessica had to be here.

Maybe even Gaspar.

Not Imogen. She wouldn't have let a sorcerer hold them.

"You weren't expecting that, were you?" Gavin said.

The sorcerer, no longer shrouded by shadows, glared at Gavin. He wrapped his hands around the sword and pushed, his strength forcing Gavin back much more easily than expected.

Gavin stumbled backward, still holding on to the sword, and blood dripped from the blade.

The sorcerer looked down. He *tsk*ed and waved his hand over his belly. The bleeding stopped. "No, I wasn't expecting that, but you're not the first person to stab me. I doubt you will be the last. It will be the only time you succeed, though."

The sorcerer started to wind tendrils of power around Gavin again, which snaked up from the ground and worked around his legs. Gavin brought the sword down, carving at them. Each time, another strange invisible tendril started to crawl around him. The sorcerer worked more rapidly, and more and more of them continued to work around Gavin until he was once again trapped.

The sorcerer took a step toward him, smiling. He didn't bother to shroud himself in shadows any longer, likely realizing that it was unnecessary now that Gavin had seen him.

"I will enjoy tormenting you," the sorcerer said.

"Come too close, and you're going to find my sword in your belly again," Gavin said.

The sorcerer grinned. "I think not." He twisted his hand, and the strange magic that held Gavin surged more tightly, wrapping around him.

Gavin could barely move. He could barely breathe. He focused on the energy deep within him and continued to call on it, trying to push outward. He felt it bulge again, but not nearly enough. The energy within him, his core reserve, started to fade.

The sorcerer watched him, almost as if he knew that Gavin had some way of accessing that power.

All he needed to do was to access that power again, and he hoped that he could shift the sword. He wasn't going to give up. He'd been through too much to give up like that.

The power constricted again, squeezing him.

The sorcerer smiled. "Yes. You will make an interesting—"

The door to the tavern thundered open. An explosion of light ripped through the room.

Gavin turned his head, the only part of him that still could move.

The sorcerer held on to the power around him as darkened figures darted into the room. They moved quickly—enchanted movement. Constables. Even enchanted, they'd be slaughtered.

"No!" Gavin yelled.

More shadows streaked into the room.

The sorcerer leaned forward toward Gavin, smiling at him. "How lovely."

They were flickers of movement, dark shadows and nothing else. The constables were getting attacked; the force of it too much, too aggressive, and much more than they could withstand. Occasional explosions of light erupted.

The sorcerer remained near Gavin, and he held one hand out, turning it slowly in place. There was a buildup of power from him, but the sorcerer's focus was distracted.

Gavin could use that and find a different way to surprise him. He pushed against the barrier.

Glancing in his direction, the sorcerer turned his hand and tried to twist his wrist, but something struck the sorcerer at the same time. The combination of Gavin pushing against him and the suddenness of the attack freed Gavin.

He could move.

He slashed, slicing through the sorcerer's leg, and the

sorcerer cried out. Gavin darted forward again, and he brought the sword around and stabbed the sorcerer through his belly. He jerked the blade upward.

The sorcerer glared at him. Once again, he grabbed the blade, gripping it on either side, and slid it out. He waved a hand at his chest, and the wounds knitted back together.

Gavin charged forward with the blade and carved at the sorcerer, but the sorcerer blocked him. Gavin lunged, sweeping the blade again.

The sorcerer held his hand up, and he simply caught it.

The blade cut through his palm, but then it stopped. He turned his attention to Gavin. "You are *most* troublesome."

He grabbed the blade and threw it across the room. He took a step toward Gavin, and he drove a magically enhanced fist toward him. The punch landed in Gavin's chest, knocking the wind out of him. He tried to take a gasping breath, but he couldn't.

The sorcerer grabbed Gavin and dragged him toward the door. If the sorcerer pulled him out of the Dragon, Gavin doubted he could get back to find Wrenlow and Jessica.

He had to break free.

I have an enchantment.

He pulled it out of his pocket and slipped it onto his wrist. He kept the enchantment on him, though never used it because he tried not to become reliant upon it. It was too dangerous for him to do so.

He drew upon its power and turned to see whether he could escape in some fashion. Everything seemed to slow.

The combination of strength and speed was enough that Gavin wondered if he would be able to overwhelm the sorcerer. He brought his arm around, chopping it through the sorcerer's arm.

There was a satisfying crack as the sorcerer's arm shattered. Gavin staggered back, suddenly freed from his grip. He raced across the room, grabbed his sword, and spun, but the sorcerer was gone.

Light exploded in the room. Gavin clutched his chest, trying to steady his breathing.

Everything hurt.

He noticed a hint of pale white glowing along his blade.

Gavin looked up and saw Davel Chan. The constables filled the entire front space of the Dragon. A dozen or so men all had swords unsheathed, and all were dressed in the simple gray jacket and pants of the constables. Even Davel held a sword, something Gavin had not yet seen him fight with, but he suspected a man of his station had considerable skill.

Davel turned to Gavin with a tight smile. "Now. About the egg."

CHAPTER TWELVE

Gavin sat in a chair near the hearth. He clutched his chest, trying to breathe through the pain. He was accustomed to handling pain, but what he now felt was something different—as if his bones had been shattered but, at the same time, as if they were also knitting back together and healing.

He didn't know if it was something he was doing, whether he had some enhancement naturally that would allow him to recover, or whether it was something that was tied to what the sorcerer had done to him. He'd always healed fast.

He held on to the sword. Gavin had refused to sheathe it, even after there was no evidence of the sorcerer attack here. He kept the enchantment on as well.

Wrenlow sat across from him. His face was bruised, and a trickle of blood ran down from his nose that he hadn't completely wiped away.

Jessica looked unharmed. Gavin supposed that he should be thankful for that. She had been injured enough times because of him.

"He was after you," Wrenlow said as Gavin approached. "I tried to get word to you, but he attacked before I had a chance."

Gavin shook his head. "You did well."

"They sealed us after that," Wrenlow said, looking over to Jessica. She was quiet, but the longer the sorcerer had been gone, the more she seemed to be coming around. "It was like they put up a blanket of darkness over us."

Jessica nodded. "I couldn't see anything. I could barely hear anything. Only muffled sounds."

"And the fighting," Wrenlow said.

Jessica frowned and nodded. She swept her gaze around her again before settling on the constables nearby. "I don't like having the constables around here," Jessica said.

"I don't either," Gavin said, "but I don't know that we have much choice in the matter."

"We could tell them to leave."

"Do you think they would?"

"You have an agreement with them," she said.

Gavin shook his head. "I *had* an agreement, but I don't know if that's been modified now that Davel had to save me."

Had Davel not come, Gavin had little doubt that he would have succumbed to the sorcerer. He would have been taken from here, tormented and killed. Given that Gavin had stabbed the sorcerer twice, the man probably wanted revenge.

Gavin got to his feet, feeling shaky. He needed rest.

The door opened, and Davel strode in, followed by three constables. His gaze darted around the tavern before settling on Gavin. He made his way toward where Gavin sat near the hearth, grabbed a chair, and took a seat across from him. The other three constables took up positions at each door around the room.

"I suppose I should thank you," Gavin said.

"That is generally what one does when their life is saved," Davel said, smiling tightly.

"You knew they were here."

"As I said, I recognized there was a sorcerer's presence in the city."

But Gavin didn't think he knew about the Captain. "You weren't aware of it when Cyran was here."

Davel's brow furrowed. "No. I'm not exactly sure why that is, only that he managed to conceal his presence from us."

Gavin flicked his gaze toward where he had been attacked. "I have a feeling this one doesn't think he needs to hide."

"Probably not," Davel said. He fell silent, and he stared at the crackling logs.

Lighting a fire was the first thing that Jessica had done after the attack. Well, almost the first thing. She had cleaned up the tavern as well as she could, tipping the chairs back into place, moving the tables back where they belonged. Thankfully, she and Wrenlow had been trapped and held by the sorcerer in one corner, and as soon as the attack started and the sorcerer turned toward the constables, the two of them were able to sneak into the kitchen and hide.

Gaspar hadn't been there.

"Who is he?" Davel finally asked.

"I don't know much about him. He called himself one of the Fates, though the only thing that I've been able to determine about the Fates is that they somehow lead the sorcerers. I came across him the night before when he killed the Captain."

That elicited a slight raise of the brow. Not much more than that. "That one preferred to risk more than he should." He shook his head. "No, the Fates don't lead the sorcerers," Davel said, sighing. "It's worse than that. Much worse. They control them. The Fates have guided the sorcerers for as long as I've been aware of it."

"As long as you've been aware of it?" Gavin was surprised that word of the Captain's death didn't hit Davel any harder than it had.

"Yes," Davel said. "We understand the dangers of magic in the city, and we take great pains to ensure that we are prepared for the possibility of any further attack. If the Fates are involved, so are all who serve them."

"From what you say, all the sorcerers serve them."

Davel shook his head. "If we have one of the Fates within Yoran, then we are in far more trouble than I realized."

"And you attacked one."

"There was always going to be a fight if one of the Fates was here," Davel said.

"What do you know about them?" Gavin shifted on the chair, and he moved the sword. He needed to know if what Zella had shared with him was true or not. It probably was, but there might be gaps in her knowledge.

"Every rumor you've heard is probably true," Davel said. "The best solution is to offer them whatever they want so that they leave."

Don't let him have it.

"You think that's all it will take?" Gavin laughed softly. "My experience with people like that is that even when they get what they want, they don't necessarily leave. They're here for a reason, and someone with that much power likely has a reason that brought them here—one that might pose a danger to all of Yoran."

"As if you care about Yoran."

"I care about several people here," Gavin said. As he said it, he knew it was true. This despite everything he kept telling himself about needing to leave Yoran. "And myself."

"That's all you care about," Davel said.

Gavin shrugged. "I've never claimed otherwise. In fact, I have been quite clear that the only person I am concerned about is myself. When it comes to an attack like this, I'm not willing to stay here and suffer."

And he couldn't hand over anything to the Fate as he didn't have anything. Could he have followed someone *other* than the Fate out of the Captain's fortress? The attack on the Captain had been brutal, and he couldn't imagine anyone *not* a sorcerer handling him—and his people—like that.

He had to figure that out.

The Fate had been near the sorcerer's lair.

"I stabbed the Fate twice," Gavin went on. "The second time should have been enough to kill him. I carved through his belly, up into his chest, and he pushed my sword away as if it were nothing."

"They supposedly have diamond-hard skin, and it's impossible to even get a knife into them." Davel glanced down at the sword. "What is that weapon?"

Gavin took a seat and held the sword over his lap, and he glanced down at the blade. "It's an El'aras sword, at least as far as I can tell. It's a little bit different than the dagger I have." He pulled the dagger out from the sheath and held it out. "This one I took off of an El'aras."

"Not the sword?"

"Not the sword," Gavin said.

"But how do you know it's an El'aras blade?"

"I don't. At least not necessarily. But it reacts the same as the dagger. It glows when there's magic used around us." Gavin stared at the sword for a moment, then twisted it in place. "Besides, it has something else about it that makes it more likely to be an El'aras blade. This writing," Gavin said, motioning to it. He held the sword out.

Davel leaned close. His mouth was pressed together in a tight line, and after studying it for a moment, he sat back in his chair. "I don't know if it's an El'aras sword. I have heard that even the El'aras cannot kill one of the Fates."

"I doubt that's true," Gavin said. "I have some experience with the El'aras, and their sword fighters are quite skilled."

"I'm not doubting the skill of their fighters. All I'm saying is that the Fates have incredibly hard skin."

"Magically enchanted," Gavin said.

"Possibly."

"Then maybe there's something that we can do to counter that." If they were going to have to deal with the Fates, then they needed more than an equal footing. "Do you think the egg can create an enchantment like that?" he asked.

"It's possible." Davel looked up. "Enchantments can only be created by those who understand them. We have to find someone who has the necessary knowledge."

He understood what Davel was getting at—he wanted to know where the enchanters were.

"I don't think I can help you," he said.

"You can help. You're just choosing not to."

Gavin looked down at the sword again, noting the symbols on the blade. If it were more than just the El'aras blade, then what was it? He had found the sword beneath Cyran's home. Within his lair.

Another sorcerer's lair.

And it had been protected. Almost as if it were something dangerous.

Of course, the sword would be. Gavin had seen how dangerous it could be, but that didn't mean it was anything other than an El'aras sword because even that would be dangerous.

Only, an El'aras sword wouldn't have been kept within a protective barrier.

The Fate had been after something.

Could it be the sword?

"Gavin?" Jessica asked.

He glanced over. "I'm thinking."

"Think more quickly," Davel said.

Gavin turned toward him, gripping the sword and suppressing the frustration within him. "Don't tell me what I need to do."

Davel smiled. "That's the attitude you're going to need with them."

"You don't know them," Gavin said.

"I know them well enough. I understand the danger we face when it comes to the Fates."

Gavin glanced down at the sword. Somehow, it was important.

He thought about the sorcerer's lair. It wasn't only that the sword had been found there, it was also how the sword had been used to help him move from one place to another within the lair.

Gavin wasn't about to give the sword to the Fate.

Which meant he needed help—the constables' help.

"Why don't we start with something more basic?" Gavin said.

"Basic how?" Davel asked.

"I think we need to better understand just what the egg can do."

Davel looked at him for a moment before shaking his head. "No."

"You don't want me to know?"

"I don't have a problem with you knowing, but I have a problem with what you intend to do when you understand it."

"First you want me to work with you on using the egg to create enchantments, and now you're telling me no?"

"I'm not going to have you arm yourself with enchantments," Davel said.

Gavin flashed a bright smile. "Seeing as how I'm the one in command of the egg, I don't know that you get to choose that."

The only problem with it was that he would have to get to the egg. That might be a challenge. For all his taunting of Davel and offering him an opportunity to access the egg, Gavin had secured it in a way that would keep it safe and ensure that no one else could reach the egg unless he allowed it. Now he didn't know whether that was going to be easy enough for him to accommodate.

"I'll return with the egg, and you bring your enchanter-type people here," Gavin said.

Davel looked around the tavern. "Here? You would have us place enchantments inside this place?"

"Hey!" Jessica said.

"I agree with her sentiment," Gavin said. "What makes you think this is any less effective than your constable barracks?"

"There are requirements within each place where the enchantments are placed."

"What sort of requirements?"

"The kind that ensures a certain stability. I'm not going to walk you through this. It will take far more time, and if you're going to secure the egg and bring it back here, then we can talk about it at that time."

"We can talk about it now," Gavin said. "Because if I'm going to bring the egg to you, I want to know I'm going to be safe. I want to know that anything I might do for you will be safe."

"It's not a matter of safety. It's a matter of having the necessary focus of the magic," Davel said.

"You don't think you can have that focus here?"

"There will be too many distractions."

"What kind of place do you need?" Gavin asked. "Other than your barracks."

"Short of having access to a sorcerer's lair, we need a place devoid of any influence."

Gavin hadn't known the lair's purpose before, but the idea that it would prevent any magical influence from escaping did make sense to him. He didn't know if that would be necessary, though. He wasn't willing to go to the constables' barracks, which meant that he would have to come up with a different solution.

"I might have a place that we can use," Gavin said. "When I return, I'll tell you. But only you."

"That's not going to work," Davel said.

"Why not?" Gavin asked.

"I have to tell someone."

"Don't you trust me?"

"No," Davel said.

"Good. I don't trust you either. I suppose that makes us even when it comes to working together."

"You're a strange man, Gavin Lorren," Davel said.

Gavin flashed a smile. "Get whoever you need ready and bring them here."

Davel got to his feet, and he made a small motion with his hand. The other constables followed him out of the tavern.

That left Gavin with Wrenlow and Jessica.

He hadn't learned what happened with Gaspar and Imogen. They'd been gone for a while. The only thing he could think of was that they were off on some job. Likely something to help protect Desarra and Olivia. That seemed to be Gaspar's greatest concern these days.

"Are you really going to work with the constables?" Jessica asked.

"If it will allow us to make some enchantments, I think I need to."

"Then I need to make sure the tavern is secured." She got up and headed to the kitchen, leaving Gavin to have a chance to talk to Wrenlow alone.

"This Fate already took something from the Captain and was after something else. Maybe the sword." He described to Wrenlow what he'd discovered in the lair, and his friend grew increasingly unsettled, shifting in his seat. "As much as I hate to think this way, I'm going to have to take on the

Fate." Going up against a powerful sorcerer again didn't sit well with him, but at this point, he didn't know if there was any alternative. "I'd love to have your help."

"You know you'll have it."

"I might need your focus, too."

He didn't want Wrenlow angry with him, but he would need Wrenlow's connections. Besides, the Fate had proven he knew how to find Gavin—and those he cared about.

Wrenlow watched him. Finally, he leaned forward, rested his hands on the table, and shook his head slowly. "I don't like it, but I also don't like the idea of leaving powerful sorcerers like that to terrorize the city."

"I'm not sure it's about terrorizing so much as it's about finding something they want," Gavin said.

"Maybe that won't be their intention, but their presence in the city would be," Wrenlow said. "We know what sorcerers can do. Even if they don't mean to cause harm, they always seem to manage to do it."

Gavin crossed his arms over his chest, looking down at the blade. Wrenlow was right, which was part of the reason that Gavin tried to avoid sorcery.

Now he was far more entrenched in it than he ever had been before.

Was it all because of Yoran?

Maybe it was all because of Cyran.

He sighed. "Let's start with one thing at a time."

He didn't want to rely upon enchantments, but Gavin wasn't sure he would have much of a choice.

"I'm going to get the egg. She's going to be busy getting

the Dragon back in order," he said, looking over to where Jessica moved the tables back into position, "so I'll hurry back."

"You don't think the Fate will return here?" Wrenlow asked.

Gavin glanced toward the door. "I have a feeling the constables will be watching."

"Which means that you think Davel will follow you when you go for the egg," Wrenlow said.

Gavin chuckled. At least he could laugh about that much. "I do."

"You don't want him to know where you're keeping it, though."

"Not really." There was value in having the sorcerer's lair to himself.

At least, there *had* been.

Now he didn't know if he could consider it safe.

"How do you intend to sneak past him?" Wrenlow asked.

"Oh, I have a few ideas."

CHAPTER THIRTEEN

Gavin kept the hood of his cloak up as he headed through the streets. The city was quiet, as far as Yoran was concerned. There was typically more of a crowd, and this was not nearly as dense of a gathering as was often found moving through the city. A dozen people were in the distance, but as they looked toward him—or, more likely, toward the constables trailing him—they veered off, disappearing down some of the side streets or alleyways.

As far as he could tell, a pair of constables had been following him for the last few blocks. The streets of Yoran quickly widened the closer to the edge of the city, the buildings getting even more spaced apart, mostly because the buildings were smaller. Gavin hadn't made any effort to sneak out of the Dragon any differently than he would've normally.

He wanted the constables to know he'd left, though he didn't know if that would leave the tavern unprotected.

Having the constables watch over the Dragon would offer a layer of protection that Jessica might need.

Gavin reached an intersection, pausing on the uneven cobbles and stepping off to the side of the street to let three children pulling a wagon toward a nearby market pass him. He hesitated before hurrying forward. The carts on either side of the street pressed toward him, as if they were actively trying to slow him. Most of them looked to be houses, though he noticed a few storefronts, all with darkened windows. In the distance, he noted three constables heading toward him. They must have been using enchantments to communicate.

Clever.

Of course, he had a similar ability.

Gavin turned into an alley, climbed up onto the rooftop, then slid forward. He didn't see any of the constables around him, though he suspected they would be following even from afar.

He wasn't entirely comfortable moving from rooftop to rooftop, but it did offer him a freedom he didn't have down on the street. He could more effectively watch the movement within the street and make out whether the constables were trailing him. There was another cluster of constables he hadn't seen when he was at street level. They were heading toward his previous location.

"Whenever you're ready," Gavin whispered, looking below.

Wrenlow popped out of the doorway where Gavin had just been, pulled the hood of his cloak up, and started to walk down the street. "Are you really sure this is necessary? He knows what you're doing anyway."

"We need some protections he doesn't know about."

"Even if the Fate knows how to find the lair?"

Gavin thought about arguing that the Fate might not know how to find *this* lair, but it didn't matter if they were connected. "Just do it."

"I don't look anything like you."

"It's not a matter of whether you look like me. It's a matter of whether you can convince them that you *are* me. At least for a little while."

Wrenlow started to tilt his head up in Gavin's direction, but he stopped. "I don't even have your size."

"You don't need my size. You're wearing one of my cloaks, and that's all they're going to see." Thankfully, he had two that were the same. He could take the one he'd been wearing off and slip into the growing crowd. Some constables could be curious about why he looked different, but he suspected they'd focus on the cloak and trail after that more than anything else. "I'm going to watch for a while."

"Fine, but I don't know how well I'm going to uncover anything going this way."

Gavin smiled to himself as Wrenlow headed into the street. The constables converged on him, keeping some distance, though not so much they wouldn't be noticeable. Could they really think that Gavin was so ignorant as to overlook them? It wasn't as if they were traveling at night.

"Take the next left," he said.

"And then what?"

"And then keep winding that way."

"What about you?" Wrenlow asked.

"I'm going to be fine."

"You don't have anybody watching over you."

"So long as I have you in my ear, you are with me," Gavin said.

He waited for a while longer, ensuring the constables were trailing after Wrenlow. Then he scrambled down from the roof and followed the alley until he reached the end of it, twisting back out into the main street.

From there, Gavin started to head deeper into the city. He took a circuitous route to make sure that there wasn't anyone else following him. It wasn't just the constables that he worried about. It was also the enchanters. And, worst of all, the Fates. If the Fates happened to find him, then he wanted to be ready.

Gavin didn't see any followers. As far as he could tell, no one was trailing after him. He followed the street, heading toward the outskirts of the city.

When he reached Byron Street, quickening his pace as he strode along it, there weren't nearly as many people limiting his movement as there had been before. Cyran's house sat in the distance.

As Gavin approached, he slowed, glancing around him and looking for signs of movement. He didn't see anything, but then a surge of shadows near him caught his attention.

There was a danger for him coming here, especially if the Fate knew about the lair, and Gavin had a hard time thinking the Fate wouldn't know about it. He just had to hope they hadn't found the egg.

Besides, without the sword, the different lairs *didn't* connect.

Unless he knows some magic trick to open the door.

He had to push that thought out of his mind.

Gavin decided to make a loop around Cyran's house. Following the road past, he didn't see anything there. He moved as quickly as he could and then circled around the block. The shadows never changed. Perhaps he was just overreacting.

Looking back around, Gavin glanced toward the forest. It was near enough to the edge of Yoran that it seemed as if the city had grown up to the forest and then stopped. It had younger trees, at least in this section, but if he were to follow through the forest, he would reach an older growth—and the El'aras. It amused him that the people of Yoran thought they were so separated from magic when they lived so close to the El'aras.

It wasn't just the El'aras, though that was what Gavin had believed when he'd first come to Yoran. Now he knew about the sorcerers and enchanters and the constables, even. Far too many people in the city used magic. Even him, to an extent, though he really had no idea how he was using magic or whether what he did truly constituted magic.

As he headed back around, he made his way toward Cyran's home. The building was darkened, as expected. When he neared, he glanced along the street, looking for signs of anyone paying attention to him, but didn't see anyone. Gavin slipped his dagger into the lock, glancing at the blade to make sure it wasn't glowing as he popped it open, and headed inside. He closed the door behind him, locked it, and then peered out the window, watching for movement.

When he was convinced the street was empty, he turned his attention back to the house. The blade still didn't glow. *It hadn't at the Captain's house, either.* He would be careful. Work quickly. That was all he could do.

As he headed deeper into Cyran's house, he glanced at the cabinets. Then he moved into the back room, pulled the rug off, and lifted the trapdoor. Once he climbed down the ladder, Gavin hurried past the broken stone that had been pulled down from the ceiling and reached the lair entrance.

He held his hand up against it, and he felt the sense of power within him, the core reserves of energy. Given everything that he'd gone through today, he needed a chance to rest and recuperate to restore those reserves of power, but he didn't have the chance to do so yet. He called on that power, and then he pulled the door open. Once inside, he closed it behind him again.

Gavin looked around the lair. Nothing seemed amiss. He searched for evidence that someone had come through here, but the triggers he'd placed to detect such a thing were undisturbed. As far as he could tell, no one had been here.

Get the egg and get back. That was all he needed to do.

Stay ahead of the Fate. Prepare for what he might do next.

He wanted something he thought Gavin had.

The sword made the most sense, especially if he were coming to a sorcerer's lair, but there was another possibility. The Fate *could* have been after the egg—only *why?* It created enchantments. Nothing a sorcerer needed.

Gavin headed toward the back of the room, where there was another cabinet. He had found this cabinet during one of his attempts at exploring and was intrigued that he had to press the El'aras dagger into it to open it. That suggested the cabinet involved magic—that it would *contain* magic.

He pried the dagger into the cabinet again and opened the door, revealing the jade egg inside. The egg was smooth and had a greenish hue to it, though from time to time, Gavin thought that it glowed. He didn't take it out of the cabinet that often, as he was unsure whether he should. As far as he knew, the enchanters had poured some part of themselves into the egg to create a weapon that could be used against the sorcerers during the war two decades prior, and doing so had changed things for those who had been involved. It was the reason that Gavin was tempted to return the egg to the enchanters, but he needed to know that he would do so at the right time. For now, he had held onto it, making sure that neither the enchanters nor the constables could use it against the other.

Gavin slipped it into his pocket.

It felt strange to have an item of such importance in his pocket, but he didn't know what else to do with it. Perhaps he should have acquired a case for it at one point. Would this place have a connection to those hidden tunnels the same as the other sorcerer's lair had? What if there was something here that he hadn't seen before?

The door.

He paused in front of the door, and he traced his finger on the symbols. Much like in the other sorcerer's lair, the El'aras writing seemed to have some sort of meaning, though Gavin couldn't read it to understand just what it was. He held the dagger up to it and waited to see if there would be some sort of hiss coming from it, but there was nothing.

What about the sword?

It had worked for the other doors. If it worked here, then maybe he could find a connection to those other lairs.

The sword didn't do anything either.

There didn't seem to be any hidden doors. Maybe that was why Cyran had chosen this place. Either that, or Cyran had built it himself, and it didn't connect to the others.

There was still one other door he hadn't managed to unlock. Maybe it would connect here, but he didn't have any way of triggering it to open.

Not now, though. He needed to head back. Stay ahead of the Fate.

Gavin opened the door and stepped back out into the hallway, sealing the door closed again. When he neared the ladder, he thought he saw shadows moving near him.

He unsheathed the sword. The blade had a faint glowing sheen to it.

Not the Fate. It would glow more brightly were it him.

There were times when he had seen the blade glow

when there had been no magic. Gavin had come to believe that this was possibly related to him. He held it out, peering along the hallway.

He had been attacked there once before. He started to climb the ladder, and then he paused again when he was partway up, looking along the length of the hallway. There was nothing other than the shadows, but they didn't seem to be anything unnatural.

He reached the surface, closed the trapdoor, and rolled the carpet back over. Then he stood there, waiting.

Gavin had no idea if something had been down there with him, though he didn't think there was. He would've seen something more.

Would it even matter? As far as he could tell, he'd searched through it enough that he didn't think there was anything of value in there.

Gavin headed to the front door and pulled it open. *Had I closed it all the way?* He thought that he had, but it didn't seem as if it had latched. If the Fate decided to attack, he wasn't about to be surprised again.

Time to show him something more.

Gavin reached into his pocket, and he grabbed the bracelet that Olivia had enchanted for him. He slipped it on and paused a moment as the enchantment took hold. He had to adjust to the sudden shift through him. There was a surge of strength that coursed through him. It was a reason he didn't like using enchantments that often. He could see how they could become a crutch, almost intoxicating in their strength. It was better to be prepared to exist without such enchantments.

Gavin stepped outside of the house. He pulled the door closed, making sure to seal it tightly behind him. As he backed along the street, he kept his gaze on the building until he reached the forest. He stayed at the edge of the forest for a few moments, watching Cyran's house. There was nothing, but he couldn't shake the feeling he had.

Something moved along the street. He shifted his attention but then saw another surge of movement. This one came from closer to Cyran's house.

Shadows—or smoke, he realized—snaked out of the door.

There *had* been something inside.

Gavin remained where he was, lingering at the tree line. He stayed concealed as long as he could, watching the street for signs of movement. The shadows were like smoke, making it difficult for him to trail them, but he could see them drift along the street and then disappear.

He stayed where he was for a little while longer. He didn't see anything more, but what if that one movement, that wisp of smoke, wasn't all that was there? His patience was rewarded when another wisp of smoke drifted out of Cyran's home.

Strange.

This one floated away, heading in the opposite direction as the first.

He continued to watch, but nothing else changed.

"Gavin?" Wrenlow's voice came in loud through the enchantment.

"What is it?"

"They caught me."

"How far did you get?"

Knowing that Wrenlow would be taking a roundabout path to the market, it wouldn't have taken long before they realized that something was amiss.

"Well, they waited a lot longer than I thought. Got to the central market and did some shopping," Wrenlow said.

"What sort of shopping?"

"A few books. Some pastries. A belt."

"A belt?"

"I needed a new one. Mine was starting to fray."

Gavin chuckled softly. "What did they do?"

"As soon as they realized I wasn't you, they disappeared," Wrenlow said.

"Did you see where they went?"

"No, but there had to be a dozen constables following me."

"They really want the egg," Gavin said.

"You won't be able to keep it in the city indefinitely."

"I know."

Gavin didn't feel as if he could take it from Yoran either. And if the Fate *was* after it, he had to keep it from him, too. The egg belonged to the city. It belonged to the people here, to the enchanters who had sacrificed so much to create it.

"When are you returning?" Wrenlow asked.

Gavin stared at Cyran's door for a little while longer. So

far, there had been no more smoke drifting out of it. Whatever had been there must have disappeared.

Had they found what they were looking for?

"I need to check on one thing, and then I'll return," he said.

"What is it?"

"Something that I saw."

"Be careful," Wrenlow said.

"Aren't I always?"

"Be as careful as I would be."

"I don't think anyone can be as careful as you," Gavin said. He stepped out onto the street, moving away from the forest.

A hint of smoke rose in the distance. It was at the far end of the street, and it was coming toward him.

Gavin turned and looked behind him. There was smoke moving toward him from that direction as well.

"Wrenlow?"

No answer. Either Wrenlow didn't hear him, or something had happened to the enchantment.

Gavin tapped on it again, focusing on the enchantment. "Wrenlow, if you're there, I'm going to need you to alert the constables. At least, alert Davel. He needs to come—"

He didn't get the opportunity to finish.

The smoke started drifting toward him.

CHAPTER FOURTEEN

If Gavin needed any proof that the strange smoke was something magical, that was it. The smoke swirled along the street, moving quickly, as if it were something alive. He'd never seen anything quite like it before. There was a soft energy within the smoke, though he didn't know if what he saw was real or not. Did he imagine it?

The smoke slithered along the street, heading directly toward a young couple making their way along the edge of the forest.

When it struck them, they both collapsed.

Gavin leaned forward, prepared to try to help, when he saw them twitching.

It was the same thing that had happened to the constables.

He started forward, as his mind managed to catch up with what was happening.

The smoke drifted toward him.

It wasn't just his imagination. It seemed as if the smoke were actually chasing him.

He debated which way he could go. If he headed along the street, he'd be caught between the two strange streams of smoke. That left only one other option: going into Jaren Forest.

Which might be exactly what the Fate wanted.

Balls.

He slowly backed into the trees. The outskirts were not nearly as mystical as the depths. There were areas of the forest that were incredibly strange, almost as if the forest itself tried to pull someone in. When he'd dealt with the sorcerer chasing Cyran, he hadn't known whether that feeling came from the sorcerer or from the forest. Maybe both.

He sheathed the El'aras dagger and pulled out the sword. He paused a moment, looking around him. No sign of the strange smoke.

"Wrenlow?"

There was silence from the other side of the enchantment. Wrenlow had been there only a moment before, and that he'd suddenly gone silent suggested something worrisome.

"Wrenlow?"

As before, there were no sounds from the other side of the enchantment.

Gavin gripped the sword, glancing down. The blade glowed softly, though he wasn't sure if it had been glowing the entire time he'd had it unsheathed or if it had only just started.

He would loop around. If nothing else, he could use the forest to conceal himself.

Gavin jogged through the trees, keeping low. There wasn't a path. Anything he did now would be creating his own path, and as he wound through the trunks, Gavin searched for anyplace he might be able to hide.

Every so often, he felt a presence near him. He wasn't sure if that presence was the smoke or some other magical entity. The first time he felt it, he thought he was detecting something in the forest, but there wasn't anything else when he paused. The second time he felt it, Gavin realized that what he detected was real. By the time he felt it again, he no longer knew what to make of it. He moved more carefully, sweeping the sword around in an arc as he moved through the forest.

There wasn't anything. Only his racing heart.

The smoke had followed him into Cyran's home. It hadn't attacked him, though it had followed him. That seemed significant, only Gavin wasn't entirely sure why.

He reached into his pocket and gripped the jade egg.

Thankfully, he had the enchantment on his wrist, which gave him the ability to move much more rapidly than he normally would. Because of that, he'd probably stayed ahead of the smoke. He'd been running and using the enchantment, but he hadn't paid as much attention to having it on.

Movement in the distance caught his eye. It seemed to

be streaking through the trees to his left. Gavin veered right.

Every so often, he felt movement on one side or the other. He couldn't help but feel as if the slipping movement were trying to corral him, guiding him.

At one point, he paused. He was in the center of the forest near a stream, and from here he thought he could fight in the open. But what if this was where this strange magical smoke wanted him to go?

If so, then Gavin had to switch things up. He had to try to turn it to his advantage. He swung the sword around, and he started moving along the stream in a different way.

"Wrenlow?" He whispered his name again, this time with more urgency, not that the urgency in the enchantment made a difference. Gavin gritted his teeth.

He looked for signs of movement, signs of the smoke, but he didn't see anything as he ran. He paused near another stream. It seemed as if he had just been here. He had to head back out of the forest.

Gavin spun and immediately began sprinting. By the time he reached the first stream, there was a strange stirring sensation as though he was getting closer to whatever it was that tried to corral him.

He jumped the stream, and he kept moving. The farther he went, the faster he felt himself going. He kept his head low, holding his arms up to prevent the branches from smacking him. He trusted that his instincts were right and that he knew where he was going. He trusted that he could use that knowledge and find his way back to where he had been before.

Gavin couldn't see the smoke. With as fast as he ran, the enchantment pulling him along, he could no longer make out anything other than the trees and the branches whipping past him. The farther he went, the more he felt a pressure that seemed to squeeze him.

The Fate. It had to be, and that fit with the strange smoke that had left the couple unconscious the way it had the constables.

The way it would leave him it if struck.

There *had* been darkness around the Fate when he'd attacked.

This had to be some part of his magic.

The enchantment gave him strength and speed, and Gavin pulled upon his core reserves. He hadn't attempted to use both the enchantment and that core energy together before, but now that he did, he could feel that power coursing through him. He felt a surge of power that was different. The core reserves seemed to work with the enchantment in a way he hadn't expected.

Gavin streaked through the forest. There was movement around him, but now he seemed to be outrunning it. Even with as fast as he went, he still felt that movement near him. The edge of the city became visible through the trees. The pressure continued to build.

Energy flowed into him, and then he burst out of the trees. He didn't stop. He let the power of the enchantment and the power of his core reserves carry him. The combination was such that he could race through the street. Then he was among a crowd.

It slowed him a little, but powered as he was, he sprinted faster and faster. Something was moving alongside him. Was it the same smoke? It was a strange energy that pushed up against him, as if trying to squeeze in on him.

It was the middle of the day, early enough where there were quite a few people out. Gavin had to twist and turn through the streets, swinging his body from side to side, avoiding the crowd—carts rolling through the cobbled streets, merchants at wagons near markets.

He jumped. Using the core reserves, along with the enchantment, the jump carried him up to one of the rooftops. Gavin scrambled along it, then slid down, landing on another street.

The farther he went, the more he began to question whether running like this was the right strategy. If he kept running, and if he stayed ahead of this smoke, would he only be drawing it back to wherever he ended up going?

He couldn't go back to the Dragon. If he did, he would put his friends in danger.

As he ran, his gaze darted around the city. There was the fortress, the place the Captain had lived. There were other enchantments there, though Gavin didn't know how to use them, but the building would be fortified. Gavin could find Zella and the other enchanters but didn't really want to put them in danger.

There was another place he could go, but he hated doing it.

Gavin jumped to another rooftop. Again he scrambled along it, slid down, and landed on another street. He ran through the city like that, up and down rooftops, sweeping through the city in a way that carried him. He ignored everything else around him. He focused on trying to get past the people, moving where he could, and getting as far ahead as possible. The farther he went, the more Gavin knew he was heading in the right direction.

And then he saw it.

The building that held the constables' barracks was not too flashy. The squat building made of stone filled an entire block near the center of the city. It was a single level and not nearly large enough for as many constables as Gavin had seen in the time that he'd been in Yoran. The windows blazed with bright light, and the people in the street tended to avoid getting too close. Strangely, he detected some soft energy in the air as he got closer to the barracks. The entire structure was compact, almost as if it were trying to remain concealed.

The constables—

Gavin stumbled. He staggered to his feet.

The strange wisps of smoke swirled around him, getting close. Gavin realized he was still holding on to his sword, and he swung. The smoke parted around the blade.

The blade glowed brightly—magic was near.

The Fate?

He didn't see any sign of him, though.

Maybe this was his way of attacking from a distance.

Gavin raced toward the constables' barracks. He had no

idea if Davel or any of the constables would help him, but he could negotiate with the jade egg.

He jumped, which cleared him over the smoke and carried him toward the entrance to the barracks. Gavin pushed open the door without hesitating and stumbled inside. He slammed the door behind him.

He tried to catch his breath, then turned and looked around him. Five constables were there, all of them with weapons unsheathed. Some were slim. One was taller than Gavin and incredibly muscular. Another man was even flabby, a rarity with the constables. He suspected that all of them had enchantments on them. They were dressed in gray jackets and pants.

Gavin glanced down, realizing that he was still holding on to the glowing sword.

"Get Davel," he said.

The constables stared at him for a moment.

"Get Davel. There's a sorcerer out in the streets."

That had the desired effect. The constables started moving. Two of them came to the door and took up positions on either side of it. Gavin backed into the barracks. The entrance was plain. Paneled wood ran along the walls, on which weapons were hung. A desk near the back corner drew his eye.

"What happened?"

Gavin swung, and Davel caught Gavin's blade with his own. He lowered the sword. "There's something out there."

"Apparently. Otherwise you wouldn't have come here."

"I don't know what it is, only that it looks like smoke chasing me."

Davel started to grin.

Gavin shook his head, flicking his gaze toward the door. "I wish I were making it up, but I'm not."

"Smoke that's chasing you?"

"That's the only way I can describe it. I saw it with one of your people—"

"What do you mean you saw it?"

Gavin should have shared that sooner, but between Davel asking for the egg and Wrenlow's need, he'd been distracted. "I saw your constables attacked by something similar." He shook his head, holding Davel's gaze. "At the time, I didn't know what it was. We haven't been on trusting terms, such as it is."

"You still should have come to me if you knew what it was."

"That's just it. I didn't know what it was. And when I saw what it did, I realized that it had to be the same thing." And probably the Fates, though why would they use smoke like that in such an indiscriminate fashion?

That didn't seem the way that he had expected the Fates to attack.

Gavin realized that he had to be careful about sharing too much with Davel. If he revealed that he had gone to Cyran's home and that the sorcerer's lair was there, then he would reveal where he had been going.

"Where did you see this?"

"Near the edge of the city," he finished. "I don't know

what to make of it, and I don't know whether it's anything to be concerned about, but the way it makes the sword glow suggests it's magically powerful."

Davel glanced over at the sword. "Come on." He turned and headed deeper into the barracks.

"Aren't you concerned that this smoke will get into the barracks?"

"You said it was magically created?"

"If it's from the Fate, then it is."

"Then we have time. Not sure how *much* time if it's one of the Fates, but the barracks are protected. You have the egg?"

It was a simple question, but one that posed challenges.

The enchanters had waited twenty years to get the egg away from the constables. Now Gavin would be the one to bring it back?

The Fate and the smoke attack lent this a greater urgency.

He *had* to do this. Not just for himself. For the city. Which he *would* protect.

"I do."

"Good. Then follow me."

Gavin headed down the stairs, descending into the barracks and feeling as if he were descending into danger.

CHAPTER FIFTEEN

The room where Davel brought him was enormous. It was cold, with stone walls rising around everything and metal tables situated throughout. Gavin had little doubt that this was the constables' version of a sorcerer's lair.

Gavin looked around the room. Unlike in the sorcerer's lairs where he'd been, this one was sparse. There were no shelves along the walls, only the stone. The metal tables, which had nothing on them, took up much of the room. Gavin suspected the tables were used when the constables created the enchantments.

"If you want me to help you with the smoke," Davel said, and there was a hint of irritation in his voice at Gavin—likely because he hadn't come to Davel sooner—"you need to do what you agreed to as well. I will have the egg."

Gavin let out a frustrated sigh. "I never agreed to do it here."

He *had* come here looking for the constables' help.

Maybe if he learned how to use the jade egg to create enchantments, he might be able to use it for himself. Except that Gavin wasn't sure he wanted to. He'd seen too many enchantments used over the years in dangerous ways.

"What do you intend to do with it?" Gavin asked.

"I told you what I intend to do with it."

"I'm not letting you keep it."

Davel cocked a brow at him. "You aren't *letting* me?"

"You can push back if you want, but if it comes down to it, I'm going to fight my way out of here." Through constables. Then through the Fate.

Not good odds.

"You came here on your own," Davel said, his voice low and dangerous.

"I did, but that doesn't mean I'm willing to let you simply abuse this."

"You seem to forget that we've had the egg for—"

"For decades," Gavin said. "I didn't forget that at all."

Davel glared at him.

Gavin debated what else he might be able to do or say, but he simply stared back, holding his gaze.

Finally, Davel turned away. "Pull out the egg, and let's get this over with."

"What sort of enchantment are you going to make?"

"It seems as if I need to see if there's anything else magical around us."

"Don't you already have enchantments for that?" Gavin asked.

"We did."

"I didn't do anything to them."

"You didn't. Others did," Davel said.

Had the enchanters been active? Gavin hadn't noticed that, but it would make sense.

Davel made his way over to the far side of the room, and he grabbed something from a section Gavin couldn't see quite as easily. He came back with a small spool of metal.

Gavin glanced at it. "Is that what you use?"

"Haven't you tried to use the egg?"

Gavin shook his head. "There hasn't been any reason."

"You really aren't interested in creating enchantments."

"I can see the value in them, but I haven't had any reason to do so."

"You are an interesting man," Davel said.

"I think that's a compliment."

Davel shrugged. He started to unwind the length of metal, and then he rolled it over the table, winding it from one end to the other. "The egg."

Gavin frowned at him. "What are you going to do with it?"

"I'm going to use it. Isn't that the entire purpose of this?" Davel snapped.

Gavin pulled the egg out of his pocket and set it on the table.

Davel stared at it for a moment before turning his attention back to Gavin. "The egg allows those with the right knowledge to push power through it. In doing so, not only can we layer that power upon the construct we want enchanted, but those with the right knowledge can force the type of enchantment we want."

"Force it?"

"There is an element of force involved."

"Why?" Gavin asked.

"I'm not entirely sure."

Davel turned his attention back to the metal. He ran his hands along the surface of it, and then he lifted it up, setting it into a different pattern. "We had to experiment with this. When they provided us with the egg, they didn't provide us with knowledge about how to use it, or anything else."

"*They* being the enchanters."

"*They* being *they*," Davel said.

Gavin shook his head. "You don't even want to acknowledge what you did to them?"

"Acknowledge what?" Davel paused and turned toward him. "You assume you know so much about the city, yet you've only been here for the better part of a year. I don't think that amount of time has provided you with any greater insight as to the workings of the city than anyone else."

"I know that the constables worked with enchanters to expel sorcerers from the city. I know the constables ultimately betrayed the enchanters."

"Do you know that the enchanters decided they wanted to rule?" Davel fixed him with a hard stare. "After the sorcerers were gone, the enchanters thought that might be their opportunity to take power. There are many cities where enchanters are allowed to take power, and in their mind, they thought they would use that opportunity to assume control."

Gavin hadn't heard that. He would have to check with Zella if that were true or not. "You betrayed them because they tried to overpower you?"

"You call it betrayal, but I call it protection."

"Protection?" Gavin looked around the room. "Is that what this is?"

"Do you really think we want to do anything that would harm those in the city?" Davel asked.

Gavin grunted. "I don't really know. The only thing I know about you is that you continue to use the kind of power you railed against."

"We railed against the sorcerers' power. Not enchanted power."

"Except you don't want others in the city to know you still embrace magic."

"The people feel better knowing they are protected from magic. Think about it. Most of the people who lived in the city during the war twenty years ago remember what it was like when the sorcerers were fighting for control. There were factions of them, all trying to overthrow the Triad."

"The what?"

"Three sorcerers who had ganged up and taken power over the city. I'm sure that with your extensive experience in the world, you have seen how sorcerers fight for power."

"I have seen something similar."

"They encouraged it here. They even had a connection

to the Academy that trained them. The students worked just as hard as their masters to fight for power."

Gavin knew there were outposts in many cities. He had seen them enough times to know. Most of the time, the outpost served as a place for the society members to reside, but there were other places where the outpost was used to consolidate power.

And then there was what he had uncovered in Yoran.

Three sorcerers. The Triad.

That couldn't be a coincidence. Gavin had found three sorcerer's lairs. All three of them were connected, which suggested that, if nothing else, whatever he had encountered had been intentionally created. There had been the El'aras symbols on the doors, symbols that had suggested a different sort of connection and a different sort of power.

Could those lairs have been part of the Triad? Was that why the Fate had come?

"Yes, three," Davel replied. "There were others in the city, though they served the Triad. After a while, they decided they didn't want to serve the Triad anymore and that it was time to overthrow them. Thus began the Sorcerers War. It was a brutal time. Those without magic—and within Yoran, that was almost everyone—were at the mercy of the sorcerers. The Triad claimed they were trying to hold their position, wanting to fight to ensure the safety of the others, but…"

"Go on," Gavin said.

"Does it even matter?"

"A little bit."

Davel sighed. "The sorcerers who served the Triad found themselves fighting a losing war. They began to brutally attack others in the city. They thought that doing so would call the Triad out into the open, but even when they did, there was nothing they could do."

"That's why the enchanters and the constables began to work together," Gavin said.

"That's part of the reason. We wanted to protect those without magic. Considering how few people had it, we thought we needed to offer some element of safety."

"Why you?"

"Because we'd always served."

Gavin shook his head. "You had always served… You were serving the Triad."

Davel glared at him for a moment, and then his expression softened. "We were, though we didn't do so happily."

Gavin started to smile.

"What?" Davel said.

"This is all about you paying penance."

"This is not about penance."

"It's certainly not about a desire to protect," Gavin said.

"You don't know anything about what happened then."

"No, but I can imagine. And seeing the way you reacted, I have a pretty good idea." Gavin stared down at the metal. "So the constables and the enchanters began working together, and then the constables decided they wanted to take over—"

"After the enchanters decided they were going to betray us."

Gavin looked at the jade egg. Every time he thought he understood what had happened in Yoran, he found out something new. Some new piece of history; some new information that changed everything for him.

Gaspar had never spoken of any of that.

What role did Gaspar have in all of this?

Gavin didn't fully understand the politics of Yoran these days. The sorcerers had led in the city up until twenty years ago, and the enchanters and the constables had worked together to push their influence out. When it was over, the constables had turned on the enchanters.

Now the constables, and Davel Chan, essentially ruled in the city, though there had to be more to it.

"Who do you serve now?"

Davel watched him. "There's a council that leads the city."

"And what's your responsibility with that?" The constables had a significant role in the city, but it was one Gavin hadn't taken the time to fully understand.

At first, Gavin wasn't sure if he was even going to answer, but his mouth tightened into a thin line, his frown deepening. "I sit on the council."

At least that answered part of the question for Gavin.

But it didn't explain everything.

They had the Triad, and they had the Fates.

What if the Fates wanted revenge?

"If the Triad ruled in the city, I have to believe they were subservient to the Fates," Gavin said.

"Possibly," Davel said.

"You already considered that."

"I would have imagined you had as well."

"Given how little I know about the history of Yoran, I don't know that I could have," he said, staring at Davel.

The two men held each other's gaze, and then Davel looked away, turning his attention back to the egg.

"The enchantments have allowed us to keep the influence of the sorcerers at bay. Over the last two decades, we've been safe, protected from anything the sorcerers think to do. Even the Fates." Davel lifted the egg, then took one end of the metal and wrapped it around the egg. He started from the bottom and worked quickly to wrap the metal around its entirety.

Curiosity overwhelmed Gavin. He wanted to know more about the enchantments. Not only how the egg worked with them, but how Davel managed to use it to create them. If he understood that, maybe he could use it himself.

"What do you have to do with it?" Gavin asked.

"We have to bind the metal to the egg. There's a transference of power."

"How?" Despite himself, Gavin couldn't help but feel curious about what Davel was doing.

"There is a certain intention to it," Davel said.

It likely involved a use of magic.

Gavin glanced down at the sword. The blade had stopped glowing, so whatever smoke and energy he had detected above seemed to be gone.

Davel continued wrapping the metal around the egg,

and then he stopped. He pressed his hands on either side of it, squeezing for a moment. Gavin watched him out of curiosity, but he also watched the sword because of a suspicion he had. There came a flare of power along the sword. It was brief, and when it was done, Gavin knew that the enchantment had taken hold.

"Did you do it?" he asked softly.

Davel set the egg down, and he carefully began to remove the metal that he'd wound around it. "It's done," he said.

"What enchantment did you make?"

"I wanted something that would allow me to know whether there is magic used around me."

"Interesting," Gavin said.

Davel looked over. "Not all of us have an El'aras dagger —or sword." He held out the metal, and then with another squeeze, he pressed the metal together and formed a bracelet.

Gavin was reminded of the bracelet he now wore. Olivia had done something different when making enchantments. She had used her own power, through her connection to her magic. This was something else, though if Gavin was right, there was more of an element of magic to it than what he suspected Davel understood—or probably believed.

Davel began to wrap another band of metal around the egg. He worked quickly and then pressed his hands on either side of it. As before, the sword surged with a bright white glow. This time, it was also met by a surge of white light from the new enchantment that Davel had made.

When it was done, Davel began to peel the metal off the egg again.

"How long have you known?" Gavin asked.

"How long have I known what?"

"That you had magic."

Davel paused, and he looked up at Gavin. "What was that?" He asked it slowly, dangerously.

"With what you're doing. Obviously, you have to have some magic for this to work." Gavin tapped on the table, pointing to the egg. "I suspect much of it comes from the egg, but for there to be a purpose behind it and for the egg to know just what you want to do, there has to be magic within you." He held Davel's gaze. "How long have you known?"

"I don't have magic. The magic comes from the egg."

Gavin smiled and shrugged. "If that's what you prefer to believe, but I don't think that's quite right."

"And you are some expert on magic?"

"Not an expert at all. I am, however, familiar with magic, and I have felt it used around me enough times that I can recognize when it's used near me now."

And he was certain of what he detected. He was certain Davel had been using magic, even though he claimed he hadn't been. As far as Gavin knew, the power Davel had been using was enough to pulse outward, pushing with considerable force and energy. It didn't surprise him that Davel would have a connection to magic, only that he didn't acknowledge it.

Davel began to wrap another band of metal around the

egg. He pulled it from the spool, and he pressed his hands on either side of it. As it surged with white light, all the other enchantments began to glow softly.

"That's the egg," Davel said.

"If you say so," Gavin responded. He'd once doubted his own magical ability, so he understood how difficult it could be to learn you had magic.

Davel continued making enchantments, working quickly. After a while, he shifted techniques, winding the metal around the egg in a different fashion. Gavin frowned as he did, trying to make sense of what Davel was doing.

"Is this a different enchantment?" Gavin asked.

"A little different."

"You aren't still trying to make one to detect magic?"

"No. I'm trying to contain it," Davel said.

"How?"

"There are certain enchantments allowed to hold magic. There is something about the enchantment that repels magic used against it."

That would be useful, if true. Gavin could easily imagine having an enchantment that would repel an attack. He could use that if sorcerers were to come at him.

"I would like an enchantment like that," he said.

"I didn't have the sense you wanted enchantments."

"Generally, no. But if you have something that can repel magic…"

"It's not so much repelling magic. It's a matter of containing it."

"It sounds like it's all about intent," Gavin said.

Davel looked down. "I suppose that's true."

"All I want is something that can keep magic from hitting me. Do you think you can make anything like that?"

Davel opened his mouth as if he were going to object, but then he closed it and began to wrap some of the metal around the egg again. He worked slowly this time, deliberately, and he turned the egg from side to side as he did, focusing on it.

There came a hint of a soft light glowing from Gavin's sword, though he didn't see nearly the same glow from the enchantments now resting on the table. Either the sword was better attuned to the use of magic, or Davel somehow prevented his use of magic from being revealed. After a moment, he pressed again, and the sword surged with a white light.

Davel glanced over at him, shaking his head.

"I didn't say anything," Gavin said.

"You didn't have to."

Davel peeled the enchantment off the egg, and then he squeezed. As before, there was another surge of light. The enchantment constricted, forming a bracelet. Davel held it out.

"Will this repel magic?" Gavin asked.

"Probably. It won't contain it, though, so if that's what you want, I would have to form something else."

"Is that how that one would work?" Gavin pointed to one of the enchantments that had been set on the table, one that probably allowed Davel to confine magic.

"That's how it *should* work," Davel said.

"Interesting."

Davel ignored him, and Gavin stood back, watching him work. He had a practiced hand. Gavin could imagine Davel down here, creating enchantments, working one after another.

"If you had all of these enchantments, then what happened to them?" Gavin asked.

"I've told you what happened to them."

"No, you said that they were destroyed."

"The enchantments don't last indefinitely. Over time, the power within them fades. They have to be recharged—or remade. We found that remaking them seems to be more effective for holding on to power longer."

Gavin glanced down at the enchantment he wore on his wrist. "How quickly do they fade?" He knew enchantments faded over time. The stronger the magic user, the longer they would last, but it was a general rule and not anything predictable.

"If they lasted indefinitely, people would carry enchantments forever."

Gavin reached up, touching his ear. The enchantment had been made by the El'aras. In the time that he'd had it, he hadn't noticed any fading, but maybe that was why it wasn't working quite as effectively. Only, the enchantment that he initially had, the one that he and Wrenlow had worked with for all those years, never seemed to fade.

"I would imagine the egg would allow you to create incredibly powerful enchantments."

"Oh, now it's the egg again, not me?" Davel asked, pausing as he wrapped more metal around the egg.

"Only because you said so," Gavin said, smiling.

"The egg has power, but again it's only enchanter power."

"I would think the enchanters would have much more capability of adding power to things."

"It's still not the same as a sorcerer placing it. A sorcerer might be able to place power that will remain with an item for years. Decades. Sometimes even longer." Davel looked down at the metal, pulling it off the egg. "Unfortunately, we don't have a sorcerer to place enchantments like that. Which means we have had to rely upon the egg to continue placing them."

Gavin grinned, yet he still didn't say anything to him about how, even though they didn't have a sorcerer, they did have an enchanter—Davel.

Gavin could see that Davel had magic every time he surged power through himself, creating each enchantment. He didn't even need the egg to do it. When he squeezed the end of the metal together, it created an additional enchantment to it. Gavin started watching the sword and noting how it glowed periodically, but each time it did, a hint of power surged from it—but nothing more than that.

Finally, Davel was done with the spool of metal, and he grabbed another one. As he started to unwind it, Gavin noticed his blade glowing more brightly.

"What are you doing?" Gavin asked him.

"I'm not doing anything. I'm preparing."

Davel wasn't doing anything with the enchantment.

Gavin turned his attention to the door behind him and groaned. "I thought you said the barracks have protections around them."

"They do."

Gavin could feel something, but it was not only that, but it was also the way the blade continued to glow brightly. Davel said it wasn't him, which meant something else. Something worse.

"Then I think we have a problem."

"What kind?"

"A sorcery problem."

CHAPTER SIXTEEN

The blade continued to steadily glow as Gavin gripped the sword. He focused on his core reserves, trying to reach for that power, but didn't want to draw on too much and risk wasting that power before he needed to use it. He had no idea what was going to come. If the Fate was willing to attack the constables' barracks, then the sorcerer truly was fearless.

Gavin hurried over to the table and grabbed the jade egg. Then, on a whim, he grabbed a spool of metal and stuffed it into his pocket. Surprisingly, the spool wasn't very heavy. It was efficient that the small, narrow bands of thin metal wrapped around the spool could simply be unwound to create each enchantment. Still, he couldn't help but wonder if there was another way to create enchantments that might be more effective.

"What do you think you're doing?" Davel asked.

"Well, I figure if we're going to be attacked, we might as

well keep the jade egg away from the sorcerers. And if we need to make another enchantment, why not have your supplies?"

Davel frowned, then hurried over to a cabinet, pulled out two more spools, and stuffed them into his pocket before joining Gavin. They both stood in front of the door.

"What do you think?" Davel asked.

"I think it's time for us to test whether or not your enchantment repels magic."

Gavin pulled open the door. A wisp of smoke slammed into him but then bounced away. He smiled. "Seems like it works."

He whipped the sword around, drawing on his core reserves of power. If the smoke wasn't coming from one of the sorcerers, then it was still something that served them.

"The sword isn't doing anything," Davel said. He had a similar repelling enchantment, and the smoke wasn't getting any closer to him—but it also didn't allow him to do anything else.

If they couldn't carve through the smoke, they needed another option.

"We need to trap it," Gavin said.

"It's a good thing I made another enchantment." Davel pulled out an enchantment and threw it onto the ground. It was shaped something like a silver bowl, with spiraling patterns worked around the surface.

Gavin wasn't sure what to make of that. Typically, an enchantment had to be close to a person, in contact with skin, to use the power within it. He didn't know what purpose Davel would have by tossing it on the ground. There wouldn't be any way for him to use that power, to summon the energy within it.

And without that...

The smoke slammed into Gavin's enchantment again, which repelled it. He continued swinging his sword, but it was as if he were trying to cut through the wind. He could do nothing to the smoke to harm it, but maybe he didn't have to.

If the enchantment on the ground worked by needing to have contact with the smoke, then maybe all Gavin had to do was to find a way to force the smoke closer to the enchantment. He swept the blade around, trying to move the smoke toward the trap.

"You need another one," Gavin said.

"That one will work," Davel said.

"If it has to be in contact with it, it's not going to work."

"It will—"

Davel stumbled.

Gavin jerked his head around, looking to see what had happened. Davel seemed to have been attacked by something, though Gavin couldn't see what it was. He darted forward, sweeping the blade.

His own enchantment allowed him to move quickly, and he forced the smoke back.

He forced the smoke creature toward the trap. When he neared the enchantment, Gavin thought about reaching for it, but he hesitated. Its purpose was to trap something magical, and *he* might possess magic. There was a possibility that the enchantment might hold him. He had to be careful and not touch it.

He had no idea what Davel was doing. He didn't dare look over to the constable, instead keeping his focus on this smoke to overwhelm it. He swept the sword through another series of movements. Then he brought it down.

The smoke streaked away, this time heading toward the ground. Gavin completed the arc, and though the smoke tried to escape, it touched the enchantment. The smoke swirled around the top of it, creating a pattern as it spiraled down closer and closer to the enchantment. Finally, the smoke stopped moving. The enchantment held it.

He nudged the enchantment with his toe. "Davel?"

Gavin glanced over at the constable, who was getting to his feet.

Davel held a different enchantment, which had another smoke ring inside of it.

"That was interesting," Gavin said.

"What are these things?" Davel asked.

"Near as I can tell, they're magical smoke creatures. Though, to be honest, I don't even know what to make of them. I'm not sure why the Fate wouldn't have used this from the beginning."

Davel shook his head. "How are there magical smoke creatures?"

Gavin could only shrug. "I don't really know. They're probably something the Fate sent after me."

Davel reached down and picked up the other enchantment, and he set them both on the table.

"You might need something more to contain them," Gavin said.

"I have an idea." Davel carried the enchantments to the back of the room and placed them in a cabinet.

There was a strange surge of power, a hiss that reminded Gavin of when he brought the dagger up to the door, then it faded.

"What was that?"

"A seal. It's an enchantment, though one made by multiple enchanters. It should hold."

Gavin raised an eyebrow. "Should?"

"Seeing as how I don't have any idea what we're dealing with."

They would have to find a way to destroy them. Gavin didn't want to leave anything lying around that might pose a danger to anyone.

He looked toward the door. "I don't know if that's all of them."

"Were there more than two?"

"Well, when I was at the edge of the city, I saw two of these strange wisps of smoke. I didn't know what they were."

Gavin started toward the door and hesitated, looking down at the sword. The blade had stopped glowing. The smoke must've been the source of the magic he had detected.

Now he had to better understand the smoke creatures and what they meant. Only, Gavin wasn't at all sure how he was going to figure that out.

"Do you have any sort of magical archive?"

"What?" Davel asked.

"A place you go to research. You have to have something."

"We have a storeroom," Davel said. "After the Triad was destroyed and the other sorcerers were expelled, there wasn't the need to keep anything."

"Did you go through their lairs to see what they might have?"

"We didn't find them," Davel said.

Even more reason for Gavin to believe that what he'd found were the Triad's lairs. But if the constable had never found them, then why was it that he had?

Perhaps a better question would be how Cyran *had found them.*

"Whatever they might have would be dangerous."

"The Triad likely had time to empty their lairs before leaving."

There had been little within those spaces that Gavin thought would be valuable. The sword. The table with enchantments. The body of the sorcerer.

Up the stairs, two constables lay immobile. Davel rushed over toward them, quickly checking for a pulse.

"This is like when the smoke attacked before," Gavin said. "Are they alive?"

"Seem to be. Help me move them," Davel said.

Gavin grunted, and he grabbed one of the men. He dragged him along the hallway. "Where do you want me to take him?"

Davel nodded toward a door. "There's a place up here."

He opened the door, and Gavin looked inside the room, which appeared to be a comfortable lounge. There was a hearth with a fire crackling in it, several chairs, and book-lined shelves along one wall. Gavin's stomach rumbled at the sight of a table with food stacked on it.

"This is… unexpected," he said.

"Why?"

"I didn't know the constables knew how to read."

Gavin dragged the man inside. He settled the constable into one of the chairs, propping him back so that he wouldn't end up any more stiff and sore than necessary when he came around. He grabbed a piece of jerky, some grapes, and a hunk of bread off the table. Though he ate quickly, it did little to settle his stomach. He was hungrier than he had expected to be.

"Help yourself," Davel said.

"Considering I helped defend the barracks, I think I've earned it."

"You defended the barracks from creatures you brought here."

"I didn't bring them here. I only brought them close by. They came in." Davel shook his head. "Besides, don't you want to make sure that you can protect the city from all things, magical or not?"

Gavin smiled in between bites, and he set the hunk of bread back down on the table. It was a little crunchy but not terrible. He expected that the constables would have decent food.

"There might be others," Davel said.

"There might be," Gavin answered.

"Aren't you going to help?"

"Help with what? If they're not dead, then there is nothing to be concerned about."

Davel ignored him and left the room.

Gavin took another bite, chewing slowly. Gradually, his strength started to return. He looked around, surprised by this room and how comfortable it was.

He headed over to the shelf, examining the books. The titles were mostly about the history of Yoran. He pulled one of the books off the shelf and started to flip through it. The book, which was an older one, had maps of the city. It suggested that Yoran was at least a thousand years old, and from the narrow streets and the structure of the buildings, Gavin suspected that was true. He put the book back on the shelf, and he pulled another one out. Like the other, this one was also about the city.

Were all of them?

One of the constables behind him started to stir, and Gavin glanced back at him.

The man sat up, rubbing his eyes. "What happened?"

"Near as we can tell, a smoke attack," Gavin said, turning to face him. He took another bite of bread, chewing it slowly.

The constable jerked his head around, eyes widening as he looked over at Gavin. "Who are you? What are you doing in here?"

"Don't worry about it. Davel knows I'm here."

"What are you—"

The door opened, and Davel dragged another constable inside. This constable's face was ashen, and she looked to be in worse shape than the others. *How badly had she been hurt?* Gavin hurried over, helping Davel.

"Now you want to help?" Davel muttered.

"What happened to her?"

"The same as the others."

"This isn't the same," Gavin said.

Davel stretched the woman out, resting her on the floor. Gavin checked for a pulse. When he had trained with Tristan, he'd learned about injuries. Hurting. Killing. Also healing. It was necessary for him to know how to identify his injuries and know what could and should be done to restore himself.

He couldn't tell what had happened to the woman, only that something seemed to be amiss. Gavin leaned forward. Something smelled *off* about her.

It reminded him of the strange smell in the sorcerer's lair.

"Do you detect that?" he asked.

"Detect what?"

"The smell."

"Now you're going to be criticizing my people about how they smell?" Davel asked.

"If they deserve it, but that's not what I'm getting at."

He took a deep breath, inhaling the strange odor coming off the woman. It was foul, though he wasn't at all sure what it was. Darkness seemed to swirl around her.

Strangely, it seemed the shadows were feeding on the woman. Almost as if they were trying to consume her. Something diminished within her the longer that it remained near her.

If he did nothing, she'd die.

It had to be the same as what happened to the sorcerer in the lair.

Gavin jumped back. "One of your enchantments. Now!"

Davel frowned at him. "What are you getting on about?"

"Get one of your enchantments!"

Davel shook his head. "I don't know what you're doing, but…" He reached into his pocket and pulled one of them out.

Gavin nodded to the fallen constable. "Put it on her chest."

Davel sighed and placed the enchantment onto the constable's chest.

There came a swirl of energy. Had Gavin not been expecting it, he might've been startled, but the darkness and the shadow started to leach out of the constable, flowing toward the enchantment.

Davel grunted. "How did you know?"

"It didn't feel right," Gavin said. If the Fate used this kind of attack, then they might be in even more trouble than Gavin realized. "We need to see how many others have been influenced like this."

"I thought you said you only saw the two."

"I thought that's all it was," Gavin admitted.

Now he no longer knew.

If there were more than just the two, how many were out in the city? More importantly, what *were they?*

The Fates had sent something new—and dangerous—into the city.

And Gavin would have to be prepared. At least he had the enchantments that repelled magic, but he had no idea how long they would work and whether they would keep him safe indefinitely. If what Davel said about the enchantments was true—and Gavin had no reason to believe it wasn't—then eventually the effect of the enchantments would fade. When it happened, he had no idea what would befall him, but he needed to be ready for anything.

"I think we're going to need to make more enchantments," he said softly.

Davel nodded once.

CHAPTER SEVENTEEN

Gavin waited in the Dragon, which was empty other than Wrenlow sitting alone near the hearth and trying to hide the annoyance on his face. Gavin had not been able to placate him about his ongoing silence through the enchantments, though what was he going to be able to say to Wrenlow anyway? At this point, he no longer knew why the enchantment only worked intermittently. As soon as Gavin had left the constable barracks, he'd begun to hear Wrenlow chirping at him through the earpiece. That couldn't be a coincidence. Either the barracks somehow shielded him, or there was some other answer.

There were other times when the enchantment hadn't worked quite right lately. It hadn't worked near the smoke creatures, and it hadn't even worked in the sorcerer's lair. Something had to be shielding it.

"He's going to come," Jessica said, sweeping out of the kitchen and handing him a mug.

Gavin looked over to her. "I'm sure he's going to come, but it's just…" He stared at the entrance, one hand resting on the hilt of the El'aras dagger.

Gaspar had others who needed his protection now. Gavin understood that.

He paced and glanced over at Wrenlow, who sat quietly, still not looking up at him. Gavin took a deep breath, headed over toward the hearth, and sat next to him.

"I don't like this," Wrenlow said without looking over to him.

"I don't either."

"Not the attack. What I'm feeling."

"And how is that?" Gavin looked to the door. *How long would Gaspar take?*

"Do you know what it was like before we came to Yoran?" Wrenlow asked.

Gavin shrugged. "I remember. We traveled quite a bit, and we never were completely safe."

"Not completely, but safe enough. And I was useful. At least, I felt like I was. I don't know whether or not I really was useful to you."

"Is that what this is about? You're questioning whether I find value in what you offer?"

"Well, ever since coming here, I don't know if I am useful," Wrenlow said. "Most of the time when I think that I can help, you disappear, or you go silent or you ask somebody else to come along with you. You have been training me, but even that isn't going to be enough. I'm trying to improve. Really, I am. I've been taking the lessons that you have been giving me as seriously as I can. It's just… I'm not you, Gavin."

Gavin breathed out slowly. He knew that, and he had been pushing Wrenlow, wanting to get him to improve, knowing that he needed to learn to fight, especially if he would stay around Gavin with everything that Gavin dealt with. But Wrenlow was right. He wasn't Gavin. He could not be.

"I don't want anything to happen to you."

"Nothing is going to happen to me. It certainly won't if you continue to feel like you need to protect me," Wrenlow said.

"Is that a bad thing?" Gavin asked.

"I can be of more assistance than you think."

"I know you can."

Wrenlow smiled at Gavin and then shook his head. "No, I don't know that you do. I shouldn't even be upset. And I guess I'm not. Not really. It's just that I want to be valuable to you. I want what I do to matter."

"You do matter. And not just to Olivia." Gavin flashed a grin, which Wrenlow ignored.

When they had traveled before, Wrenlow's role was much more important, especially as they tried to get established in different locations. He had a way with finding sources and acquiring information, and he could use that to help them build the network they needed rapidly. Ever since coming to Yoran, with Gavin operating out of the Dragon, Wrenlow hadn't needed to do that.

He'd trained, trying to understand different fighting

techniques, working with Gavin, but there was only so much that he could learn at this point in his life. Gavin had trained from near infancy to acquire his skill. There was a limit to what Wrenlow could accomplish.

"Maybe we need to find another position for you," Gavin said.

"What else do you think I can do? You've got other people who have better connections than I do throughout the city."

"I don't know," Gavin admitted. "But I'm willing to work on it."

Wrenlow leaned forward. "Maybe that's what I need."

Gavin watched his friend. And he *was* a friend. "I will do everything I can to help make sure you have something rewarding."

Wrenlow watched him and then glanced toward the door. "He's here."

Gavin got to his feet, looking over to the door. Gaspar came in. The old thief was dressed better than the last time Gavin had seen him. It felt like ages ago, rather than only a few days. His eyes darted around, almost as if he were looking for a trap. Could Gaspar really think that Gavin would try to trap him? Of course, given the way things had ended between them the last time, it was possible Gaspar would.

"You needed to pull me away for this?" Gaspar asked, sweeping his gaze around the Dragon.

"We need information," Gavin said. "We've been dealing with the Fates, and I'm concerned about what they are doing now." He filled Gaspar in about everything that had happened since he'd last seen him, including about the smoke creatures and how the constables were attacked. "Somehow, it's related, but…"

"But you don't know why?" Gaspar asked.

"I don't know why. I thought they were after something, but after killing the Captain, he went to the lair, so now I'm beginning to suspect it's tied to the Triad. Even with that, I don't know why the Fates would've waited until now."

That was the part of all this that troubled Gavin. He simply did not have the answer. And there had to be an answer.

Why now?

Could it be tied to something Gavin had done? Maybe attacking the Mistress of Vines had drawn the Fates' attention. Maybe it was Cyran, and his use of magic, or whoever he had apprenticed to. Or perhaps it was even one of the jobs he had forced Gavin to take under false pretenses.

Gaspar sighed. "I've been trying to settle the enchanters."

"That's where you've been?" Jessica asked.

He frowned at her. "Now I have you asking me for accountability?"

"I was just worried."

Gaspar grunted. "So are Desarra and Olivia. As soon as they heard the Fates might have come to the city, they started to be concerned. I tried to talk them into leaving, but—"

"There isn't any place they can go that they could avoid the Fates," Gavin said.

"That is what they said, as well. Which is why... I suppose that doesn't matter right now. We figure out what they're after, then we can get them to leave."

"I don't know if it's going to work like that. This is a city that has rejected sorcery. If the Fates have decided to pay attention to the city again, I don't know if we will be able to prevent that. If they do, the enchanters will..." Gavin realized he didn't even know what would happen.

"They know what it will be like," Gaspar said, his voice soft.

They faced each other a moment. "I learned all about the Triad," Gavin said. "And I think the Fates are here because of what happened in the past." Gavin didn't have the answers, but he felt as if he was on the right track with it. Somehow, there was something the Fate—or worse, the Fates—was after, and he had to figure that out before others were hurt. "Regardless of what we think, the Fate is here, and is attacking. And we need to do whatever we can to protect the city."

Gaspar grunted. "We? Suddenly you're one of the constables?"

There was more to the question. Both knew it.

Gavin didn't know what he felt about Yoran, but he wasn't about to let sorcery overwhelm the city. There were too many people here he cared about.

"I think the constables are more than they're letting on," Gavin said.

He watched Gaspar as he said it. If he was right, then Davel wouldn't be the only constable who had some connection to the enchanters. It might not be as strong as some, but he believed there was a connection there.

Gaspar looked back at him, saying nothing.

"Anyway, there are some strange smoke creatures that have attacked in the city. I don't really know anything about them, only that they're tied to magic in some way. There's a way of containing them," Gavin said, pulling one of the enchantments out of his pocket. He tested it to make sure he wasn't trapped by it, and it seemed as if it wouldn't hold him. Whether or not that was intentional, Gavin didn't know. "These can contain them, but we don't really know whether to be concerned about them spreading through the city."

"We?" Gaspar asked.

"Davel Chan and I."

Gaspar snorted. "This is incredibly amusing. Given the kind of work you enjoy, I thought you would be the one who would rail against the constables. Not that it's any different for me, but now you're working with them?"

"I know about the constables," Gavin said softly.

Gaspar frowned at him. "What exactly do you think you know?"

"I was with Davel when he used the jade egg. I understand what's involved in creating the enchantments."

"Then you know what they stole from the enchanters."

"I'm not so sure they stole anything," Gavin said.

Gaspar glared at him. "After everything you went through and what you've seen of how the constables will attack, you're questioning whether they've stolen the power from the enchanters they betrayed?"

"Did the constables betray them, or did the enchanters decide they wanted power for themselves? I'm not so sure Davel needs the jade egg for enchantments," Gavin said.

Gaspar stiffened. "What was that?"

"You heard me. And I suspect he's not the only one of the constables who wouldn't need the jade egg to summon the kind of power they do." Gavin forced a smile. "Did you know that the constables can place enchantments?"

Gaspar narrowed his eyes. "What are you getting at?"

"I'm sure you'll work it out eventually. Don't you like to tell me how slow my mind is? I got there."

Gaspar turned back to the door, one hand resting on it. He didn't leave. "It doesn't work like that."

"Maybe not, but the Fate is here. The smoke creatures seem to target those with magic. Which means—"

"You think they're coming for the enchanters."

"I don't know if they're coming for them or only willing to release power." He still didn't feel like he'd pieced things together quite right. "The Fate is after something. I don't know what it is, but he needed something from the Captain and then went to the lair."

"Unless he was only getting revenge," Wrenlow said.

Gavin looked over. "Why would you say that?"

"If the Fates are angry about what happened, maybe he's getting revenge. Kill the Captain who had been a part of pushing the sorcerers out and then going after the constables. You said you saw some of them attacked."

Gavin had. The constables *had* been a part of the war all those years ago. Could it really be connected to something that had happened decades ago?

"Which would put the enchanters in danger," Gaspar said.

"That's my concern. When they attack somebody with more power, they can cause more damage than if they attack somebody who has none. When I was at the barracks, several of the constables were knocked unconscious, but they came back around. There was one, though, that the smoke creature seemed to have taken a liking to," Gavin said. "It seemed as if the smoke creature latched onto her. I don't really know what it was, only that it seemed to be…"

Gavin thought back to what he had seen and realized something. It wasn't just that the smoke creature latched onto the constable. It had seemed to be pulling energy from him.

Until they had placed the enchantment upon him, the smoke creature was drawing that power, almost as if it were feeding on him. Could that be it? Why would the sorcerers have released something like that in the city? Unless they had some way of controlling them.

"It seemed to be what?" Gaspar asked.

"I don't know if the smoke creature was feeding on the constable or whether it was simply trying to harm him, but it only stopped when we contained it."

If the Fate *had* come for revenge, that would be a brutal way of doing it.

Use magic to feed off those who had it and couldn't defend against it.

The very thing someone like the Fate he'd met would do.

"There's still the issue of the Fate wanting something," Wrenlow said. "You told me that he believed you had something. And the Captain didn't want him to take one of his enchantments."

"We haven't been able to determine what he took," Gaspar said. "We've looked, but…" He shrugged.

"There's more to it," Gavin said. "There has to be."

It all came back to the Triad—to something more than that.

Something had called the Fates to the city.

He just had to figure out what it was.

"While we figure this out, we need help creating protections," Gavin said.

"What sort of protections?"

Gavin reached into his pocket, pulled out another enchantment, and tossed it to Gaspar.

Gaspar caught it and held it up, examining it for a moment. "What does it do?"

"It repels magical attacks."

"You would just give this to me?"

"I don't know how many attacks it will repel," Gavin said. "From what I've been told, there's a limit to what these enchantments will permit. With this, you'll have some protection, but it might be limited."

"Limited how?"

"How many attacks you can repel. I've already seen that

this will withstand a smoke creature attack, but I had better luck with it than Davel did. So it does protect, but it isn't perfect."

"That's all you want them to do? You want the enchanters to make more of these?"

"No," Gavin said, though that wasn't a bad idea. Having them create more enchantments like that might be better than trying to use the jade egg. But he didn't know if the enchantments made by the jade egg were more valuable than those that were made by an enchanter.

The only way to truly place a solid protection might be by getting a sorcerer involved. *What sorcerer would go against the Fates?*

"Then let's get this over with," Gaspar said.

Gavin appreciated that Gaspar didn't want to linger, though he wasn't surprised. If the enchanters were in danger, he'd do what he needed to protect them.

Before leaving, he tapped on the enchantment in his ear. "Can you hear me?"

"I can hear you for now," Wrenlow said.

"Stay alert. I might need your help."

"You said that before."

Gavin turned to Jessica. "Keep the Dragon locked."

She shook her head. "Don't worry about me. You said it yourself—the constables are keeping watch. Go with Gaspar. I'll keep an eye on him," she said, looking over at Wrenlow.

Wrenlow had turned his attention back to the book in front of him.

He followed Gaspar out of the tavern and along the street. "Where's Imogen? She could be useful in all of this."

Gaspar shot him a stern look. "She offered to protect Desarra and Olivia. Did you think I would leave them unprotected?"

"Olivia could make enchantments."

"No enchanter would be able to overpower any sorcerer." Gaspar sighed. "You weren't in the city during the war, and you wouldn't have seen that. For those of us who were, we know just what it was like and what the sorcerers can do to those who don't have their power." They stopped at an intersecting street, heading toward the west, and not where Gavin had anticipated. "How many constables do you have watching the Dragon?" Gaspar asked.

"I don't have any watching it."

"You're just going to leave it unprotected?" Gaspar paused, turning and staring at the tavern.

"I'm not the one who commands the constables."

"You can really be a pain in the ass," Gaspar said.

Gavin pointed to two constables on the rooftop and two along the street. "There are four watching the Dragon. There might be more, but those are the ones obvious to me."

Gaspar furrowed his brow as he studied them. "Good."

"How many do you think there are?"

"Well, if you're seeing four, then there are probably another four you can't see, which is at least a reasonable starting point."

They turned, heading back along the street. Gavin

trailed after Gaspar, starting to think he knew where they were heading.

"The Captain's?" he asked. Gaspar nodded. "Why did they move there?"

"Because it was safer. With the Captain gone, they figured they'd take over a larger building. Gives them a little more freedom. Besides," he said, glancing back at Gavin, "with everything the Captain took from them over the years, they figure he owed them."

If they were there, maybe Zella would be able to find the necklace that had started all of this for Gavin.

Gavin watched for signs of the smoke creatures and glowing of the El'aras dagger but didn't see anything. He left the enchantment for speed and strength on, though now that he knew it might fade over time, he wondered if he should save it for when he needed it. He had no idea if he was borrowing from that energy even while walking through the streets. Maybe he should have asked Davel for another enchantment that would work similarly.

They veered off down a narrow side street not far from the Captain's fortress lined by tall bells trees. Gavin made a point of keeping away from them, though Gaspar didn't seem to care—which likely meant he had an enchantment that protected him. The street would lead them to the back side of the yard, not the direct approach Gavin had taken when he'd come. Gaspar slowed, and he motioned for Gavin to follow him.

A nagging doubt troubled him. He had to figure out why the Fate would use the smoke creatures. Hopefully, the enchanters—and Zella in particular—would have that knowledge.

They neared the wall surrounding the fortress when a cool sensation washed across his skin. He paused.

"Keep going," Gaspar said.

"I felt something."

"Of course you did. It's designed for you to feel something."

"What is it?"

"A way for them to know if somebody who has magic has come through." Gaspar looked over at him. "So, knowing what we do about you, I'm not surprised you felt something."

"What about you? Did you feel anything?"

"No," Gaspar said. "Now keep moving."

"What are you worried about?" Gavin said.

"There are other defenses they placed here."

"What sort?"

"The kind that will prevent you from getting much farther, so keep moving."

They neared a small doorway near the wall. Gavin glanced behind him, and he started to turn back toward the doorway when something out of the corner of his eye caught his attention.

He turned back. "Move," he said to Gaspar.

"I am moving, so just wait a second."

Gavin reached into his pocket, pulling out one of the enchantments. As he looked at the faint trace of smoke in the distance, he wasn't sure if one enchantment was going to be enough. The cloud appeared to be larger than the other ones he had seen. Gavin pulled out another enchantment.

He pushed Gaspar, but Gaspar only glanced back at him.

"It's time for you to get moving before you find out whether or not that smoke creature is really going to come after you," he said to Gaspar.

He prepared for the attack. He had to figure out some way to draw the smoke creature into the enchantment, though Gavin wasn't sure how to do that. He might've gotten lucky in the constables' barracks.

Gavin pushed Gaspar forward again. "You need to keep moving."

"What do you think I'm trying to do?"

"I can't really tell. You're just standing there," Gavin said.

"Because I have to wait for the others to come out."

"I don't know if we have enough time for that."

Gaspar looked past him, his eyes going wide. "What is that?"

"That's the smoke creature."

"What's within the smoke?"

Gavin turned back, and his breath caught. Within the smoke was what appeared to be a face. That face opened a massive mouth, as if it were trying to swallow them.

CHAPTER EIGHTEEN

Gavin hurriedly held out the enchantment. He jammed it toward the smoke creature, unmindful of what might happen if it were to clamp down on his arm. The creature swirled around, but the enchantment took hold, swallowing the smoke. Gavin hurriedly added another enchantment.

Given the size of this smoke creature, he had to try something more.

The smoke creature screamed. The sound was a horrible shriek, and Gavin wanted nothing more than to cover his ears. He had to keep his hand out, forcing the enchantments toward the creature.

"What is it?" Gaspar asked.

"Get moving!"

"What about you?"

"I'm going to be fine. I have the enchantment that repels magic."

The smoke creature slammed toward him, trying to force its way through. Gavin ignored it, holding on to the enchantments, prepared for the possibility that the creature might come toward him with a renewed violence. He might need the sword, if it would work.

Gavin pushed Gaspar back, and Gaspar crashed into something behind him. Gavin hazarded a glance over his shoulder. Gaspar struggled getting to his feet and tried to unsheathe one of his knives.

Gavin shook his head. "Weapons aren't going to work against it. I've tried already, and even the El'aras dagger and sword haven't done anything to them."

"The enchantment?"

Gavin nodded. He turned his attention back to the smoke creature. As he held the enchantments out, he could feel them vibrating as if they were trying to pull power.

He glanced behind him.

There was nothing but the wall. Gaspar was gone.

The enchanters must have let him in.

There was something more dangerous about this smoke creature than the others he'd encountered. Gavin felt his heart racing as he stood close to it, fear building within him. He had to ignore that sense. The creature pressed out at him with its strange magic, forcing those emotions upon him.

They should have been careful—and Gavin should have known better.

The smoke creatures had been following *him*. The Fate was using Gavin to find others.

They weren't helpless, though. He knew the smoke creature could be captured.

He leaned forward, and the smoke creature bounced off the magical protection that he held.

"Wrenlow?" he said into his enchantment. For a moment, Gavin worried the enchantment was no longer working.

Wrenlow's voice crackled. "What is it?"

"I need you to get word to the constables."

"What kind of word?"

He told Wrenlow where they had traveled. "Send them to the Captain's fortress."

"Are you sure?"

"It's not about attacking the enchanters," Gavin said. "It's about saving them."

His arms started to grow heavy. Still, the smoke creature fought against the enchantments, struggling within the power Gavin pushed at it.

Gavin took a step toward it. He had to count on the fact that his enchantment that pushed back magic would be enough to protect him.

The smoke creature started to shriek even louder. He stepped forward again, holding on to the power within the enchantments, and moved closer to the smoke creature.

All he had to do was push.

He took another step.

The smoke creature swirled closer.

That was new.

Gavin reached into his pocket, pulling out one that was

another magical barrier. The smoke creature was repelled farther, though it started to crash toward Gavin, as if it were suddenly aware of how things had changed.

He forced the smoke creature forward, ignoring the shrieking.

What he needed was more power for the trap.

"Hold on, Gavin. We're coming toward you."

He felt a surge of relief at hearing Wrenlow's voice. The irony was not lost on him that, after everything he'd gone through in Yoran, he wanted the constables coming in his direction.

He pulled out another enchantment and used the combination to hold the smoke creature. He needed to trap it. Gavin took another step. Violence within the smoke creature intensified.

What if he added his core energy to the traps? Gavin hadn't tried that before. He hadn't even tried using it to help with the magical repellant. Now was the time to attempt it.

Gavin called that power up from within himself. When he had used it before, he had usually used it to replenish his own strength. There had been a few times where he had learned to use that power to help break the bonds around him, and Gavin had come to know that he could use that power to shatter those bindings.

But this was something different. This was a matter of trying to pour power out from him in a controlled way.

Gavin pushed that power through him and into the enchantments. All of them surged. Strangely, symbols formed in his mind. El'aras symbols.

The creature shrieked.

Power was there, and he let it flow—but there was a limit to it. He had used enough already—maybe too much—but, for now, he let energy flow outward. It struck the enchantment, and the enchantment struck the smoke creature.

Gavin could practically see a barrier form. Rather than pouring out of multiple enchantments, it poured out of only one of them, flowing from him to the smoke creature. The barrier wrapped around the smoke creature, trapping it. The creature shrieked, rising within that barrier, and Gavin struggled to keep his hand firm. Everything within him trembled as he tried to maintain his grip, holding on to the power within him, knowing the energy was still there.

His strength started to wane, but he refused to let go of it.

Gavin cried out. Power flowed from him, and weakness began to overwhelm him. He was using too much of his core reserves. Too much of the magic within him. If only he had some way to call upon more.

Fatigue dropped him to his knees, and he looked up. He was so close to the fortress, but if he drew the creatures in, the enchanters would be in danger. The creature shrieked at him, the massive mouth of smoke stretched open and wide, looking as if it were trying to consume him.

Gavin ignored it. Power continued to flow, and then it swallowed the smoke creature, pulling it down into the enchantment.

He sank down, dropping to his hands and knees. He

took a gasping breath. There was no further sign of the smoke creature. It was gone.

"What was that?"

Gavin looked up. When had Davel arrived?

"What was what?" Gavin asked, dragging himself to his feet. He could barely stand, and it took everything within him to try to focus on keeping his eyes open.

"Where did you get the sorcerer's trap?"

Gavin looked at the enchantment. "What?"

"The sorcerer's trap. Where did you get it?"

Gavin shrugged. "I don't know." It was too much to answer now. He could barely think. He needed to rest. "This one was harder to trap than the others."

"I saw it. I felt the power."

"You felt it?" Gavin asked, smiling.

Davel shook his head. "Not like that." He slipped an arm around Gavin's shoulders, helping him to his feet. "I have ways of detecting magic."

"I know you do. I was there when you made one of them," Gavin said.

He looked past Davel, and he made out several of the constables arranged in a line nearby. Gavin surveyed them, noting their swords and looking for signs of enchantments, but he didn't see anything.

"Where's Wrenlow?" Gavin asked.

"Your friend? He sent word, but he said he was going to watch from a different vantage."

"Where is he?" Gavin took a deep breath, tapped on the enchantment, and called out, "Wrenlow?"

There was silence.

Why had Wrenlow suddenly gone silent on me again?

"He's fine," Davel said.

"I'll believe it when I see him," Gavin said.

"Fine. You can be my guest."

Davel nodded toward the street, and several of the constables disappeared. It wasn't long before they returned, Wrenlow with them. Wrenlow glanced in Gavin's direction, his brow furrowed. All this time, Wrenlow had wanted more excitement, but Gavin suspected he never really intended to come out into the city. Certainly not when there were dangerous sorcerers involved. Hopefully, Olivia had provided him with an enchantment or two that would offer him levels of protection. But if not…

Gavin hurried toward the end of the wall surrounding the Captain's house where Wrenlow stood.

"I think it's something around here. Something is interfering with the enchantment," Wrenlow said.

"Either the smoke creatures or the Fate."

"I suppose, though it might be something else," Wrenlow said. He looked over at Davel. "I found the constables… Where's Gaspar?"

Davel looked over at Gavin sharply. "Gaspar is with you? Why did he bring you here?"

"I thought it was because we were going to warn the enchanters of the danger of the smoke creatures."

"They came here?" Davel asked, looking up at the Captain's fortress.

"They figured he owed them for what he took from them."

Davel's eyes narrowed. Gavin wondered how he would react to that news.

"Why would you want to warn them?" he asked.

"Because of what I learned at your barracks. I think the smoke creatures feed on magic."

"I've already told you—"

Gavin sighed, shaking his head. "I know what you told me, but I also know what I saw. And I know what I felt." He ignored the way that Davel looked at him. There was a question in his eyes, but it was a question Gavin wasn't going to answer, not now. As he looked past Davel, he shrugged. "Anyway, Gaspar left. For whatever reason, he decided to abandon me."

"He didn't abandon you," a voice said from nearby.

Gavin turned. Gaspar was stepping through what appeared to be a solid section of the wall. Not a wall at all, but an enchantment.

"Gaspar," Davel said, nodding to him.

"Davel Chan," Gaspar said. He crossed his arms over his chest and glared. "What are you doing here?" he asked Davel, then shot Gavin a look that was ignored.

"We received word we were needed," Davel replied.

"Really. And what would make you think that?"

"Your friend," Davel said, glancing at Gavin and smiling, "ran into a little bit of trouble. It's not the first time he's involved us."

"I'm all too aware of that," Gaspar said.

"Yes, well, being that as it is, we came to offer whatever help we could. You know how we feel about magic in the city."

He needed the constables and enchanters to find peace.

Gavin would have to be the one to force the issue.

He turned, then sagged and nearly collapsed. He tried to stay on his feet, attempting to keep moving, but he couldn't. Not easily. As much as he wanted to, he could feel the weakness within him and how the energy was fading from him.

He looked over at Gaspar. "Don't be fighting over me."

"What?" Gaspar asked.

"Don't be fighting over me," he muttered. "Find a way to hold this damn thing." He held out the enchantment the smoke creature was in.

With that, Gavin collapsed.

CHAPTER NINETEEN

When Gavin awoke, everything was dark around him. He listened for a moment.

Something throbbed within him, and it took a moment to realize it was his head. He got up, and everything started to spin. There was enough light for him to make out some details around him. The dresser across the room looked like a hazy shadow. There was a window, though the blinds were closed, and the curtains were pulled mostly shut. He moved carefully so that he didn't kick and spill the washbasin on the table near him.

He swung his legs over the edge of the bed, and he looked around the room. He expected to be in the Dragon, but he realized this wasn't it. He should have noticed that the window was a little bit off, the angle of sunlight coming in casting faint bands of light along the floor in ways that his window at the Dragon never did.

"Easy," Wrenlow said.

"Where are we?"

"The enchanters put you up in the fortress. From what I've heard, they placed enchantments around it to protect themselves from the Fate—and the smoke creatures."

"Hopefully, that will work better than the ones the constables used on the barracks." He breathed out slowly. "How long was I out?"

After having used that much of his core reserves, Gavin worried. One of the things that Tristan had loved about him was his willingness to push beyond where he should have, to fight beyond the point of sensibility, and to overwhelm weakness within him.

"As far as I can tell, the better part of three hours."

Three hours. Not so long.

"Why?" Wrenlow asked.

"When I've spent myself like that, I've slept for days."

"I've never known you to sleep for days," Wrenlow said.

"It's been a while." Gavin tensed every muscle, releasing each one slowly. It was his way of testing and preparing for anything.

Wrenlow rested his hand on his shoulder. "Don't get up. At least, don't get up too quickly. What happened there? Davel said you were doing something," Wrenlow said.

Gavin leaned forward, ignoring the throbbing in his head and pushing it away. He checked and realized he was still wearing the enchantments. The one for increased strength and speed was there, as was the magical barrier.

Taking a deep breath, he started to stand.

"I'm going to be fine," Gavin said.

"I'm sure. I've never seen you really hurt."

Gavin shrugged. "I've been hurt."

"Like I said, I'm sure. I've just never seen it."

When he stood, Gavin stayed still. It took a moment, but he gathered himself and pushed back the pain, dizziness, and everything else. Three hours of rest was enough to replenish his core of energy.

His magic.

As much as he was giving Gaspar a hard time about the enchanter abilities he thought the constables had, he had to deal with his own magical ability. The core reserves of strength he possessed were tied to something else. Gavin didn't know exactly what it was or how he could use it, only that what he had was more than just simply strength.

Gavin hovered there for a moment, wobbling in place, and took a few steps.

"Easy," Wrenlow said.

"I'm fine." Gavin took another step, then he stumbled.

Wrenlow slipped his arm underneath Gavin's and lifted him. He started to steer him back toward the bed.

Gavin shook his head. "Not yet. This isn't over."

"You can't fight in this condition," Wrenlow said.

Gavin chuckled. "Most of the time when I fight, I'm in this condition."

"You look like you've been beaten up."

"Do I?"

"Not much from the bruising or anything like that, it's just that you have this hollow expression in your eyes,"

Wrenlow said. "And... I don't know how to describe it. You just look like you've been beaten."

"I feel like it too," Gavin said.

He took a deep breath and then tapped into his core reserves again. It was dangerous to do so this soon after waking, but he needed to gather energy and strength and figure out how to fight off the Fates and the smoke creatures.

When he stabilized himself, he took another deep breath and then held his hands up. He'd strengthened himself, but there had been a cost. "I'm fine."

"What did you just do?" Wrenlow asked. "I felt something. It was like a tingling along my skin." He held out an enchantment, though this was different than any enchantment that Gavin had seen from him before. Probably something new from Olivia or one of the other enchanters. Obviously, something that detected magic.

"I didn't really do anything. I just tapped into my core reserves."

"Ah."

"Don't say it like that," Gavin said.

"Say it like what? You were borrowing from the strength within you."

"Yes."

"And you don't even question what that strength is from?" Wrenlow asked.

"I realize where it's from."

"Do you?"

"I do well enough," Gavin said and headed toward the door of the room.

He glanced back at Wrenlow. His friend watched him, his eyes flicking from one spot to another. He was worried.

"I still don't know what to make of all of it," Gavin said, starting slowly. Wrenlow glanced over to him. "If this is all El'aras, I don't know how I'm going to control it."

Wrenlow watched him. "Do you want to talk about it?"

Gavin smiled tightly, appreciating Wrenlow and his concern for him. He was a real friend and had been from the moment they'd met. "About *how* I'm El'aras? I don't even know what happened to my parents. I have flashes of memory. Fire. Screams." Gavin squeezed his eyes shut. "I don't know how much of it is from when they were lost." Gavin was sure that they were lost, though Tristan had never talked to him about it. He had said there was no point in doing so. He had said that he needed to move on, and that Tristan would help. "I was brought to Tristan's facility, where I was trained."

"I know," Wrenlow said.

"I just wish I knew why." He looked up, meeting his friend's eyes. "There has to be more of a reason. He taught me how to access that part of me. He made me something more than just a skilled fighter."

And Gavin was. His training with Tristan had taught him various fighting styles, techniques he could call upon when it came down to survival.

It was more than that, though. Gavin wouldn't have been able to become the Chain Breaker had he not. As he thought about it, he had to believe Tristan had known. And if he had, then what had Tristan hoped to accomplish?

Gavin looked into an expansive room. He recognized it from his last time through here, and knew it was on the main level. Tables occupied much of it, with chairs all around. There were several hearths along the walls, all of them crackling with warm flames that put out heat. A gentle smoke drifted into the room, and Gavin breathed it in, welcoming that aroma. In addition to the smell of smoke, there was a hint of incense and spice, along with a few more exotic aromas that he couldn't quite place.

Tristan would be disappointed that he couldn't recall the various smells around him. He had always wanted Gavin to be able to identify smells to detect any threat within them. Here, with the enchanters, the constables, and people he would otherwise consider friends, he didn't think there were any dangers. Perhaps that was a mistake.

Gaspar sat at a table, talking quietly with Zella.

In one corner, there were three constables. Two of them stood with hands clasped in front of them, and Davel sat at a table, his gaze surveying everything around him.

Gavin waited.

Wrenlow pressed up behind him. "Are you going to go in?"

"In a minute," Gavin said.

"They've been doing that."

"They've been doing what?"

"Watching each other," Wrenlow said, stepping forward. He nodded toward the constables. "You can see them in one corner, but there are two others over there," he said, motioning to the opposite corner.

Gavin looked to where Wrenlow pointed. Two more constables stood in the corner. They didn't make any movement, but Gavin had little doubt that they were some of the most enchanted of the constables.

"Then there are the enchanters," Wrenlow continued. "There are several different groupings, and all of them seem to be casual. But the longer they're watched, the less it seems that they are as casual as they want everyone to believe."

"Everybody's sizing each other up," Gavin said.

"That was my thought too."

"Everybody other than Gaspar," Gavin said, nodding to the old thief.

"He's been talking to her for most of the time he's been here."

"Do you know what he's talking about?"

"No," Wrenlow said. "Gaspar won't let me get close enough to listen. I think he knows I'm trying to overhear him, and he's keeping his voice down."

"He probably has an enchantment that prevents you from hearing him too," Gavin said.

"When he was at the Dragon, Gaspar never carried enchantments with him."

"That we know of. It's possible that he's had enchantments all along."

Gavin glanced over at Davel, nodding to him before sauntering through the room.

Zella looked up as Gavin joined them, and she smiled at him tightly. "You were the reason we moved, and now you've brought this upon us."

"It's nice to see you again too," Gavin said. "If you find that enchanted memory necklace, I still get paid."

She shook her head. "It's been recovered." When he held his hand out, she shook her head. "What do you think you're doing here? It's not about the necklace."

"I'll tell you once I have the necklace. I took the job. I'm going to complete it."

Zella glowered at him a moment and seemed to realize he wouldn't change his mind. She headed to the far side of the room, digging into a drawer, before coming back to him and holding out a simple silver necklace with a circular charm hanging from it. Gavin stuffed it into his pocket.

"Now. Tell me what you're doing here."

Gavin looked over at Gaspar. "I sort of thought Gaspar would've filled you in by now."

"Gaspar has shared some of what's going on, but I find it difficult to know just how much of it to believe. It seems a bit fantastical, if you ask me."

"Which part? The Fate coming to visit? Seeing as how you were there when they came, I would think you believed that part of it."

"Not the Fate," she said.

"Then the smoke creatures," Gavin said. "I'll admit that it's a bit strange, but it is what it is." He'd learned practicality from Tristan as well. He'd never seen anything like the smoke creatures before, but he knew he had to deal with them. "That's why Gaspar and I were coming here until we were attacked."

She leaned forward, locking eyes with him. "You wanted to bring them here?"

"Not exactly. From what I can tell, the creatures chase those with magical abilities."

"How do you know that?" Zella asked.

Gavin glanced over at the constables. "Because they chased me. And they attacked the constables."

Zella grinned.

"See?" Gaspar said.

"I do see," she agreed.

Gavin looked at Gaspar. "You told her."

"I told her, mostly because I can't believe it would even be possible," Gaspar said.

"Even after your experience?"

"Especially because of my experience."

Gavin started to wobble. He needed to focus more on his core power, letting it fill him. If he didn't, then he would fade even more.

"He just doesn't want to acknowledge he might have a hint of enchanter magic," Gavin said to Zella. "Most of them have it."

"Most of them?"

Gavin nodded. "Enough of them, at least. Now, whether that's true is a different matter, but from what I've been able to determine…"

Zella watched him. "What makes you think this?"

"What I saw taking place when Davel was making

enchantments. But it was more than that. It was the way the smoke creatures were coming at those constables. They wouldn't have unless there was some reason."

"You don't know that," Gaspar said.

"I don't. But I suspect it."

Gaspar leaned back, laughing. "Just because you suspect something doesn't make it true."

Gavin shrugged. "No, it doesn't, but it's most likely true." He leaned on the table, looking at Zella. "As to why I came here, I wanted to warn your people, but I think we also need your help."

"To combat these smoke creatures."

"That, and to stop the Fate. Together." He looked to the constables briefly before turning his attention back to Zella.

"From what I understand, when you faced one of the Fates, you were very nearly killed."

"Very nearly," Gavin agreed.

"What makes you think you would fare any better with our help?"

"Nothing, I guess. All I know is that there is a way to harm them. I've done that. And with the right enchantments, I think we can kill him." That had to be the reason the Fate had turned away when Gavin had gone to Zella and the others.

"They don't fear us," Zella said, looking away. "They view us as less than them. The same way the sorcerers always did. We have always been less."

She turned away, and Davel watched her, though Gavin couldn't read the look in his eyes. Could *that* be the reason for the attack? Not just revenge, but removing some element of magic the Fates didn't approve of?

"When I first came across him here, he was after something," he said. "I've been trying to figure out the reason the Fates would have suddenly started paying attention to Yoran. They had ignored the city up until now, ignoring the fall of the Triad. They hadn't been concerned about anything else that had happened, so why now?" He looked at the others. "There are only two things I can think of—the sword and the egg. The sword is an El'aras creation, so I don't know that they would care about it so much." It still didn't explain why the sword would open the connecting chamber to the lairs beneath the city, but that was a different matter. "But given what we've seen from the smoke creature attack, I have to think it's the egg."

He turned, looking across the room.

"Davel," he shouted.

The constable sat up straighter.

"I need you to come over here," Gavin said.

Davel glared at him. "I don't do what you ask."

"Fine. Come over here so that we can talk about the jade egg."

Davel continued to glower at him, and Gavin smiled to himself.

Davel got up and took a seat across the table from Gavin, positioning himself in such a way that he could look at everybody else around the table.

"I need you to tell me exactly how you acquired the jade egg," Gavin said.

"Do you really still think this is tied to events that are decades old?"

"At this point, nothing would be altogether surprising, especially when it comes to the type of magic here and the kind of magic you're trying to hide."

"The jade egg was given to us by the enchanters when they aligned with us. They told us that it was something they made."

"They *did* make it," Zella said.

"Are you sure about that?" Gavin asked.

"Why?"

"Because, for a long time, the jade egg was protected by the constables." Gavin looked over at Davel, watching him. He thought about the lower level of the barracks, a place where magic could be concealed. The constables essentially had a sorcerer's lair. "When you moved it," he said to Davel, "or when you reached out to the Mistress of Vines," he said to Zella, "I think it drew their attention."

"*We* drew their attention?" Davel said.

"Yes. I think the Fates thought the jade egg was lost—or destroyed. Knowing it survived…"

Knowing it survived would have granted them a particular type of power.

Now they could either give it to the Fate—or protect it.

"I don't think that fits," Davel said.

"No? What if I showed you the sorcerer's lairs for the Triad?" Gavin knew he was reaching. He still wasn't sure that the places he'd found were truly the Triad's, but if they were…

That might explain much more than what he already understood. He might be able to see if there was some reason for the jade egg, which might tie back to what Cyran had been after. Knowing Cyran, Gavin couldn't help but wonder if it was all part of some grander scheme.

Had I played into that? Perhaps I had been used all this time.

"We've not been able to find them," Davel said.

"And you said you've looked?" Gavin asked.

"Yes."

"And you haven't found anything."

"Did you hear what I said?" Davel asked.

"I'm just trying to get the point across that you claim you looked for them for how long? Twenty years? And in that time, you haven't found anything?" He glanced from Gaspar to Zella. Zella watched him, saying nothing, but Gaspar was shaking his head slightly.

"If you know something, then let it out," Davel said.

"I might just stay here and enjoy this feeling for a while longer," Gavin said.

"Careful," Gaspar whispered. "If you reveal what you know, you lose the advantage."

"What advantage is there to those locations?"

"I don't know," Gaspar said.

"Listen, if the constables and the enchanters are all descended from the same sort of people"—Gavin smiled at Davel as he said it and turned to Zella—"then it seems to me we need to work together to better understand everything going on within the city. And as much as you might want to claim that the events from decades ago don't matter, I believe they do. I think it's merely a matter of timing."

"What sort of timing?" Davel asked.

"I don't really know, but I have to question what happened to the Triad."

"What?" Davel asked.

"What does that have to do with anything?" Zella questioned.

"All those years ago. The Triad were powerful sorcerers, were they not?"

"They were. Incredibly powerful," Davel said.

"And because of the enchanters and the constables, you were able to overthrow their oppression."

"We were."

"Did you kill them?" Gavin asked.

"What does that have to do with it?"

"It's a matter of understanding just what happened. Did you kill them?"

"No," Davel said. "They were banished from the city. They left. There was no further danger from them, and there would've been great danger had we gone after them."

Gavin looked over at Gaspar and watched him for a moment.

"What are you getting at?" Gaspar asked him.

"It seems the enchanters believed the sorcerers were destroyed, and the constables were content with them being sent from the city."

"And?" Gaspar said.

"And that's it."

"They haven't returned," Davel said. "They won't return. It would be too dangerous for them, especially knowing what they do of our ability."

"But it's not your ability, is it? You'd borrowed that ability in working with the enchanters, and since you betrayed them, whatever protection the enchanters offered you is no longer there. Wouldn't you say that's true? Listen," Gavin went on, "if the sorcerers were expelled from the city but not killed, it's possible the Fates wanted revenge." He leaned forward. "Why haven't the Fates come before now?"

"Because we're at the edge of the forest. There isn't anything here," Gaspar said.

"And because the constables have prevented any danger from occurring to others within the city," Davel said.

Gavin looked from one to the other. "Or because they waited."

"Waited for what?" Davel asked.

Gavin shook his head. "I don't know. The right time to come after the egg?"

"If they wanted the egg, they could have come for it at any time," Davel said.

"Fine. There's another reason they might have waited." They looked at him, and he made a point of meeting each person's gaze, so what he said next would have a more significant impact. "Maybe they waited until now for revenge."

CHAPTER TWENTY

Gavin led Davel, Gaspar, Zella and a few other constables and enchanters through the city, keeping an eye out for the smoke creatures. It was almost as if the people were aware of the crowd making their way through the streets and were avoiding them. They passed businesses with storefronts darkened, homes with an occasional lantern glowing, and chimneys that spewed comfortable smoke out of them—nothing like the terrifying smoke creatures that had chased him through the city.

With as many enchanters as there were with them, along with constables who he suspected had power, Gavin worried that they were putting themselves in danger by venturing out here like this. Another part of him wasn't nearly as concerned about the possibility of an attack as he had been before. If there was going to be a smoke creature attack, he would have to be at the forefront of stopping it, using the enchantment he and Davel created. So far, there'd been no sign of the smoke creatures.

Gavin held the El'aras dagger regardless, watching for it to glow as they moved through the streets.

"Here?" Gaspar asked as they approached the building. The awning loomed in front of them, shadows around it.

Gavin couldn't help but feel as if the shadows were somehow significant. "Here. This is where I followed the Fate," he said, glancing over at Davel and then at Zella. "It's similar to what I found after Cyran attacked."

"Have you given much thought to the targets he gave you?" Gaspar asked, pulling off to the side of the street. "Presuming your theory is correct, after all. What did those targets have in common?"

"I've been trying to figure out the connection between them. So far, I can't piece it together, but I am concerned that you're right. That there is something that links all of them together. Perhaps he was going after the egg, the same as the Fates, but I don't really know."

Gaspar studied him. "What can you remember about the targets?"

"You were there for some of them."

"The Captain. The El'aras. The connection between the two of them is fairly straightforward."

Gavin wasn't entirely sure. Cyran had wanted the Shard, but what was there about the Captain?

Enchantments?

Even that wasn't a target that Cyran had given him.

"There were others." He thought about the merchant

with the children that he'd smuggled. "I thought that maybe he was trying to disrupt the power in the city. But if this was all about magic, then I don't really know how that fits."

"At least you started to see that he was using us."

Gavin started to smile.

He could tell just how hard it was for Gaspar to admit that they were a team. It was equally difficult for Gavin. They didn't always work together—and they didn't always work well together—but in his time within Yoran, they had become a team.

It was almost as hard for Gavin to admit that.

"He was using us, but I still don't know why," Gavin said.

"Get through this, stop the Fates, and we can figure out the rest."

Gavin nodded. Gaspar was right.

"Let's get moving," he said.

He reached the door underneath the awning and looked around, prepared for smoke creatures or the Fate, but he didn't see any glow from the sword. Stepping inside, he made it through the main part of the home and into the back room. He pulled open the trapdoor.

This door had been blocked to him before when he had tried to come out. Something had sealed off, likely magically, making it so that he couldn't navigate through here. There was no sign of anything here now. Gavin had no idea why he should be able to pull it open so easily.

"This?" Davel asked him.

"I know it looks simple, but this is anything but."

Gavin descended the broken ladder and headed along

the hallway. He reached the door leading into the lair and debated how to open it. He thought about using either the El'aras dagger or the sword, but he didn't know if that would reveal a different sort of truth about it. Instead, Gavin pushed on the door, holding on to that core energy within him, and it came open with a soft hiss. He tried not to think about how that hiss reminded him of what he heard when he placed the dagger against the door.

Once inside, he strode forward.

"You said you've been looking for the sorcerer's lair. This is it."

"It stinks," Zella said.

Several of the other enchanters filed in, Mekal among them. They hurriedly made a circuit of it, and the constables followed them, creating their own pattern and looking along the side. Gavin couldn't help but feel amused at how both parties investigated, as if one side would find something the other had missed.

He searched the room again, as well. Something was off.

The body.

"When I first came here, there were the bones of a sorcerer," he said, motioning toward the back of the room. "And…" He headed toward the wall. The bones were gone. "I don't know what that means," he muttered.

"You don't know what means?" Gaspar asked.

Gavin shot him an annoyed look. "There was a dead sorcerer here. If we presume that this is one of the Triad's lairs, then it's possible it was one of the Triad who died here."

"That's not necessarily the case," Davel said.

"Why not?"

Davel crouched down to the ground and ran his hand through dust. That dust had to be the remains of the sorcerer who'd died, and Gavin resisted the urge to shudder.

"The Triad had plenty of sorcerers who worked underneath them. Each sorcerer in the Triad had others who served them. It was a pyramid of power, with the Triad sitting at the top of it. Far beneath each sorcerer were the enchanters," Davel said, getting to his feet and wiping his hands on his pants. "When the rebellion came, it started at the bottom, working its way up."

"So the enchanters attacked the lower-level sorcerers first."

"Those were the easiest," Davel said.

Zella nodded.

"And when they got to the Triad?" Gavin asked.

"When they got to the Triad, I think the Triad realized that either they were going to have to use their magic to continue to attack, or they were going to have to disappear. Two disappeared."

"Two?"

"Well, there was one who decided to stay and fight. Howarth. A powerful sorcerer and one of the first to have settled within Yoran. Then there was Ilian, a man who was harder than any of the others. And Fenna." He shook his head. "She was the worst of them all. No one was sad to see them gone."

"They didn't have silly names like the Mistress of Vines?" Gavin realized he should have asked about the Triad's names before now, and the fact that he hadn't was probably to his disadvantage. "I would've expected them to create terrifying nicknames."

"I think the Triad was enough."

Gavin snorted. "You're probably right. Though I don't know. Howarth? That doesn't sound altogether terrifying. Neither does Fenna."

"It would have were you here then," Gaspar said, and he swept his gaze around before settling on Gavin.

Only one had stayed.

Gavin looked to where he'd seen the bones.

Could that have been Howarth?

There had been the same smell that he'd noticed in the barracks.

And the smoke *had* been in Cyran's lair.

Could the Fates have used their magic on the Triad?

"What makes you think this is the Triad?"

"There are three chambers like this," Gavin said.

Gaspar started laughing. "This and your friend's."

"And one more."

"That doesn't mean anything."

"I'm afraid he's right," Davel said. "Each sorcerer may have had their own chamber. It's not at all surprising they would have retreated like this. I admit it's a little bit more extensive than I would've expected, but the home above is quite nondescript and not at all what I would've expected with one of the Triad. When they were here, they were a bit… let's say, flashier."

Gavin stepped toward the door, and he pressed the sword against it. There came a steady rumble as a section of the wall rolled apart.

He pulled the sword away. "Why don't we go down here."

The others looked at the now-open corridor. Gavin stepped inside, and they followed. He hurried through it. Having been here before, knowing where he was going and what was around, he wasn't nearly as concerned as he had been the first time. He reached the branch point and turned, heading toward the other sorcerer's lair he knew. When he reached the door, he pressed the sword against it, and it came open as it had before. Gavin stepped inside and waited for the others.

"They're connected," Davel whispered.

"If you go through that door"—Gavin motioned toward the other doorway with the El'aras writing on it—"you will find that not only are they connected, but there's a similar nondescript building above this one. It's more of a warehouse and a home, but it is still protected."

"You said there was a third," Davel said.

"I can't access the third."

"Show us."

Gavin backed down the hall and followed the other corridor. When he reached that door, he pressed the sword against it, but nothing changed. It was the same as when he had been here before, when he had attempted to push on the door to try to open it. There was nothing from it.

"I can't open it, but I believe that the other lair I know is on the other side of this. It doesn't open the same as the others, but I wonder if Cyran did something that prevented it from being able to open in that way."

"Three sorcerers. Three lairs." Davel stared at the door, tracing his fingers over it.

Zella stepped forward, and she pulled something from her pocket.

"What are you doing?" Gaspar asked.

"We need to see if this will work," she said.

"If what will work?" Davel asked.

It was a slender blade, and it reminded Gavin of the El'aras dagger and the sword he carried. She pressed it against the door, but nothing happened.

She stepped back, frowning at it. "It was worth a shot."

"What about the egg?" Davel asked. "If you're right and it was a tool of the Triad, it would only make sense that they would have needed it to open their doors."

Gavin had to wonder, and he reached into his pocket. Ever since the creation of the enchantments and the time he spent with Davel, he had kept the egg on him. He had been hesitant to store it anywhere, worried he would lose it. More than ever, if the Fates were after the egg, then he would have to find some way to protect it.

He held the egg toward the door. There came a soft hiss, which intensified as he pressed it against the door. Gavin twisted the egg, and then the hiss became something worse, a sound that filled his head and echoed within his mind. The door started to glow. It took on a faint white sheen, the color of Gavin's sword and dagger when magic was used around him.

Could the door be somehow channeling magic?

What if he added his to this? It wouldn't be any different than what he had done with the enchantment by calling upon his core reserves. Gavin took a deep breath, reached for that energy, then pushed it out through the egg.

There came an increasing surge, and the door exploded with light.

Gavin was thrown back. He cupped the egg against him, shielding it with his body to ensure it wasn't damaged. He rolled over and got to his feet.

The door had been shattered.

He stepped forward.

Davel grabbed him. "Are you sure that's safe?"

"I don't think any of this is safe," Gavin said.

He waited for a moment, and the others followed him. Stepping into the room, he looked around. The awful smell struck him first.

The smoke creatures had been here.

"This *has* to be the Triad," Davel said.

"It does," Zella said.

"You didn't know about this?" Davel asked her.

She shook her head. "We've been looking, same as you, because we have long suspected that the Triad left items of power behind."

Gavin looked around the room. Of all the spaces, this

one was the most well-preserved. There was the lair he'd most recently found, empty other than the sorcerer's bones. There was the other that had enchantments, but nothing that looked dangerous. And then there was this one, a place that had the sword Gavin now carried, among other items.

"What now?" Zella asked.

"I suppose nothing. I wasn't really expecting there to be anything here, but that this actually is a lair of a Triad… The smoke creatures followed me here," Gavin said. "I thought I saw movement when I was in this space, and by the time I got up to the upper level, I could still see movement, though I didn't know what it was or what it meant. It wasn't until I got outside the house that I started to see that smoke moving along the street. I ran into the forest, but it chased me in and back out, forcing me to run through the streets until I got to the barracks."

"We can just give them the egg," Gaspar said. "If it will protect the enchanters."

Davel shook his head. "We don't know that."

"It seems to fit, though, doesn't it? Everything we've found suggests that what Gavin is saying is correct, much as it pains me to admit that. And if he's right, then we have to wonder if perhaps there is another connection we haven't identified."

"We will not give the Fate the egg," Davel said. "In the meantime, we need to make as many enchantments as possible."

"Now you want our help?" Zella asked.

"If we want to protect the city, we need to have it."

Zella looked behind her toward the other enchanters before turning to Davel. She was dressed in a long cloak with dozens of symbols worked into the fabric—each one likely an enchantment, and each one likely some way of offering her layers of protection that she wouldn't have otherwise. How many of the other enchanters had something similar? For that matter, Gavin wondered if he should have something like that. Maybe he would be better protected if he did.

"For now. A truce," she said.

Gavin had to think that was beneficial, though he didn't know if it would be in time. "We still need to understand these smoke creatures," he said. "Someone who knew the power of the Fates."

"If only the Keeper remained," Zella said.

"The Keeper?"

"The Keeper of Records. When the sorcerers ruled the city, the Keeper of Records maintained an archive of sorts. If we had the Keeper, we might be able to find what we need."

Davel sighed softly, glancing from Gavin to the enchanters before nodding. He twisted his shoulder slightly, and his mouth twisted in a sour line, as if trying to decide if he wanted to reveal some secret he had wanted to keep buried.

Davel clenched his jaw. "I might be able to help with that."

"What?" Zella said.

"Come with me."

CHAPTER TWENTY-ONE

Heading into the barracks for a second time was strange. The constables sat around at their stations and looked up when Davel entered, jumping to their feet when the line of enchanters poured in.

The inside of the barracks was not nearly as ornate as Gavin would have expected, given the level of its importance within the city. It had a low ceiling and stone walls, and somewhere somebody burned incense to push back the stale odor that still managed to permeate everything. There was also a dampness, as if some moisture seeped in through the stone. There was no upper level, as all the barracks descended far below the ground or far enough. Gavin had only seen the main entrance and the stairs leading down, though he suspected there were other rooms on this level that he had not yet observed.

"What is this?" one of the constables asked, eying Zella and Mekal.

"Easy, Thomas," Davel said.

"Easy? Look what you brought in here," Thomas said. He was a slender man with dark hair and a sharp nose. Several bracelets adorned one wrist—all enchantments. His gaze lingered on the enchanters, and his jaw clenched, as if he wanted to leap at them.

"I know what I brought here," Davel said. "If I'm not mistaken, I still lead the constables."

"Are you sure about this?" Gavin asked.

"No," Davel said, nodding toward the stairs to the back.

Gavin descended the stairs with the others, and he glanced over at Davel. "You're certainly having trouble with your people these days."

"They will see the value in my leadership soon enough."

"With too much change like this, you run the risk of rebellion."

"I always run the risk of rebellion," Davel said.

They headed deeper than they had the first time. Whereas the magical room where Gavin had worked with Davel before seemed to be quite a way beneath the ground, Davel descended even farther now. As they went, Gavin felt a sense of the walls starting to squeeze around him. There was a pressure, a buildup of energy, and he tried to fight the sense of claustrophobia pressing around him.

He'd been in worse places. Tristan had seen to that. He'd forced Gavin to experience tight caves and had even buried him alive at one point, all to try to get him over a fear of confinement. It had worked, though he still didn't care much for it.

Gavin swept his gaze along the hallway, settling on each space before realizing what it was. "This is your prison?"

It was no prison like anything he had ever seen. It had to have some magical connection, some way for them to confine those who had power and ensure they didn't cause danger to the constables or anybody else within the city.

"Such as it is," Davel said and continued descending into the depths of the barracks.

Finally, they stopped. He led them forward, and they reached a narrow tunnel with a row of cells. He motioned for them to follow.

Their numbers had dwindled. Several of the enchanters had remained out on the street, and only Zella and Mekal had come down into the prisons with them. Davel had brought two constables with him, and Gavin suspected that they were both heavily enchanted. Gaspar and Wrenlow were there too.

Gavin stopped at one of the cells. The bars were smooth and slick, and they seemed to have some energy to them. He gripped them tightly, feeling the metal, trying to identify something more from it. He couldn't.

"What sort of prison is this?" he asked.

"One that will hold anything of magical power," Davel said. "You should be thankful we have something like that."

"Something like the prison that holds those who can use magic?" Zella asked. "Such as a prison that would confine my people?"

"It does nothing to your people."

"That's not true, and you know it."

Davel stared at her, saying nothing.

"Anyway," Gavin said. "Where is this Keeper?"

"Not far from here," Davel said. "Come with me."

They hurried along the hallway, and they stopped at a cell near the back. Gavin looked in each of them as they went, but he didn't see anything inside, just the empty cells. He could imagine that, at one point, these all were occupied by powerful magical users. When they reached the back of the prison, Davel motioned for him to look inside the cell at the end.

A single person sat on a cot at the back of the cell. Long, lanky gray hair hung down into their face. A dirty brown robe—or had it once been white?—covered them but looked several sizes too large. They were curled up into a ball, and they ignored the fact that any of them were out there. Gavin couldn't even tell if it was a man or woman.

"How long have they been here?" he asked.

"Ever since the war," Davel said.

"You've kept them here this long?"

"They were with the sorcerers."

Gavin couldn't imagine being imprisoned for that long, what it must be like for this person to be held captive as long as they had been.

"What do you know about them?" Gavin asked.

"Not much. They haven't spoken ever since coming here."

"Not at all?"

"Not that any has heard," Davel said.

Gavin couldn't help but find that impressive. "So why did you bring us here?"

"You wanted to see the Keeper," Davel said.

"But if they aren't speaking, then there's no point in us coming to them," Gavin said.

"I figured somebody might be able to coax them into talking."

Gavin chuckled. "What makes you think that anybody here would be any more effective at that than you have been?"

"I do not. Why don't you ask her?" Davel said, nodding to Zella.

Gavin looked over at her, and she stared into the room, saying nothing. She looked through the bars of the cell, and she barely took a breath. Zella knew this Keeper.

"Who is this person?" Gavin asked.

"It's… my mother," Zella whispered. She looked from Gavin to Davel, her brow darkening. Her hands clenched at her sides, and her jaw worked as if she wanted to scream. "I didn't know she even lived."

"How could you not know?"

"She served the sorcerers. At that time, so many served them. They didn't have much choice. When the war came, she tried to escape."

"She didn't try to," Davel said.

"No, I heard word that she did."

"I was there when she was captured." Zella turned and glared at him. "You can blame me all you want, or you can blame your mother for her service to the sorcerers. Either way, I'm not the one at fault here," Davel said.

Zella stared for a moment, and there was a look in her eyes, a question that burned there, and Gavin wished that he could help her. He'd lost his parents, and he understood the pain. And seeing that Davel didn't seem to have any remorse for what had happened left Gavin angry with the constable.

"You captured her?"

"We had to drag her away from the others."

"What others?" Gavin asked.

"There were others with the sorcerers. They all worked together to protect the Triad."

"What if that wasn't what they were doing?" Zella asked.

"I was there. They were doing whatever they could to protect the Triad."

"My mother wouldn't have done that," she said.

"You may not want to believe that, but as I keep telling you, I was—"

"There," Gavin said, watching Zella and noting the way she squeezed the bars of the cell. "You've made your point."

"I'm not sure I have," Davel said. "She doesn't want to listen."

"Because it's her mother." Gavin joined Zella at the bars of the cell. "How old were you when she was lost?"

"Fifteen," Zella said. "Old enough that I never thought I'd see her again."

"See if you can say anything to her," Gavin said.

"What am I supposed to say?" She looked over at him.

"What do you think I can say to my mother that I haven't said in my head all these years?"

"You have questions. Now is your opportunity to get the answers you want."

Zella squeezed the bars, but she didn't say anything more.

"Let her in," Gavin said to Davel.

"I'm not opening the door," Davel said.

"Let her in. The Keeper is old. What do you think she's going to do?"

"If she's the Keeper, then there are many things she could do."

Gavin could only shake his head. "She's been here for twenty years. If she were going to do something, don't you think she would have tried?"

"She *has* tried," Davel whispered.

"What has she done?"

"We have lost many constables."

A slight smile curved Zella's lips.

"Let her in," Gavin said again.

Davel hesitated, his hand resting on the bars to the cell. He squeezed for a moment, his knuckles going white. Then he reached down, sweeping his hand across the ground and pushing. An enchantment.

A door opened. There was a small release, and he triggered it from the outside, sliding the bars of the cell open ever so slightly.

The Keeper, Zella's mother, leaped from the back of the cell, lunging toward them. She moved far faster than

Gavin would've expected, given how old and infirm she appeared.

Gavin darted forward, putting himself between the bars of the cell and Zella. He swept the sword out and held it in front of him. The blade glowed bright white.

The Keeper looked at the sword, staring at it. "You," she said, her voice a raspy whisper. It was the sound of paper tearing.

"Me?" Gavin asked.

"The Guardian should not be here."

She lunged toward him, and Gavin twisted and dropped to the ground. He reached for her arm, twisting it up and locking it behind her back. Despite how she appeared, she was still strong. She writhed in his grip and very nearly came free.

Gavin continued to hold on to her wrist, trapping her arm behind her. He shoved her toward the wall. Zella cried out, but he ignored it. He had no choice.

"Your daughter is here," Gavin whispered in her ear. "If you want a chance to speak with her, you need to calm yourself."

She stunk. It was a mixture of urine and feces, along with a foul stench of body odor. Gavin would have gagged, but the urgency of the moment overrode even that instinct.

"Zella?" she whispered.

Gavin twisted the Keeper around, turning her so that she could see the dark-haired woman standing before her. "She's there," he said. "Now, if you want to have a chance to speak with her, then settle down. Otherwise, I'm going to force you back into the cell, and you will stay here for the remainder of your days."

It was somewhat of an empty threat. Gavin wasn't responsible for keeping her here, though she wouldn't know that.

Slowly, the tension within her started to ease. When he was convinced that she wasn't going to attempt to escape again, he released her arm and moved back toward the entrance to the cell, holding the sword in front of him.

She had recognized the blade. Regardless of what other answer they got, Gavin needed to find out what she knew about the sword.

"You've gotten so big," the Keeper said.

"And you've gotten old," Zella said.

"You shouldn't have come."

"I didn't know it was you."

"They held me." The Keeper coughed, clearing her throat. Given that she had been trapped here as long as she had, and given that, from what the constables said, she hadn't spoken in all this time, she probably wasn't accustomed to using her voice.

"We need to know about the creatures made of smoke," Gavin said to her.

The Keeper turned toward him, and as before, her gaze kept darting to his sword. When she looked up at his face, she finally registered a look of surprise. "You shouldn't have that," she said. "You are not *them*."

Them? A sorcerer?

The blade was El'aras—wasn't it?

Am I wrong? Could the sword be what the Fate was after?

"What do you know about the smoke creatures?" he asked again.

The Keeper stared at him for another moment, and a strange expression lingered in her eyes. It was one of concern. "What happened? Where are the others?"

"What others?" Zella asked.

"The Triad. Where are they? When Howarth died, another would have been in line to replace him. The Triad would rule."

"They abandoned Yoran," Gavin said.

She shook her head. "They would not have abandoned Yoran."

"After they were defeated," Gavin said, glancing over to Davel, "they disappeared. For all we know, they're dead. The Fates have come."

Her eyes widened. "If the Fates are here, then they learned what the Triad planned."

"What they planned?" Gavin asked.

The Keeper's glare deepened. "The Triad will rise. You cannot stop power. We have something even the Fates could not understand."

The egg. It had to be.

Could the Triad have been planning a coup?

Davel claimed sorcerers fought for power. This could have been another play for power. And significant power.

"You would still serve the sorcerers?" Zella asked.

"As should you. That is our purpose. We have always been meant to serve."

Something changed in Zella's face. "We aren't meant to serve."

"You're wrong. That is our role. We don't have their power."

"We have our own power," Zella said. She took a step back, toward the cell.

Davel looked over to her, though Gavin couldn't tell why he watched her the way he did.

"What are they?" Gavin asked. "I need to know what these smoke creatures are."

The Keeper shook her head. "They will destroy you. They will destroy all of you. You cannot control it. Only the Triad could."

Gavin frowned. "How?"

She eyed him, then the others with him, but didn't answer.

He wasn't sure he needed her to answer.

They would feed on those with magic.

He'd seen it.

"What are they?"

She stared at his blade again before looking up at his face. A horrifying smile appeared on her lips. "They are your penance."

She lunged again, lightning quick.

Had he not been prepared for the possibility, Gavin might not have been able to react nearly as quickly. But he was ready for anything she might do. He rolled to the side, using the power of the enchantment to grant him a hint of speed. Then he grabbed her wrist, twisted it again behind her, and slammed her to the ground.

Here he'd thought her fragile, but she was not only fast but strong. She struggled against him, and he reached into his pocket, grabbing one of the enchantments.

He pressed one of the magical traps against her. She sucked in a sharp breath, and then she stopped fighting. Gavin climbed off. He left the enchantment on her, placed against her wrinkled skin.

"What did you do?" Zella asked.

"I used an enchantment that keeps her from calling upon her magic."

"But she's just an enchanter."

Gavin backed away. "Maybe, but if so, she's far more potent than any enchanter I've ever encountered. She might even be a sorcerer. And, given that she served the Triad, she could be fairly powerful." Gavin turned to Davel. "You need to have your constables come question her. We need to find out more about these smoke creatures. If we can, then we will know what we have to deal with. There was some way to control the smoke creatures. The Triad knew of it. Now we have to learn."

Davel nodded and waited near the bars of the prison cell. Gavin backed toward the cell door and pulled Zella with him. Once on the other side, Davel closed the bars, sealing it again.

The enchantment stayed pressed against the Keeper's back. Gavin didn't know how long it would work or whether she could find some way to overpower the magic within the enchantment.

"She's gone," Gavin said to Zella.

"I…"

"I understand." He took Zella by the elbow, and he urged her to come with them.

Gaspar and Wrenlow watched him.

"I lost my parents when I was young," Gavin said. He ignored the others looking, listening. "I don't remember much about them. You're lucky that you remember your mother. I never had a chance to visit with my parents after they were gone."

Zella looked up at him. "What happened to you?"

"I was taken in by a man who trained me. He turned me into the person I am today."

"An assassin?"

"I don't know if he intended me to be an assassin. I sort of fell into that by necessity. He taught me to fight. To kill when necessary. He taught me to use various fighting techniques and to be prepared."

"Prepared for what?" she asked.

Gavin shook his head, taking the stairs carefully. "I never found out."

"Why not?"

"Because others got tired of his training and rebelled."

They reached the top of the stairs, heading into the main part of the constables' barracks. Davel stayed with them.

"I'm sorry," Davel said.

Were it not such a tense situation, Gavin would've

smiled. He could see how difficult it was for Davel to admit that much.

"You are sorry?"

"About your mother. I am sorry."

"I can't believe what she did," Zella said, her voice soft. "I can't believe that she still wants to serve. After all of that."

"We could let her out. She has been held long enough, and we have secured the city now, so there is no reason to hold her any longer."

Zella looked at him. Her expression shifted, the tightness in her face fading, and her shoulders sagging just a little. "I don't think you can. Not until we know more." She glanced toward the stairs. "If she still serves the Triad, then we need to know what she knows."

Davel nodded. "I would welcome your assistance in questioning her."

"You would permit that?"

"I think that we must. We haven't got much information from her in twenty years. Maybe you can change that."

She swallowed tightly before nodding.

Gavin didn't know much about the enchanters. He hadn't the opportunity to get to know them very well. At least, not all of them very well. He knew that so much of their identity was tied up in the war two decades previously. It had changed them, essentially cursing them as their parents had poured power into the egg.

It had to be incredibly difficult for Zella to finally find her mother alive after all this time.

What would he think if he were to find his parents alive?

Probably the same as when he had learned Tristan still lived.

"What next?" Zella asked.

"I have the constables sweeping through the city, searching for any sign of magic," Davel said. "We will find the Fate and stop him."

"There might be more than one Fate, if what Zella said is true."

She nodded. "They wouldn't want another to rise to prominence." She looked to Davel. "Is it safe sending your people into the city? If the smoke creatures are out there and somehow feeding on the enchantments."

"I don't know," Davel said. "They're trained and prepared. We've given them as many enchantments as they need to withstand anything they might come across."

That might work, though Gavin couldn't help but wonder if it was the wrong approach. "We might not have time to get the answers we're after." They couldn't wait around while the creatures continued to attack the enchanters. "We may have to draw them out."

"Draw them out how?" Gaspar asked.

Gavin reached into his pocket and pulled out the jade egg. "This."

"Let's say that it's what they're after," Davel said. "Even if we do draw them out, what will we be able to do with them?"

"Either we give the Fate the egg and he leaves, taking the smoke creatures with him, or we have to fight them," Gavin said.

Davel shook his head. "I'm not certain that either of those strategies is the right plan."

"No, they're both stupid," Gaspar said. "You've seen just how powerful the Fate is."

"Short of a sorcerer…" Gavin frowned. Having fought the Fates, at least those who were here, he couldn't help but think they wouldn't be able to do anything. "There might be something else we can do."

Gaspar looked over at him. "What is it?"

"You're both right. We might not be powerful enough to stop a Fate. But what if we can call someone who is?"

Gaspar groaned.

"I'm missing something, aren't I?" Davel asked.

"He intends to call a special friend," Gaspar said. "And the last time they were here, they nearly destroyed part of the city."

Davel looked over at Gavin, his brow furrowing. "What are you going to do?"

"I think it's time I call the El'aras."

CHAPTER TWENTY-TWO

Gavin waited in the forest. He wasn't far in, though he'd gone far enough that any threat to the city would be mitigated. This part of the forest was familiar to Gavin. Not only was there a large clearing here, but it was where they had dealt with Cyran and the other sorcerer. There was a certain irony in using this place to summon Anna and the other El'aras. Magic would come to the forest once again.

The trees towered around him. As he headed deeper into the forest, it didn't take long for the trees to begin to rise ever taller around him, soon blocking out the light above. They served as his sentries, watching over him, though they did not seem to care whether he succeeded or not.

He wasn't alone, or at least he didn't think he was. As far as he knew, Davel had left several of the constables to watch him, as if he were concerned that Gavin might bolt.

Davel claimed it was for Gavin's own safety, though the

longer Gavin was here, the more he questioned whether that safety was truly for him or for something else. It didn't matter. Not really. All that mattered was that he would contact the El'aras.

It had been a long time since he had spoken to Anna or any others with her.

He thought she'd understand the need behind the summons. That by calling to her and asking for her assistance with this fight, they could use the power of the El'aras. But he didn't know if that was truly the case or not.

His call might go unanswered.

He sat there and held the enchantment Anna had given him, waiting for a response. Every so often, he reached into his pocket and touched the jade egg. The egg was smooth, and when he touched it, he felt warmth flushing through it. He could not lose it. He dared not.

"What's happening there?" Wrenlow asked, his voice coming loudly through the earpiece.

"Nothing," Gavin said.

"Nothing?"

"So far, nothing. I'll let you know if anything happens."

"I don't know if you will," Wrenlow said.

"I called you for help the last time, didn't I?"

"I suppose you did."

Gavin laughed. "Besides, I don't know if you want to be here for any of this."

"If it deals with the El'aras, probably not. I didn't have the best memory of their visit the last time."

Gavin chuckled again. Somewhere out in the forest,

Gaspar prowled, and Gavin suspected that Davel was out there as well. The enchanters with them were working to create additional enchantments to be prepared for the possibility that the Fates might attack. Gavin had to hope that he had enough time before the El'aras arrived, where he could prepare and be ready for anything else he might encounter. Only, the longer he was here, the less confident he was that he would have the time he needed. He had no idea how long it would take them to arrive now that he'd triggered Anna's enchantment.

Gavin took a deep breath, getting to his feet. "Where are you?" he whispered.

"Are you talking to me?" Wrenlow asked.

"Not you."

There was a pause. "I hope you understand that I want to be a part of this, but I don't want to get involved in the violence," Wrenlow said. "Besides, you haven't taught me as much fighting as you promised."

"I've taught you some," Gavin said.

"Some, but one of these times, I'd like to win."

"Then you have to beat me."

Wrenlow grunted. "You make it sound so easy."

"It's no different than what I was once told."

Gavin made a small circle of the clearing, looking all around. There wasn't anything else here, only the sense of the movement around him. Every so often, he could feel the energy near him. He suspected that came from the constables, though Gavin wasn't entirely sure that was what it was.

He tapped the marker, running his finger around it. The

marker was small and simple, yet Gavin suspected it was incredibly powerful. How could it not be, given that it was from one of the El'aras—and a powerful El'aras at that? He had never attempted to trigger the marker before, though he had held on to it and felt the temptation to call to Anna in the past.

Gavin paced around the forest. Davel had been unwilling to have the El'aras meet Gavin in the city, almost as if he thought that he could keep them from using their power, though Gavin knew better. And even if Davel couldn't, the El'aras weren't going to go around and use magic in ways that would be perceptible to anyone else in the city. The El'aras weren't even known there.

He made a steady circle of the small clearing. "Where are you?" he whispered again.

"Here."

Gavin spun around and came face-to-face with Anna.

She was even more beautiful than he remembered. El'aras beauty could be almost impossible. She had golden hair, crystal blue eyes, and deeply tanned skin. She wore a pale blue cloak with heavy embroidery around it. A curved sword hung from her waist, though Gavin had never seen Anna use a sword. As far as he knew, she preferred to allow others to do that.

"You came yourself," Gavin said.

"You summoned. Isn't that what we had agreed to?" She had a strangely lilting quality to her voice; a softness. The way she spoke pulled on him, as if it tugged on some deep part of himself that wanted to react, to answer her call.

Gavin shrugged. "I'll be honest. I don't know what we agreed to. All I know is that I've tried not to call for your help."

"The help was freely given," Anna said.

"I understand, but there are different types of help. In this case, I wasn't sure that you'd want anything to do with what I needed to call you for."

Before looking around the forest, he watched her searching for the others that had to be here. He didn't think that he was alone here in the forest but didn't know where the others had gone, waiting while he summoned Anna. Perhaps they were watching other parts of the forest, convinced that they would have to protect against the army of the El'aras, but that was unnecessary.

"What, exactly, is it?" she asked.

"This." Gavin pulled the jade egg out of his pocket. Of all the people he'd interacted with, Anna was one he didn't worry about taking the egg from him. Which made it even more surprising when she snatched it from his grasp. "You could've asked."

"How did you acquire this?"

"It's a long and somewhat complicated story. I take it you recognize it?"

"Recognize it? It is long thought lost." She looked over at him. "Do you even know what it is?"

Gavin shook his head. "The constables call it the jade egg. They said the enchanters used it to help them place enchantments. The enchanters within the city believed that their ancestors poured their power into the egg, granting it that ability."

He no longer knew what to believe. At this point, the only thing he thought he understood was how it had passed from one group to the other. The Triad had it first. Maybe to use it against the Fates. The enchanters had somehow gotten ahold of it. The constables had taken it from them. Now the Fates wanted it.

"This belongs to my people," she said.

"Like the Shard?"

"Exactly like the Shard."

"How did it curse the enchanters?" If it was an item of the El'aras, then what Zella and the others knew of it was wrong.

"There is danger in using an item like that without the necessary power to activate it."

Gavin could imagine what had happened. The enchanters had tried to trigger the egg. They hadn't been able to. And so, they had all worked together.

And it had left the egg changed, perhaps ever so slightly.

"They used themselves as a sacrifice."

Anna nodded. "It is possible that would be enough to activate it.

"What is it?" Gavin asked.

"It's an item of ancient and incredible power." She held it carefully in one hand, squeezing it with just her fingertips. As she held on to it, the egg glowed softly. It carried a pale bluish light that seemed to mirror the colors of her cloak.

"How did your people lose this?" he asked.

"We were betrayed," she said. There was a harshness in her words that didn't fit with what he'd seen from her before.

Gavin stiffened. "Isn't that always the case." He understood betrayal. Having a friend who had betrayed him had been difficult, but he had a sense from Anna that her betrayal had been something else. Perhaps worse.

"There was one who came among us. One we trained. Allowing to know our secrets. When he came upon this, he took it before disappearing."

"And why do the Fates think it's theirs?"

"The sorcerers stole it from him long ago."

Gavin grunted. "You were betrayed, then he was betrayed. I suppose that's fitting."

"The egg has never been theirs."

Gavin stared at the egg in her hand. "I take it that if I ask for it back, you won't allow me to reclaim it."

"Why would you do such a thing, Gavin Lorren? Have I not told you that the egg belongs to my people?"

"You've told me what you believe."

"Have I misled you in the time you've known me?"

"I suppose not," he said, frowning.

"Have I helped you when you've needed it?"

Gavin nodded. "I suppose you have."

"Then the egg is mine," Anna said.

"I think there's a price."

"A price?" She turned, clutching the egg to her chest. "What sort of price do you think you could place on an item my people hold so dear?"

"The price of safety."

"Your safety has never been an issue."

"Not my safety." Gavin turned, nodding behind him. "The safety of the city."

"The city is not your concern," she said.

"Perhaps not, but I don't want anything to happen to it. Knowing the Fates have come to Yoran and that they decided to attack, I feel I need to do whatever I can to offer it a level of protection."

"That is your price?"

"The Fates need to be neutralized," Gavin said.

"Neutralized?"

"I don't care what you do to them. I don't care what any of your people do to them. All I know is that I want the Fates to be removed from the city. Them and their smoke creature servants."

She stiffened. "What did you say?"

Gavin shrugged, turning back to her. "Their smoke creatures. They unleashed them on the city, and the smoke has been feeding on magic."

"No."

"I'm sorry, but I've seen it myself. We've barely survived several of the attacks."

"What you are describing sounds like the semarrl—and the Fates would not have released them upon the city."

Anna moved over a step, sweeping her gaze around her. She seemed unmindful of the fact that she stood here with Gavin, a man who had been trained to fight and kill—though, having been around the El'aras, he suspected that he didn't pose her nearly the same threat that he posed others.

She didn't have her usual protection, though. Why would she be so willing to risk herself by coming to him and answering his summons?

There was something more here that he didn't fully understand, something more that she either didn't want to tell him or couldn't yet tell him. Gavin hated the uncertainty, hated not knowing, hated the idea that there might be somebody like Anna who knew more about him than he did. When she had been here the last time, she had made comments about his heritage that he had denied, but Gavin had increasingly begun to question whether or not she had been right.

Gavin chuckled. "Now you're trying to convince me that what I saw was inaccurate?"

"It was inaccurate if you think the Fates would unleash that kind of devastation upon the city."

"Then what is it?" Gavin asked, turning toward her. He reached for the El'aras dagger and felt the irony as he tried to grab for a weapon that he had taken from Anna and her people. None of them had tried to reclaim the weapon, though he doubted that they would have been able to. Perhaps he could have been overwhelmed if they had made a concerted effort, but instead they had worked with him, wanting to regain the Shard. Gavin still didn't understand everything about the Shard, but he knew that ensuring its safety had protected the city in some way and had kept a sorcerer from accessing it.

"It was not the Fates," Anna said.

"Who, then?"

"Another."

Gavin shook his head. "I thought you said the egg was taken years ago."

"Centuries ago. And that is a long time for one like yourself, not so long for one like us."

"So it's one of the El'aras."

"Was," she said in a whisper.

"Where are they?"

"I don't know. I'm afraid you must find the one who commands the semarrl."

That fit with what the Keeper had said.

If not the Fate, then who?

The person I saw kill the Captain.

The words the Captain said came back to him: *Don't let him take it.*

It had to be tied together.

"I don't even know where to begin."

"If these creatures have been attacking, that is where you need to begin."

"Why?" Gavin asked.

"Because they will destroy you. Them. Everyone. They can be summoned, though. With enough power, they can be drawn. Find what calls them."

Gavin's mind raced.

The Keeper had mentioned something about the Triad's plan.

A troubling thought came to him. *What if the Triad had used the egg to create something that would summon the semarrl?*

It could be used against the Fates.

And it would make sense the Captain would have it. He had acquired many of the enchantments that had been in the city after the war. The device might even explain the dead sorcerer. If the Triad had been using the egg to create a way to control the semarrl, Gavin could imagine it getting away from them.

"An enchantment?"

"None of your enchantments will hold for long. Not against the semarrl. Everything you try will fail in time."

"Could the egg create something?"

"Not with the power we possess," she said softly. "It would take much power, and at great cost."

Gavin swallowed. Everything started to fit together. The enchanters served the Triad. The Triad wanted power. They could have used the enchanters to fuel the egg to create something that would help them overthrow the Fates but damaged themselves in the process.

"So we can't do anything. That is quite reassuring," Gavin said.

"It's not meant to be reassuring. I am telling you the truth, Gavin Lorren."

"Can you help?"

"Not with the semarrl. Unfortunately, their kind is deadly to mine."

Gavin should've figured that. Knowing what he did of the smoke creatures, the way they seemed to feed on those with magic, it shouldn't surprise him that they would feed on the El'aras.

"I have to do something," he said. "If I can contain the smoke creatures, can you be responsible for removing the Fates from the city?"

Anna considered. "The threat of the semarrl is a grave danger to both sorcerer and El'aras. If you succeed, I will ensure that the Fates depart Yoran."

"Good."

"That is all?"

Gavin smirked. "That's all? You make it sound as if it's not a problem. Like you aren't concerned this power exists, as if there's no reason to be concerned about anything."

"Not quite. There are plenty of reasons to be concerned about the power that exists, but what you must do is something different."

"You're saying that what I need to do—stopping these smoke creatures—is more dangerous than what I'm asking you to do."

"Yes."

"Great," Gavin said. He shook his head, and he looked around. "Where are the others with you?"

"There are no others with me."

Gavin frowned. "Why wouldn't you have invited the others to come?"

"The agreement was with you." She held his gaze, and a wave of something washed through him. Energy. Power. Loss. Anticipation. Dozens of emotions filled him.

"Don't." Gavin shivered.

Anna watched him. "You fight your true nature."

"I don't fight anything."

"Only, I feel your nature has been awoken," she said. "Much more so than it had been before."

"What do you mean?"

"When you were with us before, you did not possess the same strength as what I detect within you now. Have you begun to embrace it?"

"I don't know if I'm embracing anything," he said. He frowned, reaching for that power. It was there, but he didn't know what it was that she asked of him.

"You must be," Anna said, "for I feel it within you."

"You haven't said what I called you away from."

She started to look away, and her gaze swept over the forest. "My time has been challenging."

"You still have Cyran."

She nodded slowly, still not looking back at him. "He will find it difficult to escape us."

"Why has your time been difficult?"

"There are reasons that I left the people for a time."

"Because you are the Risen Shard?"

She looked over to him, and there was a brightness in her eyes, and something more. Was it doubt?

"I am the Risen Shard."

"What does that mean?"

"It means that I have a destiny."

"And what is that destiny?"

Sadness fell across her features. "One that I must face. That is what I have been doing since you last saw me, Gavin

Lorren. I have been preparing, as I must."

"I'm sorry I called you away from it."

She waved a hand. "You offer me a distraction. It is welcome."

He started to smile. He wasn't so sure this kind of distraction was what she would welcome, but as he studied her, he couldn't help but question what she was dealing with. Something bothered her more than what she was letting on.

She was El'aras. She was a mystery wrapped in mystery. He doubted that he would ever know.

Gavin reached for the core reserves within him. To deal with the smoke creatures, he would need something more. "When you were here before, you gave me something."

"I did."

"Do you have more of it?"

"It's dangerous," she said.

"It might be dangerous, but if I'm going to face the semarrl, I want any advantage I might find."

Anna watched him for a moment. "When this is over, you will not be able to function for quite some time."

She pulled out a small pouch from her pocket and shook it for a moment, then handed it over to Gavin. He sniffed the pouch, recognizing that there was a strange odor within it.

"How do you know?" he asked.

"I've seen it."

Gavin dabbed his finger into the powder and touched it to his tongue. As soon as he did, there came another surge of energy. He worried whether he could take too much, but at the same time, he might need to take as much as possible for him to succeed. Defeating the Fates was all that mattered, and stopping the smoke creatures was crucial.

"With Thomas?" He dabbed three fingers into the powder, then licked them. Another surge of energy.

Anna cocked her head to the side, frowning at him for a moment. "Thomas wouldn't dare take as much as you did."

Was that a compliment? Gavin didn't necessarily feel like it was much of one. "I took what I had to." Gavin watched as she held on to the jade egg, which continued to glow. "What are you going to do to the Fates?"

"You asked me to remove them from Yoran."

"I understand, but what are you going to *do* to them?"

"Only what must be done."

He found Anna impossible to read, like a blank slate to him. As he looked at her, trying to interpret what she might be thinking, he couldn't come up with anything. Perhaps that didn't matter. All that mattered was that he had her help, even if it took some strange form he didn't fully understand.

"I might need to use the jade egg a little bit longer," Gavin said.

She frowned. "Why?"

"If I am going to find what summons them and stop the semarrl, I'm going to need to have something that will help me call to them." He might need that to protect the enchanters—and the constables.

"No."

"I'm afraid that's my price," Gavin said.

"It will not be served as bait."

"In this case, it needs to be. This way, I can also make sure you fulfill your part of the bargain," he said, smiling at her.

"You doubt I would?"

"I don't know. Should I?"

She shook her head. "The people will honor their bargain."

There was a formality to what she said, more so than what Gavin thought was necessary, but he also worried that something he had said insulted her. He could see it in her eyes, could see the expression that suggested something else. Was it concern?

Why would she be concerned about me? She had come willingly. Freely. Why would she be concerned about anything that I said?

"I'm not trying to upset you." He looked at the egg. "I'm going to need that, though." He doubted that he could draw the semarrl to him without something that would tempt them. There was power in the egg, especially if he drew on it.

In his brief experience with them, he knew that they were tempted by the power. They would be drawn to it, and he suspected if he were able to summon enough energy, he might find something that would compel them to follow. The only other challenge was that he then would have to find some way to stop them. He didn't know what that was going to take.

Anna watched him for a few moments. "You will return it to me."

"And you will take care of the Fate?"

"I can manage a single sorcerer. It is agreed," she said.

"It is agreed."

CHAPTER TWENTY-THREE

The outskirts of the city seemed like the right place for him to lure the semarrl. He had the pouch of powder in his pocket. Gavin held on to the jade egg. Ever since Anna had taken it, there was an energy flowing within, which he could feel as he clutched it. The constables had used the egg to try to create enchantments—a misuse of its magic, especially if it truly was an item of power that the El'aras claimed.

What might I be able to do with it?

Gavin tapped the enchantment. "Wrenlow?"

"I'm here."

"I need you, Gaspar, and the enchanters to go back to the Captain's fortress. Keep them safe."

"From what?"

"I'm going to do something stupid."

"Gavin—"

"I might be the only one able to do it." He didn't know if

that were true or not, but he was determined to figure it out. And he would protect the others. "Just do it. And send Davel to me."

There was a moment of pause.

"He's coming."

Gavin and Anna didn't have to wait long. Davel strode out of the forest with two other constables who followed before pausing and waiting in the trees.

"This is her?" Davel asked, eyeing Anna.

Gavin made quick introductions. "I need traps. As many as you can make."

"Why?"

"Because I'm going to capture these things. You need to get your constables back to the barracks while I do it."

"That's not how things work in my city."

Gavin smirked. "It's your city now?"

"It's always been my city."

Gavin shook his head. "Fine. Then create a perimeter around me and make sure they come toward me. Not your people. But I need the traps."

He held out the egg, then the spool of wire, ignoring the way Anna watched him.

Davel hesitated before taking it and starting to wrap it around the egg. "What makes you think you can do this alone?"

"A hunch."

"You're risking the city on a hunch?"

"I'm not risking it. I'm going to protect it."

Davel grunted as he made enchantments, handing each

one to Gavin. When he ran out of the spool of metal, he looked up.

Gavin grabbed the egg. "I need this for what I'm going to do, too."

"Do I even want to know?"

"Probably not. Get your people out of here. I'll let you know when it's done."

"If you try anything—"

"I've done nothing but help the city," Gavin said.

Davel grunted again. "I suppose that's true," he said begrudgingly, then tapped something on his side as he strode away.

It left him and Anna to deal with the semarrl and the Fates.

It seemed like not nearly enough.

At the same time, it seemed like the only solution.

If anyone else were involved, and if Gavin and Anna failed, they would draw the attention to them. It was an unnecessary risk if Gavin intended to protect the city. Which meant that the two of them had to succeed.

He glanced over at Anna. The hood of her cloak was pulled over her face, concealing her, but Gavin still had the sense of her beauty. She flicked her gaze over to him.

"I had not expected to return to this city when I left."

Gavin reached into his pocket, and he fingered the marker that she had given him. "Are you disappointed that I called?"

There was a moment when he noticed a conflicted expression crossing her brow. "Not disappointed."

"Something's worrying you."

"That is of none of your concern," she said.

"If you are going to get in trouble coming here…" Gavin had no idea how she could get in trouble. He had a sense that she was somehow El'aras royalty, though she had not said it. She was the Risen Shard, whatever that meant. She had access to power that was beyond what he could draw, even if he were part El'aras.

"No more trouble than I was destined to find."

It was a strange choice of words, and Gavin commented on it.

"There is nothing you need to concern yourself with."

He had a sense from her that she was not going to speak on the topic anymore.

"At least help me more about what we are dealing with." Gavin looked around the forest, turning his attention to the street where he had first seen the smoke creatures. The semarrl. "I need to better understand the semarrl and what that threat is."

"They are dangerous. They are death."

She said the words so solemnly and so matter of fact that Gavin couldn't help but feel as if there was something more to it. As he continued to look at her, he suspected that she wasn't as truthful as she could be.

Gavin looked along the street. There was nothing other than a crowd of people. The forest ran near him, and he could make out Cyran's old house in the distance. "What are these creatures exactly?" he asked. "You keep saying that they're dangerous and that they're death, but what are they?"

"There are creatures in the world that few have ever witnessed. Some suspect that the creatures were created by a sorcerer long ago. Either a sorcerer or a magic user who has tapped into one of the great powers in the world." She nodded to the pocket holding the egg. "Some call those powers gods, but the El'aras know them as something else."

The energy of the jade egg filled him with power that rolled through him, and he couldn't help but feel as if there was something within the jade egg he could use. And if there was something he could use, he could easily imagine what the Fates wanted it for.

If a magic user who could tap into some greater power in the world, he wanted to ensure that the Fates could not acquire it. They already had enough power, and he didn't want to be responsible for them gaining even more magical potential. It was not with what he had seen, the dangers he had experienced, and their willingness to attack so openly throughout the city.

"Once I draw the semarrl, I can trap them, but I don't know if the enchantment will hold long," Gavin said. "Without a way of truly holding the creatures, there may be nothing that can be done unless I can find the one controlling them."

Whoever they were would be powerful.

If he were right—and increasingly, he thought he was—they had killed the Captain and all his guards to get the item that would control the semarrl.

"You will need to find the item of power and use it to bind them. Doing so requires somebody of considerable understanding of the flows of magic."

"Couldn't we just use the egg?" he asked again. It would be easiest.

"Not without making a greater sacrifice," she said, shaking her head. "While you have talent, Gavin Lorren, you are untrained. You must force the person who released them to hold them once again."

He had to draw that person out.

Gavin started moving along the street, gripping the jade egg. It didn't glow quite the same way for him as it did for her, though strangely, it did continue to glow for him. Gavin didn't know if something about him caused the egg to glow or whether Anna had activated something within it. More likely, it was the latter. He felt the warmth that flowed within it. He tried to hold on to that energy to use it.

Anna watched him, frowning.

"What is it?" he asked.

"You're holding onto a kind of power I was not expecting," she said.

He recognized that there was something within the egg that he could feel. The longer he held it, the more potent the feeling of whatever it was that he detected. Strangely, it felt as if there was a reverberation from some place deep within him, almost as if the egg were calling to that core reserve of power.

"Can you feel what it is you are doing?" Anna asked.

"I can feel something," he admitted. "I don't know what it

is, only that there's a sense within me that seems as if it's tied to the power of the egg."

"It *is* the power of the egg. It's the power of trapped energy, and it is calling to part of you."

"What part of me?" he asked softly, even though he thought he knew the answer.

He had long suspected what part of him was, some hidden and sequestered piece he still didn't fully understand. Ever since he'd dealt with the El'aras, Gavin had begun to question who and what he was. Not enough that it mattered. He didn't care. It didn't influence what he did, but there was some part of him that had to wonder.

"You understand what you are," she said.

"I understand I'm somehow tied to the El'aras." Even saying it was difficult for him, though he knew it was true. He could feel the truth within himself.

"You are not just tied to the El'aras," she said.

"What is it, then?"

"You *are* El'aras." She smiled tightly at him and glanced at the sword he now carried. She'd looked to the blade a few times since arriving. "You don't have to believe it for it to be true," she said. "I felt it the first time I met you. And then when you were able to take the sh'rasn elixir, I realized you were truly one of the people."

Gavin stared at her. "I've wondered how that is possible."

"Because it is. I don't know if you are fully El'aras or whether you are only half, though for someone who is half El'aras to tolerate the elixir would be surprising. Not unheard of, but surprising."

"Why do I get the sense that you don't care for people who are half El'aras?"

"It's not me that you need to be concerned about," she said softly.

Something that Thomas or one of the other El'aras had said to him came back. He didn't remember it in great detail. At the time, he'd been trying to stay alive, but there had been something almost derogatory about a half El'aras.

"The El'aras don't care for them, do they?" Gavin asked.

"If you take the time to understand, you will know." She smiled. "I have seen you up close, Gavin Lorren."

He waited for her to expound, but she fell silent. She smiled at him, as if she were telling him some truth that he should have known all along.

He watched her for a moment. "What does it mean?"

"Why must it mean anything? If you've chosen for it to mean nothing, then it means nothing. If you've chosen for it to mean something, then it means something. There is no reason it must mean anything to you."

"Even though it ties me to the El'aras?"

"How does it tie you to the people? The only thing it does is reveal your heritage. It doesn't make you anything you were not before." She regarded him for a long moment, and he felt a pull from her, almost a desire to reach for her. "Did you know what you were before?"

It was a simple question, but it seemed laden with so much more than what Gavin had given thought to. "I know who I am, if that's what you're getting at."

"You have known that you were the Chain Breaker, but I'm asking if you know what you are."

Gavin breathed out slowly. "I lost my parents when I was too young to remember," he said.

"Many have," she said.

He looked over. "Is that why you were in the city?"

She smiled tightly. "I was in Yoran because I am the Risen Shard."

"So you were hiding."

"Yes."

It was the most admission that he had gotten out of her, and he wondered why. "Why?"

"I'm afraid we don't have an opportunity to discuss this anymore."

A strange haze appeared in the distance. Smoke.

"They're here," Gavin said.

"Then I must leave you," she said.

"Are you sure? I could use your help."

Anna frowned, shaking her head. "As much as I might be interested in seeing what the two of us could do together, I doubt there's anything I could offer you. And I have my side of the bargain to fulfill."

She leaned toward him and gripped his forearm, and then she kissed him on the cheek. A heat washed through him. He thought of Jessica and what reaction she might have if he acknowledged that he felt waves of attraction for Anna, but he thought that Jessica would understand. Jessica knew that Gavin would leave at some point, and now that he had spent some time around Anna, even Gavin thought that he needed to leave.

It was time for him to do so. It was time for him to understand who and what he was.

Why not with Anna?

Gavin pushed the thoughts away—thoughts of Anna, thoughts of the nature of the kiss—and focused on what he needed to do: Find the source and origin of the smoke creatures. Trap them and prevent them from returning.

He took a deep breath and found the energy within his core reserves, which flowed out of him into the jade egg. When he was done, he released that energy.

Finally, he held out the jade egg.

"Do you know what you did?" she whispered.

"I could feel it," he said.

"Feeling it is different than knowing it."

"I know I pushed something through the egg."

"I thought you'd be able to better identify what it was that you were doing, but…" She smiled, and then she took the egg from him. "Focus on that pool within you. You have it. I could see it when I first met you. And think about what you want to do. That is how you control it. There is more to it, but we don't have the time to go into it. Be safe, Gavin Lorren."

She ran off, disappearing into the city. He watched for a moment but turned his attention to the smoke as the semarrl came near him.

Gavin held on to the El'aras sword and dagger. He thought he could find power within him; some way of reaching it and letting it explode out from him. It would take concentration, but it would take an understanding as well.

He unsheathed the sword and held it in front of him. The blade glowed softly, though it surged more brightly than before. He pulled one of the enchantments from his pocket. He could feel that sense of energy and the trembling within it. It was almost as if it were calling to him, demanding that he release power. Gavin had to be careful not to release it any sooner than necessary.

Some pressure built upon him from a distance. He focused on his core reserves, testing as he pushed the energy through the enchantments he carried, readying for anything. Strangely, ever since holding the jade egg, he could feel that core reserve bubbling within him in a way it hadn't before.

Gavin let that power build deep within. Then he raced toward the smoke creatures, ignoring the danger of it as they pressed upon him.

He had the enchantments. The combination of the two—one for repelling magic and the other for speed and strength—allowed Gavin to move quickly.

He hurried toward the nearest of the smoke creatures. When he met it, he thrust the enchantments forward. The suddenness of Gavin's movements overwhelmed the creature. He pushed through the enchantments, using that core energy within him, and it exploded from him. Not nearly as potently as it had before, though this time with somewhat more control.

He could feel the enchantment taking hold, sealing the creature within. The semarrl stopped writhing within the enchantment, and he backed away, no longer holding quite as tightly as he had before.

Gavin spun. He stuffed the enchantment into his pocket, pulling another out. He had to be ready. He needed to find some way to call that energy to him, to draw these creatures' owner to him.

If it wasn't the Fates, then he had to find out who it was.

Gavin continued to hold on to that sense of power, clutching it to him, focusing on it. Another creature streaked toward him. He pushed the energy outward through another trap, wrapping it around the nearest of the smoke creatures.

Once he captured it, he stuffed the enchantment back into his pocket, hurriedly grabbing another. He poured power into the next enchantment, trapping another smoke creature.

As he worked through them, he started to worry. *How many smoke creatures would there be?* He didn't have enough enchantments for as many creatures as he'd detected.

He needed to find the person releasing them. He needed to stop them. And if not that, then he needed to learn how to destroy the smoke creatures.

Gavin captured one after another, using the core reserves within him. In the distance, he was aware of more pressure squeezing upon him. He walked along the street, and it seemed as if the smoke creatures were forcing him forward. He dabbed his fingers into the pouch of powder

Anna had given him and licked them quickly before stuffing the pouch back into his pocket. There came another surge of energy, though not nearly as vibrantly as before.

He followed the way the smoke creatures were pressing him. That seemed significant. He tried calling out to Wrenlow, but there was no answer. That didn't surprise him.

The more he was around the smoke creatures, the more certain Gavin was that they had a way of neutralizing magic. A massive semarrl stretched toward him. This one was dark gray, and he could almost see limbs within the smoke.

Gavin spun, drawing upon the enchantment for strength and speed, and he darted toward it. He thrust one of the enchantment barriers forward, trapping the smoke creature within it.

How many more will I be able to capture?

Davel had made sure that Gavin had plenty of enchantments, but there was a limit to what he could do. Gavin reached for the packet of powder again, taking another dose despite knowing he could only take so much. The more he consumed, the more likely it was that he would take too much and eventually run out of power. More than that, he might eventually simply succumb to overuse.

Gavin thrust another one of the enchantments forward and trapped a smoke creature again. One after another, he continued to use the energy from the powder, pushing out through his core reserves. The powder Anna had given him seemed to tap into some greater strength, as if he were calling power he couldn't otherwise. He couldn't help but feel as if that strength tied him to some other part of himself.

The semarrl continued to guide him forward along the street. He had gone this way before. Most parts of the city were familiar to him after living here as long as he had and wandering the streets as much as he had. There was still something about this that felt different, even more familiar than it would have otherwise.

Finally, the pressure forced him to turn. When it did, Gavin thought he understood what was taking place. It was forcing him along the pathway beneath the ground.

The same path that the sorcerer's lair would take.

He started to slow. It was almost as if they were sacrificing themselves to drive him forward. There had to be some reason they were directing him in this way.

He had an incredible amount of that power, far more than he had ever had before. Holding on to it now, Gavin could feel that energy flowing up within him, rolling out through him in a way that suggested he could do anything.

He needed it. Power slammed into creature after creature, giving Gavin the belief he could do this. The resistance that pressed around him was a strange energy. It felt like a wall squeezing upon him, though he could see nothing to it. Perhaps a faint shimmer, a bit of color within the translucence, but nothing more than that. He fought against it but felt his strength failing. Resistance pressed around him.

Gavin was in a part of the city emptied of people. The pressure guided him to a clearing. At one point, the market he'd visited after meeting with the old woman about the necklace occupied much of the space, but today it was gone. He traced his way along the ground, feeling the stones, but he couldn't tell why the smoke creatures would have guided him here.

He turned and shoved his fist out, driving it toward each of the smoke creatures that attacked him. They got close, but they stopped swirling as close as they had, almost as if they realized he had a way of enchanting them and trapping them. There were too many. As Gavin looked around the clearing, he counted a dozen or more separate swirls of smoke.

Too many.

All of them were darker and much more distinct than the smoke creatures had been when he'd first seen them. Several had faces within the smoke, though they'd not opened their jaws to try to swallow him the way they had when he'd headed to the enchanters. Gavin felt an overwhelming urge to be anywhere but here.

Finally, he stopped.

If the smoke creatures wanted him here, then this was where he was going to be. What he needed was to figure out who controlled them. He moved in a small circuit, turning in place to avoid the smoke creatures.

He'd have to allow the smoke creatures to surround him. Only then could he call upon the power he needed. If he could trap them using a massive enchantment, perhaps he could end this. He didn't need to find the person responsible or find whatever method they used to release the smoke creatures. That was, if the smoke creatures were some sort of magical item.

What if they are a part of the natural world, preying upon those with magic?

Anna would have known if that were the case.

Gavin stopped in the middle of the clearing with his hands at his sides as he let power flow through him. The smoke creatures circled closer and closer, dozens of them. Too many. They attempted to slam into him, but Gavin braced himself. The enchantment pushed them back.

He feared the enchantment failing. They would swarm him, overwhelm him, and swallow him. They would consume him with their strange power.

Gavin ignored that fear. Instead, he focused on what he could do with them. If they pressed in upon him, then he might be able to contain them.

But there were too many for the enchantments he had taken from Davel.

What if there was another way?

Gavin held out the enchantments, but he also held out the El'aras sword. Squeezing the hilt, he let power pour from him and flow from that core deep within him. The blade exploded with power, and he pushed that power toward the creatures, bursting through them with a vibrant light.

When he had used the sword against the smoke creatures before, nothing had happened. This time, the creatures dissipated, dissolving under the assault. Each time he swiped at the creatures, another surge of power came, a burst of energy that flowed.

He no longer tried to use the enchantments to capture the smoke creatures. Now he swung the blade and carved through them, and the smoke creatures shrieked as the blade ripped through them. It felt strange to hack at the semarrl with a sword, but Gavin could feel it cutting through them, tearing them apart.

Why had Anna been afraid of them?

If she had this kind of power—or more—there should've been nothing for her to fear. Only, as he darted through and swung the blade at these creatures, he couldn't help but feel as if there was something that Anna hadn't shared with him. Some aspect of this power and ability that she had not revealed to him.

The smoke creatures continued to dissolve. At least, Gavin thought they were dissolving. Each time he carved through them with the blade, they screamed and cried out, then disappeared.

But each time they disappeared, he realized something. They were coming back together.

He started to flow through various fighting techniques. Gavin knew nearly fifty different ones honed over decades of training. Tristan had taught him to fight in many of those techniques, wanting to ensure that Gavin would be able to handle himself regardless of which type of attack came at him—to know the strengths of the fighting style and the weaknesses so that he could counter them.

He had learned to fight with swords, knives, and

daggers, but not nearly as much as he had trained in hand-to-hand combat.

He became lost in the rhythm of it, sliding from one technique to the next. Tristan had trained him in his movements, and though he'd never taught Gavin how to fight smoke, somehow the techniques he used seemed right.

As Gavin let the sword carry him through those movements, the end of the blade glowed with his core reserve power, and he knew he would defeat the smoke creatures. Unless the energy within him faded. There was a limit to how much power he had, how much he could push out from him. Eventually, that limit would overwhelm him, and he wouldn't be able to withstand anything more.

Gavin felt pressure building around him again. It was the first time since facing the smoke creatures he'd felt it. He could feel the creatures starting to push in upon him—the sense of their energy, the connection of magic they had. All of it started to squeeze, working their way around him.

Gavin tried to ignore it, focusing instead on the power within him and the core reserve of energy that flowed. He was bolstered by the powder Anna had given him, but the smoke creatures were pushing, pushing, pushing.

He found himself moving through much more compact motions. The smoke creatures dissolved under the sword contact, but then reformed.

This won't work.

Gavin stopped and braced himself. The creatures swirled around him, pressure continuing to build and slamming into him.

There was nothing he could do.

He allowed the smoke creatures to push in on him, and he focused on how they were doing so. Gavin reached for his core power. Then he pushed it out.

It was almost the same as what he had done when he broke free from the chains Tristan had placed around him. Only, this time there *was* something different about it.

As Gavin pushed, he could feel the pressure circling around him, which reminded him of the Fates. The Fates' power had bulged, stretching as he'd attempted to strain beyond it. This was more restrictive, as if anything he might do would continue to squeeze and overwhelm him as the energy collapsed around him.

He was the Chain Breaker.

Power filled him.

Gavin unleashed it, and the smoke creatures were thrown back.

He sagged. He'd been using too much strength.

All to do what? He hadn't done anything to the smoke creatures. All he'd done was delay them. As they continued to press around him, Gavin doubted he could withstand them much longer. Once they reached him, once they overwhelmed his enchantments…

He had no idea what would happen to him when they did.

He tried to ignore the pressure swirling around him. They circled toward him, and he drew on his core reserves, pushing out once again. He used it to explode that power out from him.

Gavin wouldn't have many more chances.

Where was the person who was responsible? Someone had stolen an item from the Captain and could use that to control them, which meant they had to be somewhere nearby.

Gavin had made a mistake attempting to fight these creatures rather than searching for the one in control. The semarrl continued circling, pressing in upon him.

Movement in the distance.

A rooftop.

Gavin frowned, though he quickly tried to make it appear as if he wasn't aware of it. He turned, again calling upon that power deep within him. He would have only a few more chances.

He drew on that power and then jumped. He exploded up, letting it carry him toward the street. Then another jump. This time, he landed on the rooftop. A cloaked figure turned toward him—the same person he'd chased out of the Captain's fortress, he suspected—holding an onyx sphere that reminded Gavin of the jade egg.

"There you are," Gavin said.

The figure backed away.

Gavin could feel the smoke creatures swirling in the distance. There was one thing he could try, though he didn't know if it would be effective. What he needed was an opportunity. Only a moment, nothing more than that.

He pushed the core energy through the enchantment to force the smoke creatures back. It allowed him to face this person alone.

"I need that item," Gavin said.

"I don't think so."

There was something in the voice familiar to Gavin. Had he faced this person before? Given what he had encountered in Yoran, he wouldn't be at all surprised if he had.

He took another step toward the figure. "I think I do. Now."

Gavin darted toward them, and the figure slipped back, twisting hurriedly away from him. When they did, the hood of their cloak fell back.

Gavin stopped, frozen in place. "Tristan?"

CHAPTER TWENTY-FOUR

Gavin continued to keep the smoke creatures at bay. Even as he did, he could feel his strength fading. He needed all his strength to face Tristan.

Am I really going to have to fight him?

Reaching—and killing—the Captain required skill. Gavin had thought it required magic though the dagger hadn't glowed when he'd been there. If it had been Tristan, he wouldn't have needed any magic.

"What are you doing here?" His gaze drifted to the dark egg. He didn't know what else to call it, but it seemed fitting. *Don't let him take it.*

Tristan looked different than the last time Gavin had seen him, with a bit more weight, though he seemed even more muscular than before. His hair had the same streaks of gray, though the lines around the corners of his eyes had deepened. Shadows circled around him, though that might've only been Gavin's imagination. He had on a heavy black cloak, one that would blend into the darkness.

Within Tristan's smile, there was something that reminded Gavin of all the times he had trained under the man standing before him—the torment, the torture, all the lessons that Tristan had taught him.

"I'm doing what you were not able to do," Tristan said.

"What I couldn't do?"

"Yes." Tristan held the egg out, and power started to batter Gavin. "Interesting. It seems as if you have an enchantment."

"I do," Gavin said.

"I'm sure you're aware that enchantments fade with the proper exposure."

"I'm aware."

"I imagine you think you can hold on to the enchantment long enough for you to take this from me."

"I hope so," Gavin said.

"And if you cannot?"

"Then you'll destroy me. Others in the city. Everything."

A strange smile twisted Tristan's face. "Maybe."

"Why?"

"Because it must be done."

"And you're the one who stole that from the Captain," Gavin said, nodding to the onyx sphere.

Gavin had so many questions when it came to Tristan's sudden appearance here, but even as he asked them, he couldn't help but feel as if there was something he needed to better understand. Until then, he couldn't begin the next step in whatever he would have to do. Almost as if this were the next step in some training.

"You cannot begin to understand," Tristan said.

"I think I can. I think you're trying to prove you can do something."

Tristan nodded to him. "Think whatever you would like."

Gavin circled around him, holding on to the enchantment. The longer he waited here, the more his strength would begin to fade. Were it not for the powder Anna had given him, he might have lost his strength already.

He worried what would happen to him when the effects of the powder faded, when his strength faded. It was possible he would lose all remaining strength and be overpowered.

Gavin moved to the side, holding on to the energy within him and bracing himself with the powder. He let that sense flow into him, through him. There was considerable power still within him. He had to try to find whatever it would take to push back Tristan.

He had to get the dark egg from him.

"All I need is that," Gavin said, nodding to the egg in Tristan's hand.

"Is that all you need?" Tristan asked, a twisted smile on his face. "You've been chasing me. All this time, you've been looking for understanding, wanting to find me."

"Because I thought you were dead."

"Perhaps you would have been better off thinking I was."

"Perhaps I would have," Gavin said. He darted forward,

but Tristan moved just as quickly. Of course he would.

Tristan had trained him, and anything Gavin might do—every fighting technique and style he'd learned over the years—had originated from Tristan. That wasn't to say that Gavin hadn't expanded on that. In the days since leaving his mentor, Gavin had continued to train, searching out others to help him augment his fighting styles.

He liked to think that he'd become a more skilled fighter, though Gavin didn't know if that was enough against somebody like Tristan. Against somebody who had taught him and trained him and proven time and again that he could overwhelm Gavin.

Strangely, now that he stood across from Tristan, there was a part of him that wanted to find out. He wanted to challenge himself, test himself against his old mentor. Wasn't that what he'd been looking for during his time in Yoran—a way to test himself?

Tristan watched him. "You don't have much time, Gavin. They're coming for you. You called them here."

"I'm not their target, though, am I?"

Tristan shook his head. "No."

"You sent them against the Fates."

"Perhaps."

Gavin had been trying to figure it out. "You used the appearance of the egg." He waited for a reaction but didn't see much of one from Tristan's face. Could Tristan have been the one to steal the jade egg from the El'aras in the first place? "You've been trying to draw them out," Gavin said.

"Perhaps."

"Why?"

Tristan backed away from him. Most of the rooftop was flat, but he started to climb a section that sloped upward. When he moved overhead, he would have a better vantage. "Because it was necessary, Gavin Lorren," Tristan said. "And you are not ready."

"Ready for what?"

"To do what I trained you to do."

"I won't be used."

"You have always been used," Tristan said with a laugh. "All of you have been. That's what made you so useful."

"Until you were attacked."

"Was I?"

"Your students rebelled. They attacked you," Gavin said.

"Or did I want them to rebel? How else would I have maneuvered them into place?"

Gavin couldn't imagine that Tristan would've wanted to be attacked the way he was. But seeing him now, the way that he looked at Gavin with a strange, dark expression in his eyes, Gavin couldn't help but wonder if perhaps that was what Tristan had wanted after all.

"Why?"

Tristan smiled. "Had you only done what you were hired for, none of this would've been necessary."

Gavin shook his head. "You haven't hired me."

"You have always been under my control."

There was something in the way he said it that made Gavin pause.

He'd been looking for a connection. Cyran in the city. The Mistress of Vines. Now the Fates and the semarrl. The connection was Tristan.

Could he have coordinated all of this?

Gavin couldn't even put it past him. Tristan was a skilled manipulator. He had always been that way.

"What are you going to do, Chain Breaker?" Tristan asked, his voice soft.

The pressure behind Gavin persisted. He was going to have to do something soon. His gaze darted toward the dark egg. He had to get that to control the semarrl and remove them.

Taking a deep breath, Gavin focused on the core reserve power within him and on the enchantments that he had. One for speed and strength. One for magical repelling. That was all.

And that was all he needed.

He slipped the El'aras sword into its sheath, and he unsheathed the dagger. As useful as the sword was, the dagger served a very different purpose, and it suited him far better than the sword.

"Interesting choice," Tristan said.

"You have no idea."

"Oh, I have quite the idea."

Gavin darted toward Tristan, using his enchantments. He twisted the blade, driving it toward Tristan, who countered and blocked him. Gavin twisted his wrist several times, jerking his hand from side to side, trying to find a way through Tristan's defenses. Tristan pushed him back.

His old mentor laughed, backing up. "And to think I wondered how much you might have learned in the time since I trained you. Not enough."

Gavin grunted. "More than you taught."

"I think not. Everything you've learned from me you're bringing to bear upon me. You don't need to fight against me. You could fight *beside* me."

"If you wanted that, you would have been honest with me from the beginning."

"Perhaps," Tristan said.

Gavin summoned a hint of strength, and he jumped. While in the air, he twisted, kicking. Tristan flipped and blocked one kick, and he spun around so that he could avoid another. He was still quick, though Gavin noticed he had a faint limp.

If Tristan were El'aras—and Gavin thought he was, given everything Gavin had learned from him and how Tristan hadn't seemed to age at all—then he would have power of his own. Hopefully, he didn't have access to the powder that Gavin did. Hopefully, he wouldn't be able to use the same power that Gavin could use.

Hopefully…

Gavin twisted again, jerking the dagger around. Each time that he turned with the weapon, he wasn't fast enough.

Gavin had been drawing on his core reserves for much longer than he had ever attempted before. He was tired. It was a different sort of exhaustion than he had experienced in quite some time. He staggered, sweeping forward, but he couldn't be fast enough. He tried, but there was no speed. No strength.

Tristan drove his blade forward and cut into Gavin's arm.

Heat flowed through Gavin, but he pushed core energy out. It was almost too much. He needed to be cautious with the power that he drew, as Anna had warned him. If he called that power too quickly, he would find himself weakened in a way that would become unusable for him. Gavin had to find something else that he could do.

He drove toward Tristan, but Tristan was too fast. Gavin backed up, twisting his blade to block anything that Tristan might do to him.

What would he need to do? Tristan would know his fighting style. He would know everything Gavin had learned over the years. But he wouldn't know that Gavin had begun to understand the core power within him. Tristan might have his own version of strength, but what if he couldn't use it?

Tristan had tried to train Gavin. Others. He had wanted to use them so that they could do what he could not. Tristan had the skill—and he probably had enchantments.

But Gavin had something more than enchantments.

He focused on his core reserves. Doing so meant he would draw upon all the strength he had remaining.

Gavin surged, darting forward. He used everything he could, pouring it through the enchantment but also calling upon that strength to help guide him. He could feel that power filling him, and he slammed himself forward.

There wasn't nearly as much technique to what he was doing now. It was more about getting to Tristan and overwhelming him. He twisted the blade, thrusting it forward.

Tristan fell back. Gavin jerked his hand around, driving the blade at Tristan a second time, who blocked again. Gavin turned, and each time he did, he shoved the dagger forward, trying to carve into Tristan. Each attempt was blocked.

Tristan's face wrinkled in concentration.

Gavin continued battling. He forced his way forward, using everything in his power to find whatever it would take to overwhelm Tristan. This was a fight different than any sparring match he'd ever had with Tristan. This was not just for himself but for others. People he cared about. For Yoran.

He needed to get that dark egg. Only then could he stop what Tristan intended.

He pulled upon that core energy again, and he jumped. When he flipped, he twisted and dragged the dagger down. It sliced along Tristan's back, cutting into it.

Tristan spun quickly and brought his dagger out. Gavin blocked, then parried Tristan's attack. Gavin jerked his blade around and cut Tristan again, and then he twisted once more.

He slammed his fist forward. Tristan blocked him, but Gavin hooked his leg, knocking Tristan to the ground. Gavin dropped down and grappled with him.

Tristan was still strong, and he knew fighting styles and techniques Gavin had yet to learn. But Gavin had something that Tristan did not. He had a connection to some deep part of himself that Tristan could not access.

Gavin called upon that. "You wanted me to be the Chain Breaker."

"And you have been," Tristan said.

"No."

"What do you think you've done?"

"I've done what I needed to do," Gavin said.

"You've done what I wanted you to do."

Tristan started to laugh, and Gavin pressed down on him. He twisted, pinning Tristan's arms beneath him, and he grabbed the dark egg. It was cold, slick, unpleasant.

Gavin stuffed it into his pocket. "How do you control them?"

Tristan glared at him. "If you want it so badly, you will have to figure it out. Trust me when I tell you that they don't like to be used any more than you do."

"How do I use it?"

Tristan laughed again. Gavin thrust his knee down on Tristan's side, and Tristan grunted.

He'd beaten him.

Over the years, Gavin had wanted nothing more than to defeat Tristan when he had been training. He had wanted nothing more than to crush him, overthrow him, and prove to him that he was enough, but had never succeeded. Gavin had landed a punch, had even bloodied Tristan a time or two, but he had never defeated him.

How had I done so now?

"Are you going to hold me, or are you going to control them?" Tristan said.

"I think I'll do both. Why are you targeting the Fates?"

"If you had paid attention, you would know."

"What is that supposed to mean?"

Even as Gavin said it, he could feel the shadows starting to swirl around him. The creatures were getting closer, near enough that he would have to try to find a way to overpower them.

"I don't think so," Tristan said. "You see, they will not react well unless you determine the key to their control."

Gavin pressed his knee down on Tristan's chest again and forced Tristan to look at him. "How do I control them?"

"I've already told you that I am not going to provide the answers to you. If you want to know, you're going to have to come up with them on your own. Much like you have come up with everything else on your own, Gavin Lorren."

Gavin slammed his fist into Tristan's head. A smile came to Tristan's face as his eyes rolled up, and he went limp.

Gavin jumped to his feet, turning to face the creatures. He held on to the dark egg. The enchantment still repelled the smoke creatures, though he wondered how much longer that would be effective.

He trembled and tipped the last of the powder down his throat, knowing that he needed the rest of the power. Gavin looked down at the dark egg. There was something within it that he needed to do, to find some way to overpower what had been done in the way the smoke creatures were controlled.

What if he pushed his core power into it much like he had with the jade egg and the enchantments? If he did that, he would be connecting to it, and he worried that it would somehow change him.

Gavin had to try. He summoned that strength, which required that he abandon the power he pushed through the magical barrier. Instead, he pushed it into the dark egg. It started to glow, taking on a deep purple hue.

Something shifted.

The semarrl were called to the dark egg.

He held it up, letting power flow from him into it.

A smoke creature flowed into the dark egg, and Gavin shuddered. The sensation was disturbing, almost a slithering feeling of a snake gliding past him. The creature filled the dark egg with its strange power.

Then another and then another and then another. One by one, the semarrl flowed into the dark egg.

Gavin held on to the power, letting that connection form between him and the egg, between him and the creatures. The energy from him flowed outward, reaching the power of the egg. He tried not to think about what was happening.

As the egg glowed with that purplish power, the shadows were drawn into it. Finally, everything around him cleared. There were no more semarrl.

His core reserve faded. He sagged, dropping to his knees. He held the dark egg and then slipped it into his pocket. "You won't win this time. I've stopped them. I've stopped…"

Gavin glanced over, but Tristan was gone.

CHAPTER TWENTY-FIVE

Gavin climbed down from the rooftop and stood in the square. His fatigue came with a throbbing headache that left him needing to rub his eyes, his neck, everything to ease that sensation. But nothing could take away much of that pain.

What if this was nothing more than a test? Tristan shouldn't be so easy to defeat. Not that he had been easy, per se, but he had not been nearly as difficult as Gavin remembered him to be.

If this was more testing...

Gavin shook those thoughts away. He needed to reach Anna.

He touched the marker, and he pulsed some of his core reserves, all that he thought he had remaining, into it.

There was no response.

When he reached the center of the square, something started to crawl around his ankles. A familiar power.

The Fates.

Gavin looked around. He was exhausted and didn't think that he could handle the Fates as well. He reached into his pocket, touching one hand to the dark egg. He didn't like the idea that he might have to use it, but if the Fates came to him and attacked, then what choice would he have but to defend himself?

If he were right, then it was how the Triad had intended to use the dark egg, only Gavin didn't intend to use it to gain more power. Just to keep the city safe from a dangerous power.

He couldn't fight. Everything within him was overwhelmed. Gavin stood in place and looked around, waiting for them to reveal themselves. The air took on a shimmering quality, and it started to glow.

It was as if everything tilted around him, and where there had been nothing, suddenly there was something. Someone.

Several of them.

Not just one Fate.

The Fates.

The Fates were older-looking sorcerers, though they seemed almost ageless. One of them strode ahead of the others, a dark-bearded bald man he had fought before. The others were an older woman with pale eyes and graying hair and a thin man with a severe smile. Their crimson robes flowed down to the ground as they watched Gavin.

Gavin had only faced one of the Fates before. He had not

seen the others. Much like Zella had suspected, three were here. That might be all there were.

And they wanted the egg.

Given his weakened state, he doubted that he would be able to face them, and he certainly didn't think that he would win.

The lead Fate was dressed in a flowing crimson robe, and he was not the man Gavin had fought before. The robe reminded Gavin of what he had seen when he had headed into the sorcerer's lair. The only advantage Gavin had was that he had to believe the Fates could be divided. If they wanted the same item, maybe he could leverage it against them.

"You have been most difficult here, Gavin Lorren," the nearest one said.

Gavin grunted. "And you have been most annoying coming into the city."

"You have created quite a dilemma for us."

"Really? And what is that?"

"The question of what to do with you."

"I don't think you get to do anything with me," Gavin said.

"That would be unfortunate. You could be of much use."

Gavin tried not to think about how he could be of much use or why. It was the same way that he had tried not to think about why Tristan had trained him to use his magic. Eventually, he was going to have to face those questions and find those answers.

"I don't want to be of use to the Fates."

"Then you would prefer an alternative arrangement?" the leader asked.

The three Fates took up positions around him. The strange magical energy he had detected when they'd attacked continued to sneak up and around his ankles. He could feel it sliding up along his legs, working around his chest.

"Release me, or you'd better be prepared to face me," Gavin said.

The Fate smiled at him. "You have already seen how little you can do to us. Even one of us."

"I have," Gavin agreed.

"What makes you think this will be any different?"

"Because I have something you do not."

The bearded Fate smiled and walked toward him. "And that something is what we will take from you."

The female Fate flashed irritation as the bearded Fate came toward him.

"I'm not talking about the jade egg," Gavin said.

The Fate paused, watching him. "What is it, then?"

"Something else."

Gavin squeezed the dark egg. He didn't have much power left within him. The only thing he thought he had left was the chance of releasing the semarrl upon the Fates.

"You're going to leave the city," Gavin said.

The Fates shared a look. "This city has been without the proper guidance for long enough," the leader said. "There are many such places, though perhaps not so difficult as this. The others thought to extend their power beyond what we would have permitted. It required a firm correction."

Could the Fates have known what the Triad had planned and how they would have used the egg?

"This city already decided that it had enough of sorcerer influence. Or don't you remember what happened?"

"Oh, we know quite well what happened. Those who were involved were punished most severely."

Gavin suspected what happened to the rest of the Triad, not that it mattered to him. "You would come in here and offer your guidance, then?"

"Perhaps," the Fate said.

"No," Gavin said again.

The woman started to chuckle, her voice slightly pinched and a hint of shadow swirling around her. Not smoke. Maybe there *had* been more of the Fates here than he'd realized. "What makes you think you can defy us?"

"Because I can."

"Unfortunately for you, you have already proven incapable of countering our strength. You are formidable, but you lack focus, and you lack training," the lead Fate said.

Gavin smirked at him. "I lack training?"

"The kind of training that would make you dangerous."

Gavin grunted. "Interesting."

"Why is that interesting?"

"Because it is," Gavin said with a shrug. "Anyway, I grow weary of this conversation." He looked at the Fates. He could feel the energy they were using around him, and it started to constrict, making it so that he wouldn't have much longer.

"We will take the jade egg back. It belongs to us." This came from the angry-looking female Fate.

"It didn't always," Gavin said.

"Correct," he replied.

"What will you do when the El'aras come for it?"

The Fate laughed derisively. "The El'aras pose no challenge to us."

"Are you so certain of that?" Gavin asked.

The Fates watched him. "Yes," the Fate Gavin had stabbed said. There was an irritation in his tone that matched the way he'd seemed when Gavin had faced him in the Dragon.

The energy flowing around him started to constrict.

"We will have the jade egg," the first said.

Gavin didn't know if any of them was their leader—or if they were all here to make certain the others didn't succeed. Maybe he could use that against them. "I don't have it."

The power constricted.

Gavin focused, staring at them. "If you keep at this, I will release the semarrl."

The pressure on him eased for a second. He could see tension within their faces.

"You recognize that term," Gavin said.

"He's bluffing," the woman said. "Somebody like him could not control the creatures. He would not have the necessary power."

"I'm not bluffing, but if you'd like to take that chance,

that doesn't trouble me one bit. I can only imagine what would happen if the semarrl were released near the Fates. How hungry do you think they would be?"

He suspected the Fates would have a way of fighting off the semarrl, but it would likely take power and preparation. Given what Gavin had seen, as many as there were, he doubted they could fight them all off.

"The Triad thought they could control them, as well." Gavin tried to sound casual. "They used the egg to create the means." This time, he saw the tension in each of them increase. "Perhaps I should direct them at one of you, rather than all of you." Gavin smiled darkly. "Which would I choose? Perhaps you," he said, nodding to the woman. "Or you?" He nodded to the older of the men. "Or you," he said, looking to the man closest to him, the one he'd fought before. He'd attacked the Dragon, so maybe he was the one Gavin should release the semarrl upon. "Or perhaps all of you. As many as there are, they will likely have little difficulty with you. I'm sure you've heard they are active in the city, unless you don't fear them."

"All with power fear the semarrl."

They no longer squeezed him the way that they had, which Gavin felt was a small victory. It wasn't much, but enough that he could push against what they were doing, the way they were trying to hold him. He resisted, sending power out from him, holding on to that core reserve.

As he connected to that, he could feel the energy within him starting to wane. He didn't have much left. Before long, he wouldn't have enough strength to be able to release the semarrl. Instead, Gavin used just a bit, enough for him to resist that pressure upon him, little more than that.

Gavin scanned the distance.

Where was Anna? He'd called her after defeating Tristan. *She'd promised she would help with the Fates.* All he needed was to find a way to bide his time.

"You seem to be waiting for something," the Fate said. "Do you believe that help is coming?"

"I do."

The older Fate smiled at him. "Do you believe *she* will come?"

Gavin tensed. They knew about Anna. The comment about the El'aras had meant something. "Where is she?"

The Fate chuckled. "Did you really think that one of their kind would be able to challenge us? We are the Fates. We are those who lead. She is nothing."

Gavin resisted the urge to give in to his rage. She was more than nothing. She was the Risen Shard, even if he didn't know what that meant.

She was Anna.

"What did you do to her?"

The Fate smiled tightly. "We removed her as a threat."

Anger built up within him. He let that simmer, filling him with that agitation, the sense of what he had felt before. They had attacked Anna? The only reason she was here was because of him. The only reason she had gone after the Fate was because of him.

But she'd thought she would be facing a single sorcerer. Not all the Fates.

"You will release me," Gavin said.

"I think not. If you no longer have the jade egg, then you are of no use to us."

Power started to snake around him, even more than before. It wrapped around his throat, squeezing. Gavin could feel his strength waning as he drew upon a hint more of his core power.

He pushed outward, resisting the way that they constricted him, trying to fight back. He needed only a little bit more. Just a hint of power. As he held on to that, he could feel the pressure around him beginning to release. The energy started to ease.

If they had Anna, Gavin had little choice as to what his next step would be. Although it was what he had to do, it wasn't what he wanted. None of this was what he wanted.

He glared at them, and he let himself be filled by that power within him. He embraced the core power, and for the first time, he recognized and could feel its limit. The energy wasn't going to last long. If he lost that, then he would not be able to do anything more. He had to act quickly.

He didn't want to release the semarrl, and if he did, Gavin worried that he wouldn't have the strength to summon them back to the dark egg. It was possible that another could do so, though he wondered if there was somebody in the city who could. Better yet, if there was somebody who *should*...

Who would he trust to release and hold the power of the dark egg?

"I will give you only a few more moments to undo the

magic around me," Gavin said. "If you don't, I will unleash the semarrl, and then you will discover which of you I targeted." He locked eyes with each of them.

Finally, the power began to ease.

"Good," Gavin said. "Now, you and I will have a conversation. You may want to believe that I don't have the power of the semarrl, but I can assure you I do. Where is she?"

"You do not get to direct us," the bearded Fate said.

Gavin swung his gaze from one to the other. "Actually, I do. You've already proven that I do. If you didn't fear the semarrl, you wouldn't have released the power around me." Invisible bands of magic started to snake around him, and Gavin clenched his fists. He pulled the dark egg out of his pocket and held it out. "Do you question me now?"

The Fates stared at the dark egg, and Gavin held it up close to his face, forcing their eyes up. He needed them to know that he was the actual threat, not the dark egg.

"The Triad created this to control them. Do you doubt that it's effective?" No one answered. "I didn't think so. If you don't want it used against you, then you'll release me."

"You wouldn't dare," the older Fate said.

"I would if you continue what you're doing. Release the power around me now."

The pressure eased.

"You will release her as well."

The bearded Fate shook his head. "That is not going to happen."

"It *is* going to happen."

The Fates stared at him and did nothing.

Gavin shrugged. "It's your choice." He started to push power into the dark egg, and it took on a purplish glow.

The Fates stared at it, and Gavin couldn't tell if it was a look of hunger in their eyes, anger, or fear. They were skilled at maintaining their neutral expression. He continued to push power into the egg, using as much as he had. All he wanted was for the egg to glow, nothing more than that, and he certainly didn't want to release the semarrl, as Gavin had no idea if he would have enough power to contain them again, but he could use this as a way to scare them.

The egg continued to glow, increasingly brightly.

"Fine," the bearded man said.

"We should not—"

"We have no choice," the bearded Fate said, cutting off the woman. "We have not readied the protections. We would be a feast, and you know it."

There came another shimmer, a tilt. Within that was another figure.

Anna.

He waited, and she strode quickly across the ground toward him. Her skin almost glowed, and she had a determined step to her. She looked as if she had not been confined by the Fates. The tension in her eyes was profound, though, and her anger evident. Gavin was thankful he was not the source of her anger.

"You will leave Yoran," Gavin said to the Fates.

"Yoran is under our protection," the Fates said.

"Protection? I think you intend to keep it under your

control." Gavin inhaled deeply. There was one way to ensure they left Yoran alone. "The city is not under your protection any longer. It is under mine." He pointed the dark egg at each Fate. "If you return, I will release them. They will hunt for you. *I* will hunt for you. I may not be able to withstand you now, but I will learn. I will grow stronger. The next time will be different."

The Fates watched him, and power within them surged outward. It targeted Gavin.

He felt that power circling outward, swirling toward him, and he reacted.

He thought about what Anna had suggested.

Focus on what he wanted his power to do.

He wanted to push them back.

He drew upon as much of his core reserves as he could. Next to him, he could feel Anna doing something similar. It was strange to be aware of it, but he could feel that energy within her and feel how it flowed outward, and it struck him, but it also pushed beyond.

Gavin created a barrier. Their power struck his, and surprisingly, his power held.

Another burst of power came from him, and the dark egg glowed even more, the purple light streaming off it.

The Fates' eyes widened, almost as one.

Another blast of power exploded.

When it was gone, so were they.

Gavin sank to his knees. "I didn't know how much longer I could hold on."

Anna helped him to stand. "You have done well, Gavin Lorren."

"They aren't going to leave us alone."

"For a while, they will."

"Which means I have to stay here," he said.

Anna nodded. "For now."

Gavin took a deep breath, trying to maintain his strength. He looked around, but he couldn't see anything or anyone around him. "What about the others?" he asked.

"What others?"

"The constables. The enchanters."

He had to hope that they could keep the enchanters, and others Gavin cared about, safe from the semarrl—and from the Fates.

"I distracted the Fates before anything happened to them. And you drew off the semarrl in time."

Gavin breathed out in a heavy sigh. He had succeeded. Now, he had to rest. That was what he wanted more than anything else.

"Can you help me back to the Dragon? I might have taken all of your powder. I don't know if I can stay on my feet for too much longer."

"All of it?"

Gavin held the pouch out to her. "I needed it. I don't know what would've happened otherwise."

"It will be difficult for you, but I will make sure that you arrive safely."

He took a step. As his strength faded from him, Gavin collapsed.

CHAPTER TWENTY-SIX

Coming around slowly, Gavin opened his eyes and looked around him. It took a moment to realize he was lying in his bed within the Roasted Dragon. Everything in him hurt as he eased himself up. He rubbed the back of his throbbing head, and muscles that he didn't even remember working ached and trembled with each movement. At least his head wasn't throbbing the way that it had been before.

Even after having a good night of sleep—or perhaps even more than that—he was still tired. Gavin wasn't surprised.

He reached for his core reserves and took a deep breath, letting it out slowly. He felt refreshed. That served as a warning to him. The fact that he was refreshed meant that he had been out for a long time—possibly days.

Gavin got to his feet and dressed as quickly as possible,

strapping on the El'aras dagger and the sword. He studied the dark egg, the strange onyx sphere that rested on one of the tables, and decided to stick that into his pocket, as well. It was better than leaving it here and unprotected. He made his way out of the room and down into the tavern.

He paused at the door. A musician strummed a lute in one corner, singing with a rough voice. A fire crackled nearby, heat radiating out of the hearth. The tavern was filled with people.

It was a strange sight to see. At one point, it would have been commonplace. The tavern had been busy, a popular place for people to gather when Gavin had first come to the city, but that had started to change in the last few months. Jessica hadn't nearly the same business she had before Gavin had come.

He wound his way into the tavern. He took a seat, resting his elbows on the table and looking all around him.

"There you are," a voice said.

Gavin looked over as Jessica approached. Her hair was braided today, with small pink ribbons woven in patterns into her hair. She glanced over at him briefly. Her hands were empty, and she slipped into a seat next to him.

"How long?" he asked.

"How long what?"

"How long was I out?"

Jessica looked around the tavern before her gaze landed back on him. "A little while."

"A little while?"

She shrugged. "About a week."

Gavin grunted. "That's more than just a little while."

"She warned that you would need time," Jessica said.

"She?"

"The El'aras woman."

Gavin sighed. Anna was gone. It had been a week, and now he didn't even get a chance to say anything to her. That bothered him more than he had expected.

"Thank you," Gavin said.

"For what?"

"For giving me a place to stay. For making sure I was cared for in my incapacitated state."

Jessica chuckled. "I didn't have much choice."

"Why is that?"

She reached across the table, squeezing his hand. "I've always known you were special, Gavin. The first time you came to the Dragon, you've been…" She smiled and squeezed his hand again. "I think it's time for you and me to no longer be you and me."

His throbbing head made it difficult for him to focus, but those words stuck with him. "Why?"

"Everything has changed," she said. "Including you."

"I haven't changed that much."

"Perhaps not that much, but you've changed. And I can see you need to find yourself."

"At my age?"

"At any age," she said. She got to her feet, and she wrapped her arm around his neck in a hug. "It's good to see you back up. I'll get you some food."

Gavin frowned.

"You're up," Wrenlow said from behind.

Gavin twisted so that he could see him. Wrenlow's eyes were hollowed, with dark rings around them. He looked as if he had suffered, almost as if he had been beaten the way that Gavin felt. Ink stained his green shirt, and he offered a lopsided grin.

"I am," Gavin said.

"I didn't know how long you were going to be resting, but we were warned it may take a while for you to come back around. I didn't know that you would sleep for a week. Damn. That's a long time to sleep."

"Anna warned me that the powder she gave me might have consequences," Gavin said.

"That's what I understand."

"Jessica was acting strangely."

"I'm not surprised," Wrenlow said.

"Why?"

"Well, after what happened…"

Gavin sat up, and he looked around before settling his gaze on Wrenlow. "What happened?"

"When you returned to the Dragon, she made sure you were safe."

"I know Jessica did."

"Not Jessica," Wrenlow said. "The other woman. The El'aras."

"Anna?"

He nodded. "She stayed with you for the first day, making sure you had food and water and ensuring you weren't alone. She didn't leave you."

"She wasn't there when I awoke."

"No. I don't know if she's been here for the last few days."

Gavin looked toward the door. "Oh."

"I think Jessica realized she had to let go. She knows you'll leave."

Gavin reached into the pocket of his cloak, feeling for the dark egg. It was still there, the slick surface leaving his hand feeling oily. Unpleasant. He supposed that he should be thankful it was still there and that no one had taken it from him.

"Unfortunately—or fortunately—I won't be going anywhere." Gavin didn't know which it was at this point. "Because the Fates left the city." Gavin explained the events which had led to the Fates leaving Yoran.

"How?" Wrenlow asked.

"With this." Gavin pulled the dark egg out of his pocket and set it on the table. The dark egg reminded him of the jade egg. It was cooler to the touch and had a slick surface, whereas the jade egg had more of a sticky texture. There were markings along its surface, probably El'aras writing, though Gavin couldn't read it.

Wrenlow looked at it. "What is that thing?" He started to scoot back, moving away from the dark egg.

"This is what's used to control them," Gavin said. "And I think the Triad used the enchanters to create it." He would have to question the Keeper, but everything he'd learned made him think he was right. "The Captain held it, and Tristan... well, he might have manipulated me into helping him get to it." With the enchanters and the constables no longer at odds, the Captain had opened his vault to move enchantments.

Which would expose *this* one.

"At least I was able to convince the Fates to leave the city."

"So they're gone?"

"For now."

"And you fear they'll return," Wrenlow said.

Gavin took a deep breath, nodding. "At some point, I suspect the Fates will return. When they do, I guess…" He shook his head.

"You intend to stay."

There was a part of Gavin that didn't want to stay, but if he had to protect the city, what choice did he have? The Fates would return. He didn't think the constables and enchanters were powerful enough to push them back, regardless of what Davel believed.

At least, not yet.

"For a little while," Gavin said.

"I wonder how Jessica is going to handle that."

"Why?"

"Having you here," Wrenlow said. "I think she expected you were going to leave and go with the El'aras. If you stay, then she will have to come to terms with it."

Gavin looked over to see Jessica making her way through the tavern. There was a sadness about her, which left him sad as well. He didn't like being responsible for that sorrow, especially not with Jessica. She was a friend—and had been so much more.

He sighed, getting to his feet.

"Where are you going?" Wrenlow asked.

"I have something I need to do," Gavin said.

"But you just woke up."

"I know."

"Are you going to tell me?" Wrenlow said.

"I thought you might come with me."

Wrenlow cocked his head to the side, watching him. "Why?"

"Because I might need your help."

Wrenlow grinned and got up, and they made their way to the tavern entrance. Gavin could feel Jessica's eyes on his back. They reached the door, and he paused, looking behind him. She had turned away.

He headed through the streets, with Wrenlow following alongside him. Gavin had thought himself recovered, but he still felt tired. He staggered, and Wrenlow looked over at him but didn't say anything. Gavin appreciated that. There were other people in the street, but they paid them no mind.

They reached the constables' barracks.

Wrenlow laughed. "*This* is where you wanted to go?"

"I need to talk to Davel."

"This should be interesting," Wrenlow said.

Gavin stepped inside the barracks and paused. The barracks were busy. The last time he'd come here, there had been a half dozen constables who all jumped to their feet. They paid him little attention this time, other than a man sitting behind a narrow wooden desk near the door. He looked up at them, a lazy expression on his face. He straightened suddenly and twisted a bracelet on his wrist. An enchantment.

Gavin chuckled as he approached the man. The entrance to the barracks was not all that large. He looked around and spoke to the nearest constable. "I need to see Davel Chan."

The constable's eyes widened, and then he hurried away. Gavin had to wait only a moment before Davel came out of the back room.

"He lives," Davel said.

"You didn't think I would?"

"You were out for quite a while. I checked on you the last few days, but I wasn't allowed to see you."

"Jessica can be like that," Gavin said.

"Not her. She was welcoming enough."

That meant Anna. How long *had* she stayed with him?

"I wanted to let you know that the jade egg won't be returning to the city."

"I understand," Davel said.

"It needed to go back to its owner."

"That's what we were told."

"By the El'aras, I presume?" Gavin asked.

Davel nodded. "She can be quite emphatic."

"We will have to find another way for you to make the enchantments you need."

Davel smiled tightly. "That is not necessary."

"Why not?"

"Because I have already found another way to make enchantments."

Gavin looked around, and this time he *really* looked around. There were more than just constables here.

Enchanters.

He smiled to himself.

When he had dealt with the Mistress of Vines and stopped the Captain, there had been a part of Gavin that had hoped that the enchanters would be able to move and operate more freely within the city. And they had. They no longer had to fear the constables pursuing them, but there was still a difference between fearing pursuit and working openly.

What he saw here now was the possibility that they would be able to work openly.

When he saw here was a progress that he had not expected.

It had to be Davel and Zella. The connection they had formed.

Kegan was talking softly with one of the constables. There were several others that Gavin recognized, though he didn't know their names.

"The constables are working with the enchanters again," Gavin said.

"For now," Davel said. "So if that's your reason for coming, you don't need to be concerned. We will keep the city safe from the Fates."

Perhaps they would. Despite everything that Gavin felt like he needed to do, perhaps it wasn't necessary at all. He still needed to question the Keeper, but that would happen later.

"Is that all you wanted to say?" Davel asked.

Gavin tapped his pocket, feeling the dark egg. Perhaps Davel didn't need to know about it. "For now," he said.

Davel grunted. "You're a strange man."

"I know."

"Will we be seeing much more of you?"

He'd promised to protect Yoran. Seeing the enchanters and constables working together intrigued him, not only for what they could do for the city, but it might even give Gavin the sparring challenge he'd been looking for.

Besides, if he had to face Tristan again, he might need any advantage he could find.

Enchanters were that advantage. The city was that advantage.

"Perhaps," Gavin said.

"Great," Davel said with a grin.

"Why?"

"Because with you in the city, we keep facing unique new challenges," Davel said. "I am ready for a little bit of calm."

"It doesn't look like you're preparing for it."

Davel shook his head. "I know better than that. I might be ready for it, but with what's been going on, I fear we won't have calm for quite some time."

He met Gavin's eyes.

Gavin didn't look away. "I fear you're right."

He and Wrenlow left Davel behind, departing the constables' barracks. There was nothing else for Gavin to even do or say. The Fates were gone, though not indefinitely. They might've been defeated for now, but there was a real danger that they would return, and when—and if—they did, Gavin couldn't simply sit back and do nothing. He had never intended to claim Yoran as his own, but perhaps that was what had to be, at least for now.

Then there was the issue of Tristan. Gavin had to understand more about him. Tristan was still a skilled fighter. His fighting skill had not changed much in the years since they'd parted ways, but Gavin's had. More than that, Gavin now had access to something within him that he could call upon and use.

He truly was the Chain Breaker.

He wanted to go after Tristan, know what he intended, and learn how much he knew about Cyran. Tristan had shown himself to be something more than what Gavin had believed, whether or not it was that he was part El'aras or something else. Either way, Tristan had known far more about magic than he had ever let on when he had trained Gavin.

The streets were quiet. Wrenlow walked next to him as

they made their way back to the Dragon. Something caught Gavin's eye. Or, rather, someone.

He chuckled. "You can go over to her," he said to Wrenlow.

"I don't need to."

Olivia headed down the street with Desarra. Olivia was obvious with her dark hair, youthful features, and the bounce in her step. She was lovely, and her skin seemed to glow from the sunlight shining down. He understood why Wrenlow would pursue her, and why Yoran had become much more of a home for him. She might be the reason he wanted to improve his fighting skill.

Then there was Gaspar. He was walking behind Desarra, who had on a bright yellow dress, carrying a basket, and paused at a street vendor, leaning forward and laughing before turning to Gaspar.

"Go to her. We'll probably be here a little while, anyway."

"Are you sure? I know you, Gavin. And I thought you were ready to leave."

"Maybe the city is growing on me. Besides, don't end up like him," Gavin said. He nodded toward Gaspar, who trailed behind Olivia and Desarra and did a poor job of trying to remain hidden.

"Gaspar still cares about Desarra," Wrenlow said.

"He does, but he's too foolish to do anything about it."

"I don't know. I think him following her is a start."

"If he wants to do something about it, he should go after her," Gavin said.

Wrenlow cocked a brow at him. "The same way that you did?"

Gavin grunted. "I'm not so sure that there can be anything between Jessica and me long-term. She enjoys my company, and I enjoy hers, but I—"

"I'm not talking about Jessica."

Gavin grunted again. "I'm not so sure anything can happen there either."

"Why not?"

"She's El'aras."

"You say that as if it has some grand meaning to me," Wrenlow said. "As if you have no right to the same title."

"I'm not sure what to make of it."

"You could find out."

"Not without leaving the city," Gavin said.

"You still have her marker, don't you?" Wrenlow asked.

An older man jostled past him, and Gavin instinctively tensed. The man continued on, chatting with the others walking with him, all of them too loud—and intoxicated.

"I still have it," Gavin said.

"Then you could use it."

Gavin chuckled, pulling the marker out of his pocket and squeezing it briefly. "She already answered me once. I don't need to force her to come again."

"I'm fairly certain she isn't going to feel any irritation with you calling out to her. Come on, Gavin. She stayed in the city while you were recuperating."

"Maybe after I finish the job."

"The job?"

Gavin patted his pocket. "The one that started this whole thing. I'll meet you back at the dragon."

Wrenlow took off, skipping along the street. He passed Gaspar, clapping him on the back, and hurried up to Olivia. The two of them started murmuring, and they disappeared around a distant corner.

Gavin pulled the necklace out of his pocket and hurried through the city toward the old woman's home, passing several patrols of constables—each time with an enchanter with them. Things really *had* changed in the city.

With crowds gathering in the market near the old woman's home, there was more activity, stores with doors open to the street, and minstrels playing on several intersections. Yoran had come alive.

Or maybe *he* had.

He was still tired, but this needed to be done.

Gavin reached the woman's door and knocked.

The old woman pulled the door open, and her eyes widened. "You. I heard what you did."

"What was that?"

"Killed the Captain."

Gavin grunted. "Then you heard wrong. And maybe you don't want this." He held out the necklace, and her eyes widened even more.

She reached for it, taking it slowly and delicately. "I can't believe you found it." She looked over to him. "It's worth every bit of the gold I promised you. Let me get it—"

"No," Gavin said.

"I can't pay more. Not that it's not worth it, but the gold is all I have."

He made sure to get paid on his jobs, but something about this didn't feel quite right. Maybe he *had* changed more than he'd realized. Then again, he hadn't actually been the one to find the necklace. "I'll get what I'm owed from the other enchantments the Captain had stolen."

She stared at him for a moment. "I don't have much, so I won't refuse the offer, but if you're ever in need of supplies, might I suggest Eserra's general store. I know the owner and can help with whatever gear you might need. Just ask for Holva." She sniffed. "That's me, by the way."

He smiled. "I'll take you up on that."

Gavin started to step back when Holva hurried toward him and hugged him.

"Thank you for this. I thought I'd never have those memories back. Now…"

She swallowed and stepped back into the home, clutching the necklace as she closed the door. Gavin stood in place a moment.

Could he make a home in Yoran?

As he started back toward the Dragon, he reached for the El'aras marker and squeezed it.

The coin started vibrating in his hand.

That was unexpected.

Gavin held the El'aras marker. Anna had given it to him for a reason. Perhaps he needed to keep that fact in mind. And now she was using it. Or she was using him.

He followed the vibration within the marker, noting

how it increased in frequency. Unsurprisingly, it guided him to the forest outside of the city, where he found her waiting in the shade of some of the towering trees.

She looked lovely. Her golden hair caught streams of sunlight, and the deep green jacket and pants she had on hugged her figure and made her blend into the forest.

"I wasn't sure if you would recognize the call," Anna said, stepping toward him.

He took a deep breath. She smelled of lilacs, along with a pleasant aroma that reminded him of the forest. There was something to it that struck him as similar to a home he barely remembered. "I wasn't sure that you were calling to me," Gavin said.

"I went back to check on you. You were gone."

"You didn't have to stay."

"You returned the egg. I did have to stay," she said.

Something went unsaid. Gavin wasn't entirely sure what it was and wondered if he would ever learn. Maybe not from her directly. She had been hiding. That was the reason she had been in Yoran before, and now she was preparing.

But preparing for what?

The warm wind whispered along his cheeks, giving him a faint flush, though some of that might've come from his proximity to Anna. "If it was yours, then I was only giving it back."

"Not mine, but the people's."

"Still."

They fell silent for a moment.

"I don't know what to make of what happened," Gavin said.

Gavin looked up at her. Since coming around and since learning Anna had disappeared, he had feared he wouldn't have answers. Having her stand across from him now, with the opportunity to ask those questions, left him uncertain how to proceed.

"Why didn't you tell me about Tristan?" he asked.

"I told you that he still lived," Anna said.

"Yes, but you didn't tell me that he was El'aras."

She watched him. "To be of the people, you must accept your place."

"And he has not accepted his place?"

"He has not."

"But he's not full El'aras, is he?"

That mattered somehow. Gavin didn't completely understand the intricacies between someone who was full El'aras and someone who was not, but he recognized that there was something to it. Somehow, it mattered that Tristan—and, for that matter, probably Gavin—was not fully El'aras.

"I'm not certain," Anna said.

"How can you not be certain?"

She smiled. "It's not so easy to know."

There was more to it, Gavin was certain, but he didn't push. "What happened?"

"That is something he will have to tell you himself. Unfortunately, I do not know the details."

"But something happened."

"Something happened," she agreed.

"Did he steal the jade egg from the El'aras?"

Her mouth tightened slightly.

Gavin grunted. "He did. Then how can he be as old as you say?"

"You must have learned that our kind lives for a long time. Even you, Gavin Lorren."

He should have known that he was not what he had believed his entire life. He had always healed quickly. When he was younger, he thought it good luck more than anything else. As he had grown older, he had believed that it was simply his training. Now it made a different sense. It wasn't only good luck—it was tied to some part of him that he didn't fully understand. One that he needed to better understand.

"Are you saying that I'm not as youthful as I look?" Gavin asked.

"You know that you are not," Anna said.

He chuckled. "All this time, I've been used by him."

"Did you think it would be otherwise?"

After escaping from his training and thinking that Tristan was gone and dead, Gavin had believed that he made his own choices. Perhaps he had, to a certain extent, but there was also some part of it that left him thinking that perhaps he had not. Maybe he had truly been used all this time.

"I think he's still planning something," Gavin said.

Gavin couldn't move past the idea that it had been

nothing more than a test. Whatever Tristan had been after had been a way to push him, but push him how?

He wanted the Fates gone, though Gavin didn't quite know why.

He would have to do something more, and somehow, he would have to do it from within Yoran while keeping the city safe from the Fates.

"Most likely," Anna replied.

"I might have to stop him."

"You might," she agreed.

"What about you?"

"I called you to offer you my help."

Gavin smiled. "You already offered me your help."

"A different kind. One that you weren't ready for when I was here before, but I suspect you are now."

He knew what she was asking, and had she offered it even a week ago, it would have been difficult to refuse given everything that he'd learned about himself. He *wanted* to understand the power he could use.

Now Yoran needed him.

And he wanted to help.

"I can't."

"I haven't told you what my help entails," she said.

"You want me to go with you. To learn from the El'aras."

Anna said nothing, but the slight flicker of her pale blue eyes suggested that he was right.

"But I can't," Gavin said. "The Fates are going to return. They're gone for now, but I have offered the city my protection. I need to remain to ensure that the people in the city are ready for their possible return."

"You could serve them better by understanding what you could be."

"If I leave, the Fates will know. The city will be in danger."

Anna smiled sadly. "Then perhaps another time." She leaned forward, kissing him lightly on the cheek again. Heat rose within him, along with a surge of longing. In that moment, Gavin wanted nothing more than to go with her, to follow her. Did it stem from some El'aras power she possessed, or was it truly his attraction toward her?

"I fear that whatever started in Yoran is not over. I fear that we will meet again," she said.

"If I call…"

"I will answer."

Anna watched him for a long moment, then spun and slipped into the trees. She disappeared quickly, and he watched until she was gone. He felt her presence within the forest long after she left. He stood there for a length of time, waiting, watching, wishing that he could go with her but knowing that he could not.

This was his city now. He had to help it. He had to offer whatever protection he could.

And he was going to train and be ready. The next time he faced Tristan, it would not be a test. The next time he faced Tristan, Gavin was determined to defeat him, to destroy him if needed. He was not going to be used any longer.

Pick up the next book in The Chain Breaker series: The Stone Wolf.

A new magic threatens to destroy Gavin—or change him forever.

Gavin has secured the city, preventing the deadly Fates from bringing their terrible sorcery back to Yoran, but Tristan remains at large. Their fight had been a test, and Gavin knows he can't fail the next one.

When a strange attack pushes him to reveal the depths of his magic, Gavin knows Tristan has returned to finish what he started. This time, he's working with a power greater than any sorcerer—and something Gavin has never faced.

A friend's abduction forces Gavin to take action he never would have considered in order to save them and stop Tristan. He must use all his connections in the city, but even that might not be enough to save them—or stop a plan that's been in play for years.

The Chain Breaker will not be enough.

He must find a way to become something more than he'd ever trained to be.

SERIES BY D.K. HOLMBERG

The Dragonwalkers Series
The Dragonwalker
The Dragon Misfits

Elemental Warrior Series:
Elemental Academy
The Elemental Warrior
The Cloud Warrior Saga
The Endless War

The Dark Ability Series
The Shadow Accords
The Collector Chronicles
The Dark Ability
The Sighted Assassin
The Elder Stones Saga

The Lost Prophecy Series
The Teralin Sword
The Lost Prophecy

The Volatar Saga Series

The Volatar Saga

The Book of Maladies Series

The Book of Maladies

The Lost Garden Series

The Lost Garden

Printed in Great Britain
by Amazon

40519103R00219